WHAT IT LOOKS LIKE

WHAT IT LOOKS LIKE

MATTHEW J. METZGER

jms books

WHAT IT LOOKS LIKE

JMS Books LLC
10286 Staples Mill Rd. #221
Glen Allen, VA 23060
www.jms-books.com

Printed in the United States of America
ISBN: 9781535376068

For Sara Beth. This is exactly what it looks like.

CHAPTER I

ROB HAWKES WAS a god.

That was Eli's first coherent thought of the morning, and largely for the way Rob was inelegantly sprawled in the bed, the sheets twisted around his waist and the morning sun pooling gold over his skin. His physique—those hard lines of muscle, the breadth of his shoulders and the narrow taper down to flat abs to his hips—was nothing short of mythological divinity.

And *fuck*, Eli wanted him.

But Eli was loathe to disturb him when he looked so peaceful. Rob didn't look peaceful, as a rule. He had a hard face with scowling brows and a tense jaw; to see those harsh angles softened was a treat, and one Eli wanted to enjoy for a little longer.

Carefully, biting his lip for fear of disturbing the sleeping dragon, Eli twitched the sheets down.

Rob mumbled, but didn't stir, and Eli sat up against the pillows to drink in the sight of the sleeping, naked body. Long legs with taut thighs smattered with dark hair, large but narrow feet hanging at strange angles from thick ankles and calves like concrete. Even relaxed, there was nothing but muscle there. The left leg was covered from hip to toe in dark, intense tattoos, not an inch of skin left naked from the ink, even if the whole body was naked from clothes. A chain coiled around the ankle, buried in the skin and created out of ink instead of iron. Eli wished fervently he were able to get a real chain, tether Rob to the bed, and never let him leave.

The tattoos rose beyond the hips, but less crowded—a serpent hissed along the ribs, a mechanical heart beat over a breast and rose and fell gently with Rob's breathing, and a galaxy, vivid purples and reds on a space-scape of black, disguised one powerful shoulder. His arms, one slung across the mattress towards Eli and the other tucked under the pillow, were as coated as his left leg in crowded sleeves, fire and skulls jostling for attention, the faces of loved ones immortalised in ink, dates and quotes hiding between leaves and eagles. Across his back, Eli knew more, but the sheets and mattress hid them from the morning.

For now.

Miles of inked skin stretched out in the sun like this was too much to resist. Eli sighed in disappointment at his own weakness, even as he bent low and dragged a dry, tempting kiss across slightly-parted lips. They were still swollen from the night before, the scar at the corner puckering the bottom lip a fraction. Eli buried his teeth around that fleck of white damage, and tugged.

Rob's groan was primal.

"Morning," Eli whispered, bracing himself with arms either side of Rob's head. He nudged his nose against Rob's face, pressing plucking, nipping kisses against the man's chin and cheeks, nuzzling the harsh rasp of stubble and smelling the stale remnants of lager and wet leaves. Eli ached in memory, but the soreness was a welcome reminder. He dropped a hand down the bed to find idle, sated flesh and squeeze it.

That got Rob to open his eyes.

Just a crack, mind, but open was open. Eli—girly as it was—loved Rob's eyes. The rest of the man was a hulking wall of dark, brooding temper. The body could have been cut from a men's fitness magazine, but the *eyes*…

Rob's eyes were so startlingly pale the contrast against his pupils was almost violent. The grey irises were barely a shade darker than the whites, and it made his gaze ferociously intense, no matter the mood he was actually in. It made him look dangerous, like a feral animal or a predator on the hunt. Made him look alert and watchful even when he wasn't, and never failed to get attention from whoever was near him.

And, like every other time those incredible eyes fixed on him, Eli felt a jolt in his stomach, and leaned fractionally towards them, as though falling blindly—and uncaringly—into some abyss.

He caught himself—almost literally, splaying his fingers across the broad muscles below the gentle curve of collarbones under skin. A lazy blink and lazier smirk served to promote Rob from merely a sleeping god to one of the arrogant overlords of ancient Greco-Roman mythology.

"You look," Eli whispered, "like Zeus. A beautiful, powerful, arrogant *fuck*."

He did—even lying down, Rob had so much physical power that it could almost be smelt on him. The idle way those eyes tracked Eli's movements spoke of someone who knew his own ability to control the situation; the rough thumb that came up to rub at the corner of Eli's mouth and push demandingly past his lips and teeth showed his quiet arrogance.

And *God*, was it fucking true. Eli would—did, had—bend over and grab his ankles for this man at just the twitch of an eyebrow.

The watery warmth of the sun on Rob's skin, the almost imperceptible ebb and flow of blood under the flesh, and the way he simply lay and waited, as though knowing what Eli would do before Eli himself...

It brought a smile to Eli's face as he pulled away from Rob's intruding thumb, a kiss to be placed over Rob's heart just shy of the nipple, and made him drop his hand from where it had idled on Rob's inner thigh to more important places. Rob's cock was soft, warm in Eli's hand when he took it, and pale against the dark bruise Eli had bitten into Rob's thigh the previous morning.

"You want me?" Eli whispered, even as he shifted away from Rob's heavy hands and blew gently over the head.

Rob was uncut, and it had been one of Eli's favourite afternoons, quite literally tying Rob to the bed and *thoroughly* exploring him.

But not this time. This morning, Eli wanted one thing and one thing only—he shifted to throw his leg over Rob's shin and settle over his legs, bracing both hands on those narrow hips and taking the swelling cock in his mouth.

Eli was still a little unused to this—the sharp taste, the odd angle of his jaw, and the trick of trying to anticipate Rob's movements. But at the same time, Eli enjoyed it, the way Rob's smell would surround him, the guttural groan Rob would make deep in the back of his throat, the way his hand would—

Fingers fisted in Eli's hair as he rasped his tongue up the hardening shaft and rubbed his lips around the head. He rolled his throat, deliberately lathing Rob in as much spit as possible, because Eli had designs on more than just opening his throat for the god in his bed. He was going to get that cock as deep as he could, so deep it fucking *hurt*, and if Rob wasn't going to move, then Eli could fuck his own brains out on him anyway.

With a last parting suck, Eli pulled off and rose from the bed to drop his boxers without fanfare or finesse. Rob was watching, eyes raking Eli's body with something unfathomable in the ice-white gaze. Eli smiled, biting his lip in the way he knew Rob liked best.

"You look," he whispered, trailing a single finger up the wet shaft jutting out from Rob's still-prone form, "like you're just *waiting* to be served. Like you're the master of some decadent Roman villa and you're just waiting for some flexible slave to come and finish you off."

A smirk pulled at that stern mouth, and Eli grinned, bending over Rob's face to kiss him with open lips and a demanding tongue.

Rob would be able to taste himself, Eli knew, and the return of a fist to clutch at his hair was no surprise.

"You want to fuck me?" he whispered in a breathy tone. "I want to feel you. I can still feel you from last night, but it's fading. I'm still loose, but it's going to sting, just how I like it—"

The fist tightened, and then Rob was sitting up. His gaze was feral, and then both hands were around Eli's head and his jaw was being forced open by something that could have been termed a kiss, or a plundering. He smiled around it, hands fumbling for purchase on Rob's broad shoulders, closing the kiss into something softer when one huge paw let go. Eli loved this, the aggressive attraction in Rob's movements, the way he left no fucking doubt as to his opinion of Eli's body...

Something crinkled, and Eli groaned.

"Oh, Rob, c'mon..."

Rob's face was stern, and the condom packet cool against Eli's fingers.

"We don't need it," Eli coaxed. Rob's expression didn't so much as flicker. "Oh c'mon, Rob, the test would have come back with something by *now*, surely?"

Not a twitch. And Eli knew the rules—question too much, push too hard, and the opportunity was taken away. And this morning...fuck, *this morning...*

"Fine," he grumped, and took the packet. He tore it open with his teeth, and got his lip bitten for his efforts before the lube was handed over. "You know my bedside drawers too well."

The grin was nothing short of lecherous, and Eli kissed it away before perching on the edge of the bed and wrapped his hand absently around Rob's cock. He hadn't softened in the slightest.

Eli sighed.

"I want to feel this," he breathed, "*properly.*"

Rob raised a dark eyebrow, then tensed and closed his eyes entirely when Eli rolled the condom on. He gave a sadistic squeeze at the base of the shaft before reaching for the lubricant, silently willing next month—and next month's test results—to hurry the fuck up already.

But for now...

"There," Eli breathed, pushing Rob back into the pillows, straddling his waist with fluid ease. "Stay. I didn't get to see a thing last night—you were too busy shoving me into alley walls and fucking me *raw*—"

Rob's chest tensed and pushed against his arms; Eli gave a little shove to make his point, and carried on blithely.

"—and last night and all the lager, that was good for a seedy fuck, but this morning...God, I woke up and you looked like a fuck-

What It Looks Like   5

ing god, like something completely out of this world, so *you*—"

He shifted up on his hips and wrapped a hand around Rob's cock beneath him. This was going to sting. Loose was loose, but Eli's plan required something a little more involved. And Rob was going to kill him. *Later.*

"—are going to lie there and let a mere mortal *worship* you."

In one motion, Eli pressed down onto Rob's cock. It wasn't graceful; it wasn't even seamless. The stretch burned, the edge of pain distinct, and Rob's hiss and jerk didn't help, his hands suddenly like vices on Eli's thighs and his head thrown back in an arch of muscle and sinew. His sheathed cock was slick, but Eli was not, and even the vague catch hurt. The ache from the previous night exploded anew—and yet it was also ecstasy, the sensation of being completely filled, of taking Rob so deep Eli felt as though he'd been seized by the back of the neck and was being held in a choking, possessing grip.

"Oh my God," he groaned, his little speech forgotten. "Oh fuck. *Rob*, fuck…"

Rob's hands cupped his hips. Eli took deep lungfuls of cool air before opening his eyes—and when had he closed those?—and taking in the messy hair, piercing gaze, and heaving chest. His thighs were clamped around Rob's waist, and Eli watched in near-distant fascination as he tensed them and felt rather than saw Rob's grunt of too-close, too-intense satisfaction.

"You feel amazing," Eli blurted out, and rolled his hips. The slick slide of the condom was unpleasant, but the heavy push of Rob's cock as Eli sank back down onto it again was dizzying and quite literally breathtaking. "Fuck, Rob, I could fuck you every day and it wouldn't be enough. I want to feel you proper, I want those fucking test results, I want you to hold me down and just fuck me open with nothing between, I want—"

Rob moved so fast it was a blur—his arm was suddenly tight around Eli's back, the room was spinning, and then Eli hit the mattress. Rob drove into him so hard Eli saw stars. He yelled, digging his nails into Rob's shoulders like claws, arching under the thrust until it felt like he could take Rob to the root, until the headboard smashed against the wall with deafening force, until—

Someone shouted downstairs. Rob's grin was feral in Eli's neck before he bit down. The mattress was shaking with the force of those powerful, painful, driving thrusts.

Eli didn't give a fuck.

ROB WAS ALREADY dressed when Eli snuck back in from the shower. Sitting on the edge of Eli's bed, he was shrugging into the T-shirt he'd worn to the pub the previous night, probably still stinking of beer and barbecue chicken wings.

"You *could* start leaving clothes here, you know," Eli chided, kissing the top of his head before rummaging for his own clothes.

Rob's answer was to resoundly smack his arse. The blow stung, and Eli bit his lip against the jolt of red-hot pleasure.

"Hey!"

Rob rolled his eyes and leaned back on his hands. He openly watched Eli dress, the scrutiny both a little embarrassing, and a lot arousing.

"That's not fair," Eli grumbled. "You can fucking turn me on by *looking* at me, and I can't even walk straight."

Rob offered him a toothy grin.

Eli huffed.

"Mean," he whispered, bending to kiss the smile away.

"Eli!" a voice bellowed up the stairs. "I want that—vehicle moved!"

Eli rolled his eyes. Rob guffawed. "Fucking coppers," he rasped.

Rob had a very deep, very hoarse voice, like the rumble of a gravelly engine, and it drove Eli crazy. If Rob was a voice actor, Eli wouldn't be able to watch any of his films for fear of having a fucking orgasm in the cinema. As it was, he seized Rob's face and kissed him hungrily, tugging Rob's bottom lip between his teeth in a vicious bite until the tang of blood warned him off.

"I suppose you have to go?" he whispered.

"Uh-huh," Rob said, both hands clasping the very tops and backs of Eli's thighs, right under his arse. It was oddly more intimate than if Rob had just groped a cheek and been done with it. "Shit to do."

"See you later? Or tomorrow maybe?"

"Eli!"

"Tell him to fuck off," Rob grumbled, and stood.

Eli didn't back up, and ended up draped over Rob's front.

"Mm, no." He kissed Rob's stubbled jaw before stepping away and shrugging on a T-shirt. "Okay, okay. Come on, then, out the door."

Rob cut a huge and rough-edged figure in Eli's family home. The house was all white carpets, white walls, and expensive decorations of no use but a lot of worth scattered on various shelves. They had doilies, for goodness' sake—a man wearing yesterday's clothes, hair on end, and smelling like the floor of a dive bar didn't fit in.

Especially not under the glower of the man standing at the bottom of the stairs, in full, gleaming uniform.

"Dad," Eli said warningly. Then, as an afterthought: "*Rob.*"

Both ignored him.

"What?" Rob demanded aggressively.

Chief Inspector Samuel Bell's lips tightened.

"Your…car…is blocking the end of my driveway," he said coldly.

"Musta been when I drunk-parked it," Rob returned flippantly.

Eli huffed and gave Rob a shove in the back towards the front door.

"Lay off, Dad," he ordered, shoving Rob outside. "And don't antagonise him."

"Bloke's a fucking twat," Rob grumbled, but rolled his eyes and softened under Eli's scowl. "Alright, alright. Jesus."

"Get yourself gone," Eli scolded, walking Rob to his battered old 4x4. It was a Suzuki Jimny from the late nineties, and about as respectable on their tidy suburban street as Rob himself. Eli loved that car.

"Alright," Rob said, swinging himself into the driver's seat. It took two goes to slam the door, then he wound the window down and caught Eli's chin in one huge hand to kiss him soundly. "You still up for coming to Scotland for Christmas with me and Danny?"

"Yep," Eli said, smiling against the press of Rob's finger and thumb. He darted back in for another kiss.

"Tart. You've scratched holes in my shoulders."

"You love it."

"I fucking do an' all," Rob agreed, and that belligerent face eased into a wide, crooked grin. "Call you later, babe."

Eli smacked his hand. "Babe? Fuck off, savage."

Rob laughed and started the engine. The Suzuki jerked and rolled backwards a little before realising it had an accelerator, and then it and Rob were gone in a clattering cacophony of metal and smoke. Eli stood at the end of the drive, one hand absently rubbing at the deep bite-mark Rob had left in his neck, and smiling like a fool.

"Eli! I need to go to work."

Eli sighed, and moved aside to let his father's BMW out of the drive. Not that his father had even gotten into the thing yet—he was still standing, brass and all, in the open doorway.

"I don't like that man," Dad said firmly as Eli approached.

Eli didn't much care. He'd heard it all before, and right now, his priority was going back to bed for a few hours before getting up and going to work for the afternoon. So his response was as flippant as Rob's, though not—quite—as rude.

"Tough," he said. "Because I do."

CHAPTER 2

ELI FIRMLY BELIEVED that whole 'how you were raised' stuff was a load of crap. And the reason for that was Jenny. Sitting on the wall by the shopping centre entrance and watching his sister carelessly swinging her gleaming Audi into a too-narrow space, Eli idly wondered—as he had often—how they'd turned out so different.

They *looked* like peas in a pod. Similar height, same slender build, same waviness to their hair—although Jenny's was nearly black like Dad's, and Eli's a sandy blond like Mum's. They even had the same ears and jaw. But while Eli was all baggy T-shirts and heavy jeans, hunched shoulders and hiding behind sunglasses whenever the weather was warm enough to allow it, Jenny was...

"Eli!"

Well. *Jenny.*

"Hey, Jen."

She flung her arms around his neck in a stranglehold, and her handbag hit him in the back. Because this was where Eli and Jenny had *nothing* in common—Jenny was all about looking good, and Eli...wasn't.

It had been that way growing up, and it hadn't changed now they were adults. Jenny had always preened. She was only a year younger than Eli, but Eli could remember her caterwauling even at five when Mum hadn't done her hair *exactly* the way Jenny wanted it. She'd been getting in rows with Dad about make-up and heels when she was just twelve. And she'd nearly given him a coronary when she was fifteen, marched into the kitchen, slammed a pregnancy test kit down, and announced that Mum and Dad were going to be grand-parents. God, *that* had been a bad Christmas. Eli had been tempted, for the next eight months, to ask his grandmother if he could live with her. He'd have taken the smell of cat piss and church incense over the toxic atmosphere in the house any day.

"How's my favey bro?"

"Favey?"

"Favourite, idiot."

"I'm your *only*."

She snorted and kissed his cheek. "Same diff."

Still, despite their differences, Eli didn't much mind Jenny. She was self-centred and vain, yes, but she was also…nice. She loved him. She'd never really had a problem with him—oh, she didn't *understand* him, but she also hadn't had a problem with him. She hadn't questioned every last thing about him the way Mum and Dad had.

"How's the folks?" she asked, tucking her arm into his and leading him towards the shops. Christmas shopping, Eli's least favourite thing.

"Mad at me again."

"Why, what'd you do?"

"Who says I *did* anything?"

"Um, they're mad at you? Ergo, you did something!"

Eli rolled his eyes and complained at her judgement; Jenny laughed at him, and demanded to know what he'd done. It had been that way growing up, too. Eli had been the—not problem child, exactly, he hadn't been a bad kid, not like Rob must have been for his parents—but the difficult one. The complicated one. Jenny was easy, Jenny was just a tart swanning her way through school and boys.

Secretly, given as how Jenny was twenty and had a four-year-old daughter, Eli suspected it was that Jenny was just smarter than he was, and kept her complicated-ness away from Mum and Dad.

"Rob came over last night," he admitted finally.

Jenny groaned.

"What? I'm allowed to have my boyfriend over!"

"When your boyfriend gives Dad a heart attack, you might want to rethink that," Jenny said snottily.

Eli rolled his eyes as they wandered into Mum's favourite shop for their usual Christmas present, an expensive angora jumper in some sickly pastel colour. Despite Mum being even harder than Dad work-wise—he was a chief inspector and sat in an office making strategic decisions; Mum was head of forensics and had been shot by a drug dealer at a crime scene when Eli was six years old—she was dead mumsy at home. Jumpers, nice necklaces, and chocolate were the automatic gifts for Mum.

Dad was harder though, and Eli said as much as they found a pink jumper in Mum's size and took it to the counter.

"Dump your boyfriend, that'll make his Christmas *and* next birthday," Jenny said, then pursed her lips. "God, is Dad fifty next birthday?"

"Forty-nine," Eli corrected. "And I'm not dumping my boyfriend because Dad doesn't like him."

"Oh, thank God, I won't have the cash by February for a big five-oh," Jenny grumbled, then rolled her eyes. "I'm just saying it would be good timing. It won't be as special if you dump him in March."

"I'm not dumping him at all!" Eli said hotly.

Jenny pulled a face. "Thanks," she added to the shop assistant, taking the bag and steering Eli out by the arm.

"I'm serious," Eli said coolly. "Dad can shove it. Rob's not a—"

"Rob's a criminal," Jenny said firmly. "And that—"

"Oh come on, Jen, you know better than to look at things like that. Being a criminal just means...it just means you broke the law, it doesn't make you *bad*."

"Bad people break the law."

"Rob's not *bad*..."

"He's been to *prison*, Eli!"

"Yeah, for—"

"For?"

Eli stopped, and bit his lip. In truth...in truth, he didn't actually know. He could guess—both parents in the police gave you a pretty decent grasp of what got people sent to prison and for how long, and he knew Rob had long been what Mum would call a petty offender. Eli privately suspected he'd burgled one-too-many houses, or been caught for the twentieth time with a spliff.

But he didn't know. He'd only found out because Rob admitted to having developed an affinity for weight-lifting 'inside' and Eli had asked what he meant by that. Three years in prison, from when Rob was twenty. He'd only been out six months when Eli had met him, so it was about a year now.

"Whatever it was can't have been *that* bad, he only got three years."

"*Got*, or *served?*"

"Got," Eli said firmly. "I know that much."

"That's still three years in prison, Eli—I mean, can't you see why Dad's worried?"

"He's not worried, he's being a dick."

"He's *worried*," Jenny insisted, and squeezed Eli's arm as they wandered into an odds-and-ends, sort-of-joke-shop construction that had been slung up in the space left by the independent bakery closing down. "And can't you see why?"

Eli swallowed. "Rob's not like Greg," he said eventually.

Jenny snorted at the name of her on-again, off-again boyfriend. Currently off, after he'd punched her in the stomach at finding out she was pregnant. Dad had hit the roof. "Rob probably *knows* Greg. Seriously, ask him. They probably shoot pool together."

"Rob's not like that," Eli insisted. "For fuck's sake, Jenny, don't you think I'd know?"

"After six months with him? No," she said flatly. "He's still reeling you in."

"You're being paranoid and ridiculous."

"Am I? Come on, Eli, where's your evidence? Where's your proof he's such a nice guy, eh? He's aggressive, we've both seen the way he starts for Dad, and one day—look, Eli, that's all we're worried about. That one day he's gonna turn that on you."

Eli swallowed. He *had* proof, but he couldn't offer it. He couldn't exactly explain their sex life to Jenny, could he? The way

Rob was so accepting of what Eli wanted, even though he didn't get it. The way Rob was accepting of *Eli*, even when Eli was way outside of Rob's experience zone. The way Rob was turned on by Eli taking control—the way that Eli could dominate Rob, could cuff him and make him crawl on the floor, could collar him and order him around, could tie him down and fuck him with fingers and toys until Rob *shattered*—

He couldn't explain any of that to Jenny, vanilla Jenny, who'd gone into fits of giggles when there'd been an off-screen blowjob on *Game of Thrones* and called it kinky. She'd be horrified if she knew what Rob and Eli did, and the way round they did it.

Rob had called Eli a switch once. Eli just knew he liked to fuck and be fucked, and when he did the fucking, it was all about control. And he knew, with just as much certainty, Rob *seriously* got off on that.

How was that guy going to turn abusive? When it was Eli handcuffing him to the bedframe and beating him with a belt when he got out of line?

"Can we just accept," Eli said quietly, "that I'm not stupid?"

Jenny's face tightened; her hand dropped to her swollen stomach, pushing insistently at the confines of her dress.

"You don't have to be stupid," she said quietly.

Eli winced, held up a T-shirt with a rude slogan, and tried to change the subject. "How about this for Uncle Harry?"

"YOU *CAN'T!*"

"But it's perfect!"

"Oh my God, Dad'll *murder* you!"

"But Rob'll love it!"

"And he'll wear it round the house and Dad'll kill the both of you and bury you under the patio!"

Despite her protests, Jenny was bright red in the face and giggling. The sombre mood had lifted after buying for all the family and having lunch. Now they were working on friends—and Eli and Jenny had a similarly sadistic sense of humour when it came to friends and other halves. *Nice* presents were for family and fusty old aunties. Totally inappropriate presents were for friends.

And Eli had found the *perfect* T-shirt for Rob. *Fuck the police* in bold white letters on the front of a black T-shirt…and then *because who doesn't like a man in uniform?* on the back.

"It's," Eli insisted, "perfect." He put the T-shirt back and started rummaging for one in a large. The short sleeves were clingy, too, so there was a totally selfish element to it. Big biceps and tight black T-shirts? Yes. Just yes.

"You're dead. You're *so* dead."

"It's worth it," Eli insisted, finding the right size and beaming at his sister. "Come on, help me find one for his brother."

"What's his brother like?"

"Like Rob but a stoner," Eli said.

Jenny winced.

"Give over, Jen. Help me look."

She started to pick reluctantly through the rails. "Should I…should I get Greg something?"

"Not unless it's a restraining order," Eli said firmly. "You don't need that guy in Flora's life or yours. Or Baby's. Are you going to tell me if it's a boy or a girl yet?"

"*I* don't know," Jenny said. "And anyway, why do *you* care? I would have thought—"

"Because I want to think up names," Eli interrupted.

"Well, I want a surprise," Jenny said. "Though I'm hoping for another girl, because Greg's not interested at all in Flora and I reckon he won't be interested in a daughter."

"Greg's a shit. What about names?"

"Oh, Rose if it's a girl, but I don't know about a boy," Jenny said, waving a hand airily. "You know, you would be a great—"

"No, Jen."

"You'd make a great father," Jenny insisted. "Eli, seriously, don't blow it off! You could find a nice guy, and—"

"Already did."

"Not *Rob*, someone like—"

"I *want* Rob," Eli snapped. "Jenny, seriously, drop it. You don't know Rob. You—"

"I know enough."

"You sound like Dad."

Jenny scowled and dropped the sleeve of a T-shirt she was reading. "Grow up, Eli."

"I'm not the one who—" Eli started, then thought better of it.

"Who *what*?"

"I just don't get why everyone's ragging on at me for Rob, because he's got a bit of a history—"

"A *bit*?"

"—and he looks…okay, like he looks—and nobody's putting, you know, two and two together to make four and remembering that you were dating that good-looking, successful, totally average guy who turned out to be a girlfriend-beater? I mean, come *on*," Eli implored. "People aren't what they seem. Aren't I evidence enough of that?"

Jenny was quiet for a long time, staring absently at the shirts. Her face was vacant, her eyes seeing something in the middle-distance.

Eli moved away to peer at more shirts. He hated having to say it. He really did, but it was *true*. They were all so paranoid about Rob, and yet Mum and Dad had *loved* Greg until the first time Jenny had turned up on the doorstep with Flora, both in their pyjamas and Jenny with a huge shiner covering most of her face.

Eli just wanted them to know *better* this time. Rob wasn't perfect, Rob was nowhere close to perfect, but Eli loved the fuck out of him and he *knew* Rob. He was soft and sleepy first thing in the morning, he would break your arm for suggesting he cuddled but he *did* cuddle, he kept white bread in his cupboard for Eli's morning toast even though he couldn't stand it…

Jenny shrieked. A pair of arms slammed around Eli's shoulders and chest, seizing him in a bear hug, one huge hand coming to grip his throat and a wall of muscle smashing into his back so he was left pinned and helpless in the hold.

"Eli fucking Bell," a deep voice snarled in his ear, "fancy seeing you here, you fucking bender!"

CHAPTER 3

THEN THE VOICE laughed.

"Danny, let go!" Eli protested. The hands slackened, and he shook them off, only to be spun by the shoulder and bear-hugged from the front instead. "Jesus, and you call *me* a bender. Get off me before I catch something."

Danny Hawkes, Rob's effusive younger brother, beamed. It was all Danny did, in Eli's experience. He had a huge, stupid smile, chin-length dark hair roughly twisted into the beginnings of dread-locks, and calculating dark eyes.

"What'cha gonna catch that you reckon Rob ain't got!" Danny jeered, and Eli called him a twat and smacked him in the shoulder.

Danny simultaneously looked a lot like Rob, and nothing like him. All his features were recognisably Rob's, but subtly shifted—the dark eyebrows were less severe, the mouth crooked up instead of down, the set of his shoulders slightly narrower and his build more wiry than purely muscular. He was the same height, and probably weighed a metric ton due to the fact that Eli knew perfectly well both Hawkes brothers were all muscle and bone. He wasn't tattooed, as far as Eli knew, but metal glinted in his eyebrow and from the ring in the side of his nose.

It was when Danny moved—or talked, or laughed, or frowned—that he became Rob's twin. Their mannerisms were near-identical. They had the same huffing way of laughing, where the noise emerged before the smile. They had the same way of smiling, ducking the head before letting the mouth move. They had the same way of stilling right before getting angry, that momentary freeze when a calculating stare would be levelled on the enemy.

And they lounged on Eli the same, Danny draping an arm across Eli's shoulders and pressing his weight down, grinning at a still-startled Jenny. "Who's the bird?" he asked. "Don't tell me a pouf like you pulled a pussy?"

Jenny drew herself up. "I'm his *sister*," she snarled.

"Oh right, yeah, same bitchface," Danny snorted, and stepped back, shaking Eli's shoulder. "What you doing, eh? Didn't think to see you out 'ere."

"Same to you—shoplifting?"

"*Working*, y'berk," Danny said, and smirked. "Though if you fancy a smoke, I got a bit here somewhere…"

"Explains the smell," Eli said dryly. "And I don't do weed, you know that."

"Suit yoursel'. How about you, miss?"

Jenny's answer was to give him a withering look.

Danny chortled.

"Ne'er mind, then."

"You work?" Eli asked, trying to distract him. "Where?"

"Christmas job at the cinema," Danny said, shrugging. "I owe Rob rent and weed money so figured I needed to go legit for a while."

Eli rolled his eyes. Rob was an extremely casual dealer—if he had a bit extra, or was in need of a bit of cash, he sold weed. Danny, on the other hand, Eli was fairly sure was growing the damn stuff. He constantly smelled of it, and had way too much money for someone who had a different job every month.

"Speaking of our Rob, what've you done, eh, he was selling the last of his last night and said he weren't gonna be buying any more!"

"Good," Eli said. "I told him I don't like the drugs."

"It's just weed, t'ain't chang or—"

"I don't care," Eli said flatly. "I don't want him smoking it." Danny's words warmed him though—because he'd mentioned it to Rob rather than tried to get him to quit proper. He hadn't wanted to push his luck, or make Rob think only six months in that Eli was trying to change him. And it *was* just weed—Eli was more afraid Rob was rubbing shoulders with proper druggies, proper smackheads and the like, and would get drawn into it. Weed Eli could tolerate. Harder stuff...no.

Danny snorted again and cuffed Eli lightly around the head. "You're a good influence, an' that's a *bad* influence. You'll have him getting a proper job next, or doing some course!"

"I'd prefer it," Eli admitted, and ducked the next cuff. "Sod off, you great oaf!"

"Watch it, midget, I could wipe the floor wi' you." Danny smirked.

"Nah, 'cause then Rob'd kick your arse," Eli mock-grumbled.

Danny's face lit up in a laugh.

"Prob'ly right," he admitted.

"What do you want, anyway?" Danny had seen him around plenty in the city centre—Danny was a noticeable guy, with the short dreads and the spliff-smell—and didn't typically do much more than bellow Eli's name and wave.

"Need you to stash this," Danny said, producing a box from within his jacket.

Jenny audibly sucked in her breath.

"What is it?" Eli asked warily.

"Rob's present," Danny said, then rolled his eyes. "It's *legal*, you twat. Open it if you want. Only I'm shit at wrapping stuff so tape it back together if you do. Guy's like a fucking bloodhound for shit he ain't meant to find, so I want it out the way, yeah?"

Eli shook it gingerly. It rattled. "What's in it?"

"New watch," Danny said, shrugging. "Like I said, look f'you want. Just keep it hidden."

Eli nodded, shoving it in his backpack haphazardly.

"So," Danny said, the ear-to-ear grin reappearing. "What you getting him, then? Something fucking disgusting, I bet."

"No, actually. Something he'll enjoy for a bit longer than a half hour in his room."

"Half an hour my arse, way he walks after you're done with him!"
Jenny went a funny shade of pink.

Eli decided not to dignify Danny's jeer with an answer, and
showed him the T-shirt.

"*Nice*," Danny said approvingly. "But give me a bird in a sexy
nurse outfit any day."

"The tragedy of being straight," Eli quipped. Danny sniggered.
Then—to Eli's horror—he dropped the bomb.

"Still coming up to Scotland for Christmas, then? Rob's been
tellin' our Stella all about you."

Jenny stiffened. "What." Her voice was like ice, and suddenly—where she had been lurking five or six feet away—she was
right by Eli's elbow.

Eli groaned.

"Eli's coming to our Aunt Stella's with us for Christmas,"
Danny said cheerily, then side-eyed Eli suspiciously. "You *are*,
right? Don't you fuckin' flake out on us, Bell."

"Eli," Jenny said.

"Yes," Eli replied—to Danny. He avoided looking at his sister.
"Yes, I'm still coming." Danny's face lit up, and he started chatter-
ing about how good it was going to be—and only then did Eli dare
raise his eyes to his sister's face.

His sister's cold, shuttered face.

Because—well…he hadn't actually told his family yet.

"*WHAT!*" MUM SAID.

She looked almost comical, the horrified expression topping
her flowery apron and her arms wrist-deep in a bowl of dough.
Her gaze was piercing though, and Eli squirmed uncomfortably
against the counter.

"Thanks, Jenny," he said sourly, and Jenny glowered at him.

"Oh, fuck off," she said coarsely.

"Jennifer!"

"He's going to spend Christmas with *them*!" Jenny cried, and it was almost in a wail. "Christmas is for *family*, and—"

"And Rob hasn't got much family, so it's the perfect opportunity for me to meet them," Eli said coldly.

"In Scotland?"

"That's where his aunt and uncle live. He's my boyfriend, it's perfectly normal to spend Christmas with your b—"

"What about his parents?" Mum demanded.

Eli swallowed and ground his teeth. "I don't know."

"Right," she said. "So you're going to spend Christmas with this boyfriend that you know so very well—"

"I'm *going*. I'm an adult, I can decide where I spend my time!"

"And we are all adults and can voice our disagreement!" Mum snapped. "Eli, for goodness' sake, you're going to the other end of the country—no, a *different* country—with…with a…"

"A *what*?"

The kitchen door banged. "What the hell is going on here?" Dad. Of course. It was the weekend, and he'd been gardening.

"Eli's spending Christmas with Rob in Scotland!" Jenny blurted out before Eli could stop her.

"Jen!"

"What?"

Dad's boom was identical to Mum's aside from the pitch of it, and Eli groaned.

"Eli, for God's sake, you're not—" Dad started.

"Yes I am," Eli said firmly. "Rob is my boyfriend and—"

"Of *six months*, and quite frankly, I am not happy about my—my son going God only knows where with someone like Hawkes!"

Eli ground his teeth and hunched his shoulders, feeling the usual sting when Dad stuttered over *son*. How many years did he need?

"I know it's your first Christmas and it feels special," Mum said, a bit more diplomatically, "but you and Rob haven't been together all that long, and—"

"And I'm going."

"No you're bloody well not," Dad snarled.

"What you gonna do, arrest me?" Eli demanded, jutting his

chin out. "I'm not a child, I'm not mentally retarded, I can make my own fucking decisions and when Rob asked if I'd like to go, my decision was yes! And it's still yes, so you can all—"

"Don't use that tone in my house!"

"Don't talk smack about my boyfriend all the fucking time!"

"Eli!" Mum scolded.

"I'm *sick* of this!" Eli exploded, throwing his hands up. "I'm sick of it, all you ever do is rag on him and tell me to leave him and how he's bad news, you all freak out if I have him here overnight or I stay at his flat, you don't want me going *anywhere* with him, and you don't even know him, you don't—"

"I know enough," Dad snarled.

"You know a record on a computer screen," Eli snapped. "You know rumours and hearsay around your stations—and if you *did* look up Rob's criminal record, that's a *total* violation, you had no—what is it, no policing purpose?—no good reason to."

Dad went scarlet. "Are you accusing me of—"

"Should I be?"

"Stop it, both of you!" Mum shouted, banging the bowl of dough on the counter loudly to get their attention. "Now calm down. Everyone just *calm down*."

Eli stared at the oven, and willed it to explode.

"Right," Mum said, rinsing her hands off. "Eli, you must understand why we're upset. Christmas is a time for family, and we don't feel you've known Rob long enough for him to be family…"

"Because you won't let him be!"

"Quiet!" Mum barked.

Eli curled his lip.

"Christmas is for family," Mum repeated into the ensuing silence. "And yes, Eli, I would prefer you were home with us. At the end of the day, we don't trust Rob yet. No, *quiet*! But we also have to accept that you are an adult and free to make your own choices, however much we disagree with them."

"Louise!" Dad protested.

"No, Samuel, that's the truth," Mum snapped. "Eli, we aren't happy about it, but of course you can do what you feel is best for

Christmas. Just…think hard about it, yes?"

"I have," Eli said coldly. "I know Rob better than any of you. I want to go, I'm thrilled he's asked me, and I'm going. End of story."

"For how long?" Dad demanded. "Scotland's not exactly the other side of Huddersfield!"

"For a week," Eli said, and bit back an angry retort when Dad visibly swelled. "We're staying with his aunt and uncle and cousins. His brother's coming, too, so you don't have to worry about him beating me up in the car on the way there," he added viciously.

"Eli, stop it," Mum scolded.

"No. You fucking—"

"Eli!"

"—stop it, all of you! Rob is a nice guy. Yeah, he's a bit rough around the edges—"

"Oh, right, yeah, a bit," Jenny said acidly.

"—but he's good to me, *really* good to me, he's good as gold and he's kind and supportive and funny, and he—he *supports* me, he really does, he's really accepting of me, and if you'd just…just stop judging him on the other stuff and—"

"The other stuff? Eli, that includes violence. He's a drug addict and a—"

"He's not an addict, he smokes the odd spliff now and then, that's it," Eli snapped. "And he's never once even threatened me—" He didn't think it would be a good time to mention that Rob *had* threatened him, in the bedroom while playing their sex games, and Eli had enjoyed the fuck out of it. "—and if you would just stop staring at his police record and actually get to *know* him, get to see how he is with *me*—"

"Then let us."

Eli was brought up short by his mother's words. "What?"

"Let us," she said. "Invite him to dinner. Let's meet him properly, as a family, instead of you smuggling him in and out like stolen goods and getting at your father's throat about it."

"That's not *my* fault, I—"

"I have had enough of arguing about this, Eli!" Mum said sharply. "You keep insisting we're wrong about him, so let's see the proof.

Have him over, and let's actually sit down and talk to him."

Eli nodded jerkily, mind already spinning. "Fine," he bit out. But it wasn't, because there was no way Rob was going to agree to this. Eli was going to have to force him, or manipulate him. Maybe give the order in a scene, or promise a scene after the dinner. Or—

He turned on his heel and headed for the door.

"Eli!"

"I'm going to Rob's," he said.

"Oh for God's sake—"

"How else am I meant to tell him he's coming over?" Eli shouted over his shoulder, jogging upstairs. His brain was turning it over in earnest. He'd need time, that was the big thing—he'd need to get Rob well and truly under control before telling him to come to this dinner, or Rob would throw the idea right out.

He tossed his overnight bag onto his bed and started to stuff it, sending only a perfunctory text to Rob as warning, without a single emoticon, kiss, or explanation. Just the bare bones fact—and that should be enough to warn Rob all on its own.

Coming over.

CHAPTER 4

ROB LIVED CLEAR across the city in a run-down area of Parson Cross, in a grubby but spacious flat he shared with his brother Danny. The drive was unpleasantly long, in Eli's esteemed opinion, but Rob had a reputation locally, and, by daring to block his Suzuki in, Eli could label his car as belonging to someone in Rob Hawkes' social circle. So at least he'd have all his tyres and glass intact when he came back to it.

The flat was on the top floor, up a narrow and dirty stairwell that usually stank of piss and weed. Eli hated the jog up, for the risk of some druggie thinking he'd have cash, or the local fucknut kids hanging about by the bins at the bottom—but the early evening created an odd lull at this time, and he was undisturbed.

Except by the music blaring from behind the door, the brass number nine—hanging by a single nail, and upside-down—shaking with the force of it.

Eli sighed, and hammered his fist on the wood. Repeatedly. And as loudly as possible. "Rob!" he shouted, in feeble hope Rob would do that thing of hearing your own name across a noisy, crowded room, but not convinced he would.

"Oi!"

Eli rolled his eyes and turned as the door to number ten flew open.

"'E's been playin' tha' fuckin' crap all fuckin' day!" the neighbour shrieked. She was a woman in her mid-forties, perhaps early fifties, with crooked yellow teeth and a fag end permanently attached to her lower lip. She'd once come right up to jab her finger in Eli's chest, and she'd faintly smelled of piss herself. Uncharitably, Eli wondered if she was the one responsible for the stairwell.

"Yeah, well, I'm not his handler," Eli grumbled, still knocking.

"'E's a fuckin' nuisance!" she shrilled. "You tell 'im, you tell 'im tha' I'll—"

The door jerked away from Eli's fist; the music spilled deafeningly onto the tiled landing, and Rob's frame loomed in the open doorway. "You'll what?" he sneered. He was wearing his T-shirt and boxers, a remote control dangling from one hand and a beer bottle cold and half-empty in the other. He'd gained a black eye from somewhere, and a dark mark on his lip that might have been a split. But more importantly, those long, muscled legs were on full view, and Eli unashamedly ogled.

"Turn it tha' fuck off!" the neighbour bellowed.

Rob snorted, the remote control clicked, and the music stopped.

"There, you fucking happy?"

"I'll 'ave the cops out on you!" she squalled. "Tha' racket all day and night, tha' friend o' yours, tha' smell—you're growing canny i' there, don't you think I don't know!"

"Oh, fuck off, you old bag," Rob scoffed, stepping aside and drawing Eli in by a hand on his shoulder.

"I see your neighbourly relations aren't any better," Eli remarked tartly as Rob shut the door on her complaining and turned the music back on—albeit at a less deafening volume.

"Couldn't get better if I killed her."

"Uh-huh. Is that what happened to your face?"

"Nah—local got a bit lively," Rob said flippantly. "So Danny's out. Just you and me. You know the rules."

Eli snorted, dropping his bag on the hall floor. The flat was a two-bed, with a narrow hall and what it lacked in being just about the dampest, draughtiest flat Eli had ever seen, it made up for in space. For a top-floor job in Parson Cross, it had sizeable rooms. "I'm not even here five minutes and you want me to take my clothes off?" he said testily.

Rob raised his eyebrows. "That's the rules. You agreed to them."

"Yeah, well, I'm really not in the—"

"If they were suggestions, I'd call 'em such. Now you gonna do as you're fucking told, or do I have to—"

"Red."

Eli's voice was sharp—sharper than he'd intended, and he winced.

Rob's jaw audibly clicked shut, then he turned and vanished into the kitchen. Eli groaned, rubbing both hands over his face and through his hair before exhaling heavily.

"Rob," he called. "I—"

"Here." Rob rematerialised with a can of Carlsberg, Eli's usual poison here, and steered him into the living room. The TV was paused on a scene from Full Metal Jacket, a couple of dumbbells on the floor testimony to what Rob had been doing when Eli had shown up. Then Eli was walked right past the debris and pushed to sit on the sofa.

"I'm—*oh-my-fucking-God,*" he groaned as Rob's hands clamped down firmly on his shoulders and *squeezed.* The pressure burst the tension like a boil, and he sagged in Rob's grip, groping for the arm of the sofa to steady himself.

"What's up." Rob's tone was flat and factual.

Eli bit his lip.

"I didn't mean to snap at you," he admitted.

"Not what I asked."

Eli blew upwards into his hair and rolled his head back into Rob's hands as the massage migrated up his spine to the base of his skull. "So Danny ambushed me and Jenny shopping, and let slip I was planning to come with you for Christmas…and I hadn't, you know, actually got round to *telling* them yet…"

"Ah."

"Yeah. There was a huge row," Eli mumbled. "Dad just about flipped his shit and tried to ban me from coming to see you again—"

Rob snorted and laughed. The deep sound brought a reluctant

smile to Eli's own face, and he reached over his shoulder to squeeze one of Rob's wrists.

"I didn't exactly take that one well," he admitted. "And then there was all the usual crap about you and everything, and I just— urgh, I had to get away."

Rob shifted on the sofa until Eli was bracketed by his legs on either side. Sighing, Eli allowed himself to be pulled back into Rob's chest, the heavy weight of his arms comforting and the enclosure formed by his raised thighs either side of Eli's hips like a shield.

"I'm sorry I snapped," Eli mumbled.

Rob just hummed and butted his chin lightly against Eli's ear in an oddly nuzzling sort of motion.

"I didn't mean to use a safeword."

Rob huffed. "We've talked about this," he said, his voice rumbling deep in his chest. "Rules are only rules as long as you *don't* safeword. No safeword, no option."

"Yeah, but—"

"No," Rob interrupted firmly. "If you hadn't used it, I would have forced you to strip. You know I can."

Eli shifted, the memory of the first time he'd played *that* game with Rob still a hot flush in the base of his gut. "Yeah," he murmured lowly. "It was fucking hot, too."

Rob smirked against his ear. "Aye," he agreed, "but this time you didn't want to play, and as it's one of the rules, it's the only way you've got of telling me you're not fucking kidding and you're genuinely not up for it. Otherwise I'm just gonna think you're fucking with me again."

Eli pulled a face, stroking his hand along Rob's arm. Both arms were locked around his chest, and Eli traced the patterns of ink under the hair. "It just feels stupid, safewording outside the bedroom, for fucking *clothes*," he grumbled.

"Shut it." Rob's voice was suddenly harsh and sharp.

Eli flinched.

"I mean it. If I can't fucking trust you to use them when you don't want the rules to apply, then it's all off."

Eli winced, and broke Rob's hold to turn around and clasp his head between both hands. The kiss was gentle, Rob barely responding, and Eli pressed his nose into Rob's cheek, closing his eyes to whisper, "Don't fucking *say* that."

"It's true." Rob clasped both hands around the back of Eli's neck, pulling him back until all Eli could see were those incredible, intense grey-white eyes. "I *have* to be able to trust you to use them, Eli," Rob said slowly, his voice deep and rolling, the words cut and deliberate. "Any rule, any place, any time, when*ever* you are genuinely telling me to stop. Use. Them."

Eli felt pinned by Rob's eyes, unable to breathe under the sheer weight of his gaze. He swallowed dumbly before pressing forward to kiss Rob's lips again and whisper, "I will," there like a fervent prayer.

Rob's expression didn't flicker, and Eli grimaced.

"I *will*," he insisted. "I did, didn't I? I just blurted it out and felt stupid *after*, I still said it. And...and anyway, I know I'm being silly, it's just...I was grumpy and...I think I meant to use amber instead of red. Just put you on hold for ten minutes?"

Rob raised an eyebrow; Eli kissed it, and looped both arms around Rob's neck.

"You were hugging all the grumpiness out of me," he murmured. "Do it again."

Rob chuckled then. Eli smiled into his cheek, pleased with himself for lifting the sudden severity that had settled. Rob's grip tightened and he shifted until they were lying down, Eli wriggling into the hard contours of muscle and powerful joints until he found a comfortable place. Rob clicked the film back into life, and Eli hummed as he felt a kiss being pressed to the top of his head.

"Sorry," he whispered. "I'm still getting used to you and your rules."

Rob snorted. "You're the one who fucking needs 'em, you kinky shit."

"Oh, like you can talk!" Eli protested, smacking Rob's chest. "I have handcuffs, Rob, not a whole *chain*!"

"It's a bike chain!"

"With a *collar*!"

They were both laughing by that point, Rob's deep guffaws

rocking Eli's upper body against his ribs and chest. Eli kissed the tattooed heart affectionately and pulled himself further up to nuzzle Rob's stubble with his nose.

"You need them, too, the words," he said. "Or you'd not have been able to stop me that time with the flogger."

Rob grimaced. "Oh, fuck, I forgot about that. Fucker *stung*."

"Do I *ever* get a second chance with that?"

"Nope," Rob said in an easy drawl. "No way was that going to turn hot. There's pain and then there's *pain*, you know?"

Eli chewed on his lip, studying Rob's face, then said, "Can I try something else?"

"What, now?"

"Yeah."

"After you already safeworded once?"

"I mean try something *to you*."

Rob's wary expression eased. "I guess so."

Eli slid off that rock-solid body to perch on the coffee table.

"I want you to go and get that collar and chain," he said lowly.

Rob raised his eyebrows, but nodded and rolled off the sofa in one fluid motion. His steps were heavy on the boards, and Eli listened to him rummaging in the next room for a near minute before coming back with a cardboard box. The chain was a dark coil inside, a simple brown collar attached to one end—a dog collar, Eli suspected, and when he picked it up, it was made of a strong, rough leather.

"Take off your clothes."

"All of them?"

"All of them. And don't ask questions."

A fleeting smirk crossed Rob's face, but then his T-shirt obscured it. He wasted no time, and in about half a second, was standing in full naked glory in front of the coffee table. He wasn't entirely soft either.

Eli stroked his fingers lightly over that flushed cock.

"Kneel."

Rob knelt. Eli fisted a hand into his hair and kissed him roughly, forcing his mouth to yield to it. The taste of cheap Grolsch was unpleasant, and Eli wrinkled his nose.

"You'll have to have something else," he muttered. "Neck." The collar slid shut satisfyingly around Rob's throat, and Eli kissed the skin above it before sitting back and surveying him coolly. Or at least, trying to—the sight of the collar was unexpectedly hot, and Rob just kneeling there in front of him, completely naked...

"Anything else?"

Eli slapped him. Rob's face snapped to the side, and he didn't move. His cock twitched, and Eli licked his lips before grinning. "I said don't ask questions," he whispered, pitching his voice as slow and low as he dared.

Rob could only be teased so much. He could—and Eli knew it from experience—come without being touched at all. And Eli didn't want to give him that pleasure *too* soon.

He tested the weight of the chain in his hand before standing up. Rob's head turned back towards him, but didn't lift, and Eli took an experimental pace away, wondering if Rob would dare to stand, or—

He shuffled forward on his knees, one hand dropping to the carpet. Eli beamed.

"Good," he praised, raking a hand through that dark hair gently. "Now listen. For the next hour, you will do exactly as I tell you. You will agree to anything I ask of you, no matter what it is. The *only* way out is a safeword. Repeat them."

This—technically—was Rob's rule, the repetition of safewords. Initially, it had been to drill them into Eli's head so he'd remember them in the middle of a game, but since...well, Eli rather appreciated them since. He knew his own kinks could get a bit...heavy. Rob was all about *how* they had sex—when and where and if he could tie Eli up or not. But it was all about *sex*, the act itself. Eli's, his *real* kinks, not his little exhibitionist streak or his thing for being fucked bent over the bathroom counter, were more about control and dominance, either being dominated, or...or getting Rob on the other end of a chain and crawling naked across his own carpet because Eli fucking told him to.

So *since*, Eli kind of liked this rule. It wasn't a kink rule, as Rob called it, it was a real-world rule. One that had absolutely no opt-out clause. If Eli didn't ask, Rob would stop the scene anyway. And Eli, knowing his own kinks could go too far—and indeed, Rob had stopped him before, with the flogger *and* the choker— now appreciated them much more for what they really were.

"Red," Rob said.

"For?"

"Stop. Immediately."

"And?"

"Amber—for a pause, or slowing down."

"And?"

"Green if prompted for permission to continue, or agreement to an activity."

Eli nodded, smoothing Rob's hair before leading him back to the sofa. "Sit there, between my knees," he said softly, pointing at a patch on the carpet. Rob obeyed. "This is what we're gonna play for the next hour. I'm going to tell you what's going to happen about sorting it out this crap between you and my dad. You're going to agree to it, and then you're going to put that mouth to use and relieve the last of my...tension, exactly the way I like it. If you're good, I'll let you play, too. You argue with me, you disobey me, then I'll punish you—and you *won't* like it. Understood?"

Rob nodded, those bright-white eyes fixed on Eli's face.

"Colour?" Eli prompted softly. The question he needed more than Rob did, really—the question...

"Green."

...an answer that told Eli he wasn't going too far. That even when Rob pulled faces or argued or made sounds of distress or pain, he *was* enjoying it and he *did* want it, and Eli wasn't...wasn't *forcing* him. Not *really*.

Eli kissed him, soft and open, and tapped the end of his nose. "Alright," he said. "Here's the deal. You're coming to a family dinner with my folks."

Rob's face *instantly* turned mutinous.

"Don't," Eli warned, jerking the chain sharply and forcing Rob to break eye contact. "You will attend. You will behave yourself. You will not antagonise Dad, and you will not make a fool out of me. If you do, I *will* beat you."

Rob's gaze shifted and hardened.

"Question?"

Rob opened his mouth, then appeared to think better of it, and lowered his face. He kissed Eli's knee through his jeans instead.

"Rob."

"No question. I won't disappoint you."

"Then you'll come?" It was a false question. They both knew what would happen if Rob refused. And apparently Rob wasn't in the mood to play rough, for—

"I'll do as I'm told."

The stilted reply made the pulse in Eli's crotch a little too powerful. He popped the button on his jeans with a snap.

"Good," he praised softly, petting Rob's hair again. "You fighting with my dad makes me angry, Rob. You *know* it does. You're hurting me, you're acting out against me, when you do it."

"I don't mean to."

Eli jerked the chain again. Rob grunted harshly, face downturned.

"You *do* mean to," he said sharply. "You do it on purpose."

"I don't mean to hurt you by doing it," Rob explained in the softest voice Eli had ever heard him use. "I don't mean to make you angry."

Eli felt himself softening, too. Rob's contrite voice was a weapon, and one Eli was defenceless against.

"You're not *bad*," Eli said softly, tugging on Rob's hair and guiding his face to Eli's crotch. "You will come to dinner, you will be a model citizen and boyfriend, you will show them that sweet, caring side of you that *I* see. Then after—if you behave yourself, and I'm not forced to punish you *again*—then we can play whatever game you like."

Rob's hands curled into the edge of the sofa cushions. "Whatever game?"

"Whatever game," Eli promised, pulling on Rob's hair. "Right now, I want your mouth being used the way it's *made* to be used."

Rob's gaze was open, for once, not the stern and calculating stare he usually offered. The brush of his lips over the denim was as searing as though they were on Eli's bare skin before his teeth caught the zip and began to pull.

The flat door slammed. "Oi, faggot! I'm home!"

Rob jerked back; Eli dropped the chain barely in time to let him.

"I wouldn't come in here if I were you, Danny!" Eli yelled hastily, seizing Rob's hair and pressing a kiss to his forehead, pulled wide by his nervous laugh. "Red," he whispered. "End scene."

"Thank fuck for that," Rob muttered, grabbing for his jeans.

A fist hit the living room door. "Are you two doing something fucking vile in there?"

"Yes!" Eli shouted.

"Oh my God! On the *sofa?*"

"Not quite, I'm on the floor!" Rob shouted, pulling his jeans up over his thighs. His cock was still half-hard, and he grimaced as he tucked himself in.

Eli laughed, kissing Rob's neck as he removed the collar.

"Another time, maybe," he said, folding it back into the box.

Rob grinned.

"No shit, you kinky bitch. You were gonna go off the minute I got my tongue on you."

"Maybe," Eli teased.

"You're both fucking disgusting!" Danny bellowed through the door. "Pervs! And who's gonna pay to dry-clean the sofa? *Me!*"

"I'll dry-clean your fucking *face* if you don't shut the fuck up!" Rob yelled, switching the telly off, and wiggling his eyebrows at Eli. "Bedroom?"

"Only if you've fixed the lock."

Rob smirked.

"I *have*, actually," he said, before jerking the living room door open. Danny's horrified face was stuck in a twisted grimace. "Oh, fuck off, like you haven't had one of your hookers on that sofa."

"I fucking haven't!"

"Yeah? Oh shit, no, that were me an' all," Rob said, snapping his fingers.

Danny slapped Rob around the head, and Eli ducked past the bickering brothers to nip into Rob's room and kick the box back under the bed. After a moment, the door snapped shut behind him, and he turned in time to see Rob's grin as he rolled the new lock over and the bolt slid into place.

"I know that face," Eli said, eyeing Rob sceptically. "Unfortunately, that scene's over, and I don't much feel like just spreading my legs for y—"

The sentence was cut off, partly by Rob's teeth around Eli's jugular, and partly by the impact of being tackled bodily onto the bed.

"Fucking spread your fucking legs," Rob snarled, his voice barely high enough in his throat to count as speech at all, "or I'll spread 'em for you."

Eli laughed, tangled both hands into Rob's hair, and spread his fucking legs.

CHAPTER 5

THEY'D MET IN a bar, and it had been fuck at first sight.

Eli would like to claim it was all eyes meeting across a crowded room, and that intense gaze luring him in, but in fact, Rob had started it. The first Eli knew of the man's existence on the face of the earth was the heavy hand on his hip and the body grinding up against his arse. He'd offered a drink; Eli had downed half of it, towed the hulk into the bathrooms, and blown him in one of the cubicles.

Only after, wiping his mouth on the back of his wrist, had Eli looked up and seen those incredible grey-white eyes.

"See you 'round, babe," the man had grinned, tucking himself in and bending to roughly kiss Eli. And then he'd been gone.

Eli hadn't seen him at the bar for nearly a month—and then he'd gone to a different club, and there he'd been with some blond twink in a tight T-shirt. Eli had spent a month dreaming about those eyes and that cock, and had quite literally snagged the stranger by the cotton of his T-shirt and kissed him. Hard.

There'd been another blowjob—in an alley near the club—and then Eli had found out the man's name. And his phone number.

Six months later, and Eli still hadn't tired of this—lying in tangled sheets, sweat cooling on his skin, tracing the tattoos that laced

Rob's skin like pictures of his very soul. The mechanical heart was Eli's favourite, sitting right above Rob's real heart. Eli's fingers strayed there whenever they simply...lay, like this.

Rob usually slept after sex, especially if Eli had wound him up before. And the collar and chain had *definitely* done that, by the way he had fucked after they'd retreated to his room. Now, he dozed, sprawled in the dark sheets like a ghost, skin hot and damp from their exertions. There'd be a shower later, and—Eli shifted in vague discomfort—the sheets would have to be changed. But for now...

Carefully, Eli slid free of the messy nest and made for the desk. Rob used it as a shelf, but there was one drawer Eli had claimed ownership of in those early days of being hauled into Rob's room and simply *possessed* for weekends on end.

He slid the sketchbook and packet of fineliners out, and flipped the book open.

Rob stared back. Or rather, sketches of various parts of his body did—his jaw, his hands, his arse. There was a series of sketches of his right shoulder blade, for which Eli was still trying to design a tattoo. There were even pages upon pages of Rob's cock, fully erect and glistening, from one exhausting Saturday night when Rob had demanded to know why Eli kept following him around 'with that fucking weird book' all the time.

Eli loved to draw. He always had and he always would, one of the few things about him that hadn't changed irreversibly over the years. He had been drawing before he could write, before he could properly hold pencil to paper, and had devoted time and energy to art lessons he couldn't bear to apply to any of his other subjects. Mum had always found it sweet; Dad less so. Neither had really encouraged him beyond calling it a nice hobby, something to be pursued in his spare time and never with any thought to a career.

It was only since—

"What're you—?"

"Ssh," Eli murmured, settling back into the warmth.

The sleepy stir was abated, Rob's arm falling over his knees in a heavy, possessive embrace, and a nose tucked into the edge of his hip with a contented mumble. Eli stroked that messy dark hair, affection pooling in his stomach where desire had prickled earlier in the evening.

Eli turned to a new page. The arm was Rob's right, that naked shoulder exposed, and he decided to try again.

It was Rob who had put the idea in his head one lazy evening watching telly in their underwear when Danny had been elsewhere. "You draw on paper too much," Rob had said.

"Well, what else?"

"I dunno. Walls. Floors. Skin. More fuckin' interesting places than in sketchbooks."

"Skin?" Eli had asked, amused.

"Sure, why the hell not? All tattooists do, and they're artists."

It had been surprisingly good logic from Rob, and that evening Eli had taken the pen and gingerly drawn the silhouette of a hawk on the inside of Rob's wrist. It had been messy, made messier by Rob's hungry attack halfway through, but in the morning Eli had drawn it again and declared it perfect.

When Rob had come to pick him up the following Saturday, the hawk was still there, swollen and beginning to heal.

Ever since, Eli had been trying to design more. His target was the bare skin of Rob's right shoulder—his left had long since been painted over. Most of his back was devoted to a clash of fire and water in a violent and colourful war, but his right shoulder lay naked, and Eli would, when he found the right design, repair it.

"Ch'y'dr'w'n?"

"Sorry?" Eli murmured, pen forming the first splits of skin. Rob had no skin tear design, and Eli was fond of them. What lay beneath, though? The typical cogs and wires? Or something—

"What you drawin'?" Rob slurred, still clearly half-asleep.

Eli paused to scratch Rob's scalp and smile at him, then took up the pen again.

"Just ideas for your shoulder."

"M'see?"

"When I've actually drawn some."

"Too slow…"

"Oh, shut up and go back to sleep."

"Can't," Rob retorted with a distinct note of petulance. "You moved."

"Newsflash," Eli said dryly. "You're really fucked if me moving sets you off."

"That'd be *you*."

Eli laughed when the arm across his lap tightened and Rob's nose began to move from Eli's hip to his thigh to his crotch. "*No*," he said sternly, bending nearly double to kiss Rob's ear. "Stop it, you pest. Let me draw. And if I'm not all fucked out, you certainly are, you've not even got your eyes open."

"M'appreciating your voice."

"Sure," Eli drawled. On a whim, he widened the split on his page and etched an eye into the gap. Not a human one though—something more...feral. Something wilder.

"You should go to school."

"You *what*? You got a teenager fetish? I'm twenty-one!"

"*College*, fuckwit."

"Then say that!"

"Fuck off."

Eli laughed, tapping Rob's nose with the fineliner. He got a scowl for his troubles, and decided, while Rob was in a playful mood..."On your front."

"Already?"

"Shut up, I'm going to draw."

Rob smirked, but shifted back and settled onto his front obediently enough, sliding his arms under the pillow and burying his head in it, the picture of a tired and contented man waiting for a massage.

Or that demi-god again, because *that* pose only highlighted his biceps. Eli paused, chewing on his lip, then thought better of it. Best to let Rob rile *himself* up, rather than do it for him. A man couldn't be allowed to just expect a handjob whenever he looked good, after all.

"Why didn't you go to college?" Rob asked, that sleepy slur back in his voice. "Your old tos—"

"Rob."

"—your dad must've wanted you to."

Eli shrugged. "Not art college. It's just a silly hobby to Dad. And after school…yeah, well, after school I didn't want to go anywhere near college. Mum and Dad wanted me to go to university, but I thought it would just be more of the same shit, so I didn't go."

"Stupid." The word was smothered in the pillow.

Eli laughed and put pen to skin, soothing the shiver with the pads of his fingers before beginning to sketch.

"It's not stupid, it's just…Dad's practical," Eli said. "He wanted me to go off to university and become an accountant—you know, something dull that would keep me in a well-paid job forever. But after the nightmare that was school, I just couldn't face trying uni. So I didn't go."

"Still stupid," Rob mumbled. "Y'r good. Y'should go. Be a proper artist'n shit."

Eli smiled, kissing the nape of his neck before finishing the tears. A few of them, like his shoulder had been shredded. He added an experimental claw peeking out of one, and decided he liked the look of it. But multiple claws were needed, like some horrible alien crab-spider-thing was going to come wriggling out, maybe—

"M'serious," Rob breathed, the exhale long and peaceful. "You're wasted in th'shop. You're bored, I've seen you. Y'should go to college and do what you like. Fuck other people."

Eli chuckled. "You're good at that."

"Fuckin' people?"

"Making them fuck off."

"Mm."

"Were you always?" Eli asked on a sudden whim. "Good at making people go away?" Jealously, it suddenly occurred to Eli—and how hadn't it before?—that Rob mustn't understand what it was like to be bullied, to be beaten up by other kids when you were just seven years old because they found out you were a total *freak*—

"Nah."

Eli jumped, the pen going awry. He sighed but continued. "No?"

Rob shifted. His face, twisted to the side, creased.

"Rob?"

"Never told you much about me mam, did I?"

Eli licked his lips. "I—no."

He knew, really, nothing. Beyond Danny, and an aunt and some cousins in Scotland, he didn't know the first thing about the Hawkes, and the way Rob had muttered 'nah' like that...

"Rob?"

"Mam were shit."

Eli blinked and paused in his drawing.

"Five kids, five blokes, total fuckin' mayhem. Two of 'em taken off her, 'cause she couldn't kick the smack habit. One bloke got glassed in a pub and died, and the social were sniffin' around her three kids, so she packed 'em up and moved down t' Leeds, and then she met Liam. And Liam...fuck, man, Mam weren't nice but Liam were a right nasty shit. Only bloke she stayed with any length of time, and only then 'cause she were scared."

"He was abusive?" Eli whispered.

"Whole fuckin' family were abusive, Eli, don't go thinking my mam were innocent. But Liam were a nasty bugger."

"You...you remember him?"

Rob smirked. "Remember him? He's me fucking father."

Eli stilled. "Oh."

"Yeah. Me an' Danny, only two of Mam's seven to have the same old man. I was four when Danny showed up, and I were old enough by then. Older lot bullied me, but I looked at Danny and I thought, fuck it, this one's mine. He were my baby brother, not theirs, they couldn't have 'im. So it were me and Danny, right from the beginning."

"What...what happened to...to your mum? And Liam?"

"Fuck knows about him, he fucked off years ago. I was about ten, I dunno. And Mam's in the slammer, en't she? They put 'er away when I were about fourteen, fifteen. Can't even remember what for now, but every time she comes out, she does shit again and goes right back in. Your old man thinks I'm a thug, he ought've met me mam."

"So you went into care? You and Danny? Or did you go back to Scotland?"

"Care," Rob said. "Social didn't think our Stella were right good for kids herself. Weren't for long, though, I bailed when I were seventeen and took Danny with me. They couldn't keep him, he kept running away to my flat. Left, too, just…to get outta Leeds, you know? Away from all the crap."

Eli started to draw again, softening the edges of the tears. The monster seemed macabre now, and not what he had hoped. He switched back to his original idea, drawing a new gap further up and beginning to outline the edges of an eye.

"Do you still see any of them? Your parents and your siblings?"

Rob's laugh was a harsh bark.

"Is that a no?"

"S'a fuck no. Cunts. S'just me an' Danny, way it oughta be."

Eli kissed the back of Rob's head, shifting so he was straddling the backs of Rob's thighs. "And me now," he said quietly, tapping one of the existing tattoos with his pen before returning to his task. "Not just you and Danny anymore."

Rob's smirk softened into a smile. His eyes were closed, and his back began to relax again under Eli's hands.

"You know, I'd have probably hated you if we'd met in school."

Rob snorted. "I'd've ignored you."

"You'd have bullied me."

"Maybe," Rob said, "but then, a weedy girly kid two or three years below me, even for me that were a bit low. Danny might've, mind, he liked punching above his weight."

Eli scoffed. "I could've taken Danny."

"You shittin' me? Kid was fuckin' feral. Worse'n me as a teenager, I woulda sworn t'you then he'd have been locked up, not me."

Eli filled in the eye and spoke as carefully as he drew. "You never told me what you went to prison for." In truth, he hadn't quite dared to ask. Part of him hadn't wanted to know.

"Assault."

"Assault?"

"Yeah. Pub brawl. Glassed a bloke, put him in a coma for a week. Judge made an example out of me."

Eli grimaced and stared at the eye. After a moment, he said, "Why?"

"Why what?"

"Why'd you hit him?"

"'Cause I was pissed. Pissed up and pissed off."

"So he didn't—"

"Look, Eli, I'm not gonna defend it. There's no heroism, there's no excuse, no...justice abortion or whatever."

Eli snorted and smiled despite himself. "Miscarriage of justice."

"Yeah, whatever."

Eli hummed, stroking his fingers over his decision. It was off. He didn't like it anymore, so dropped the pen back onto the abandoned sketchbook, heaving himself off Rob's thighs and settling back into the sheets. Rob lifted an arm, and Eli drew it over himself, allowing the wriggle and the warm nose that settled in the crook of his neck.

"If you do anything that puts you back in prison," Eli whispered, "I'll leave you."

The words sounded final—and they were. Thing was, Eli didn't believe in long-distance relationships, especially when the separation was by choice. And as much as Rob made him feel...made him feel like anything and everything was possible, like he'd never been born wrong or been an outcast at all, made him feel like he was the most confident, incredible, beautiful man on earth—

"I won't do that."

Rob's arm tightened. Eli waited. And then, finally, the deep voice washed across his neck, heavy and promising. "Then I won't go back to prison."

CHAPTER 6

ELI BARELY GOT home in time for dinner, and judging by the sour look his father gave him when he arrived, they all knew where he'd been.

Fuck it, was Eli's opinion on the matter. If he wanted to spend the night with his boyfriend, then he could. He was twenty-fucking-one, for God's sake, he was well past old enough to make his own decisions about who to date.

He meandered upstairs, noting Jenny's absence by the open door to her room and the basket of clean laundry Dad had put in the doorway. Rob would piss himself laughing if he knew how house-husbandy Chief Inspector Bell really was. Eli was fairly sure Rob still had to read the manual to operate the washing machine in his flat.

Not that Eli minded. It meant Rob never offered to wash his clothes before he went home, which meant—

He dropped his bag on his bed, and lifted the neck of his T-shirt to inhale the leftover smell of Rob. Pure Rob—the man didn't bother with deodorant, referring to it scornfully as 'perfume for poufters.' A statement Eli found hilariously ironic, really.

"Eli!"

Eli jumped and whirled on his heel; Mum beamed at him from the landing, an armload of crumpled towels in her arms, obviously destined for the next wash.

"When did you get home, dear?"

"Just now."

"Just in time for dinner then—your father's decided to experiment again, thinks he *can* master the art of a decent paella…"

"Why doesn't he just buy it out the packet like everyone else?" Eli grumbled.

"Oh, you know what he's like," Mum tutted fondly, and shooed him ahead of her. "Go on, help him set the table. Jenny's had to stay at home, she's not feeling too well and little Flora's got a tummy bug, bless her…"

Eli really thought he ought to film Mum's…mumsing one day for Rob. He'd never believe it otherwise, he'd scoff at the idea of the head of forensics saying things like *tummy bug*. Still, Mum was in a good mood, which meant Dad couldn't be in too foul of a one, so Eli just nodded, made the appropriate agreeing noises, and did as he was told.

He found Dad in the admittedly impressive kitchen. It was a cavernous room at the back of the house, big enough to comfortably fit the dining table and utility corner. The table had already been set for three. Eli had been expected, at least, so he guessed he'd staved off a row by showing up at all.

"Back, then?" Dad grunted, peering into the giant wok he had appropriated for his cooking mission.

"Mm," Eli said, deciding tiredly he didn't really want a fight. He opened the fridge instead and hunted for orange juice.

"Been at Hawkes'?"

Eli rolled his eyes at the grapes. "Yes," he said flatly.

"Oh, don't you two start," Mum scolded, scurrying in with the towels and stuffing them unceremoniously into the washing machine.

"I'm not starting anything," Eli protested. "Dad asked if I was at *Rob's*, and I said yes. That's all."

"Did you have a nice time?" Mum asked, shooting his father a stern look. Eli rolled his eyes and took his juice to the table. A nice time? What was he, six?

"Yes," he repeated stonily. "How was your day?"

"Fine," Dad said brusquely, clattering the cutlery as he dished up. "Long time to be over there. Been there since you left yesterday, have you?"

"Yes."

"Long time," Dad repeated.

Eli ground his teeth.

"Yes, I actually enjoy my boyfriend's company, thank you."

"There's no need for that to—"

"Stop it," Mum interrupted sharply, rapping her knuckles on the granite countertop. "I'm sure Eli's had a lovely time—"

"For goodness' sake, Louise, he's not a child. And near enough twenty-four hours in that man's flat—"

"Was perfectly enjoyable, thank you very much!"

"Sit down! Both of you!" Mum snapped, sweeping two of the plates up off the counter. Dad sighed and retrieved his own. "Dinner. Now!"

"Thanks, Mum," Eli said grudgingly, prodding the dubious-looking paella with a fork. "Actually," he said, firmly turning towards his mother, "we had a date this morning. That's why I've been out so long."

Total balls, they'd lounged around Rob's flat all morning, and Eli had blown him in the shower when Rob had tried to wash the new tattoo designs off. Eli could dress that up as a quiet morning in, though, right?

"Oh?" Mum's smile was polite but small. "Where did you go?"

"We stayed in," Eli said. "His, uh, his brother went out, so we—"

"Lives with his brother, does he?" Dad interrupted.

"Yes."

"Typical."

"What?"

"Criminal families stick together."

"Dad!"

"Samuel!"

"Oh for goodness' sake, Louise, the man's in his twenties and he's not living independently yet?"

"Neither am I!" Eli pointed out hotly.

"That's for financial reasons, Eli, it makes no sense for you to waste so much money on renting when—"

"Danny and Rob live together for financial reasons!"

Dad's lip curled. "Oh, I see. Has the bottom dropped out of the cannabis market?"

Eli banged his fork down; Mum hit the table again. "Quiet!" she barked. "Samuel, not another word!"

An uneasy silence fell.

"I will not," Mum said coldly, "have another row about this. Samuel, for God's sake, everyone knows you disapprove. I must admit that…from the little I have seen, I'm not best enamoured with the man—with *Rob*—myself, but Eli is not a child anymore."

Despite, Eli thought grimly, Mum's constant talking to him like he was.

"So, Eli, dear, what did you do?"

"Stayed in, like I said," Eli said. "Made more plans for Christmas—" Dad's face tightened, but he said nothing. "—and Rob had some household stuff to do so we chatted while I did some sketching."

"You took your sketchbook?"

"No, Rob keeps one for me at the flat," Eli said, and seized on the opportunity. "Actually, he likes my drawings." *Really* liked them, but he figured telling Mum the extent of how much Rob liked them wasn't a good call. "He was saying today I should go to art college, pack in that dead-end job and make something of myself."

Mum's face brightened, as Eli knew it would. "See, Samuel, the man's not a complete idiot. Eli, dear, I agree with him. You're wasted in that shop, you really are, and you have a wonderful talent."

Eli squirmed uncomfortably. A talent he'd been bullied for in school, because of what he liked to draw and that, of course, he'd still—he'd had problems in school. There was a reason he hadn't gone. But maybe now things would be different, especially now he had Rob to back him up. Lots of different types went to college, right? And they were more mature than high school bullies anyway. They didn't even have to know if he didn't want them to.

"He's absolutely right," Mum said firmly. "Isn't he, Samuel?"

Dad looked like she was extracting one of his teeth. He grunted, scowled, grumbled, then muttered, "Art college sounds like a good idea."

It didn't, not to Dad. Eli wouldn't voice it—because despite all the clashing and headbutting, he *did* love his father—but Dad's scoffing at what he wanted, like drawing pencils and sketchbooks, had been the start of Eli's insecurities about his talent in the first place. What was the point of it, if your own father thought it was a silly hobby?

Really, even though he'd grown older and realised his father just wasn't the type to enjoy or appreciate art, that scorn had never left him until Rob's incredulous face on flipping through the sketchbook—of portraits-from-memory of Rob himself—that Eli hadn't hidden well enough. And Rob's look of awe, and demand as to why Eli wasn't hosting exhibitions and tattooing people at weekends…

It had shifted something inside. Eli had drawn more in the last six months than he had in the last six years. On paper *and* on skin.

"Rob's really supportive of my art," he said quietly, pushing the paella around his plate. "He's really encouraging. Says I'm scary good."

"You *are* good, dear," Mum said. "And good on him for recognising that."

Mum was warming. Eli bit back a triumphant grin.

"He even said," he continued, keeping his eyes down so the expression inevitably on Dad's face couldn't throw him off, "that I should quit the shop and find a job in some artsy place so I can make contacts and get inspiration and stuff."

"Well, you've never liked the job, dear, and there's no future in it. You're lucky enough to have your family's support, you're a lot freer to make those kinds of decisions if you wish. You know your father and I will support you."

"Well, Rob said if I wanted, if I went to college I could stay with him and—"

"Over my dead body," Dad snarled.

Eli's head snapped up to glower at his father. Dad glowered right back, his face mottled purple and red, his fork shaking in one paw of a hand.

"That man," Dad growled, "is nothing but a dangerous, brainless criminal. I will not have my own son putting himself in such a vulnerable position as to *live* with the man!"

Eli completely dropped his own fork. "I don't think that's *your* decision to make," he snapped. "And Rob isn't *dangerous!*"

"He's been arrested countless times for *violence*, Eli!"

"Not against his partners!" Eli protested. "He gets into drunk brawls and he lets idiots at the pub piss him off! That's not like…wife-beating or anything!"

"He has a proven predilection towards vi—"

"Oh, big word, did they teach you that at senior officer school?" Eli sneered.

"Eli!" Mum scolded.

"Rob's not dangerous—certainly not to me!" Eli insisted. "He's trying to support my interests and my skills, even though he's not got the first bloody clue about art except when he thinks it looks good or it doesn't, and he has no interest in ever going to any exhibitions I would ever magically put on, but he's supporting me anyway! And he's—"

"I don't bloody care if he's offered to buy you a yacht, Eli, the man's nothing but a con!" Dad raged. "His record speaks for itself—how much more proof do you want than three years in *prison,* for God's…"

Eli's phone buzzed in his pocket; he worked it out with fumbling fingers, desperately trying to tune his father out before he re-enacted the other day and stormed out in a hissy fit. Thankfully, Rob's name blinked up at him, and he slid open the message.

Guess who babe? ;) u done with diner yet?

Eli swallowed. *Not yet. Another fucking row.*

I no ;)

Eli blinked. His father was still ranting, but—*how would you know?*

Do i get super strt cred 4 this?

For what?

Brakin into the cheef inspectors house? guess whose in ur room.

Eli froze.

"…absolutely foolhardy to trust someone with…"

"Okay, I've had enough of this," Eli said, rising from his chair. "I'm going to bed early," he added in a lie. "I didn't get much sleep last night and I'm tired, so—night, Mum."

Mum looked exhausted, pinching the bridge of her nose and closing her eyes. "Goodnight, dear," she murmured faintly.

Eli didn't bother wishing his father good night. He left the kitchen slowly, knowing to dash upstairs would just make Dad think he was going to pack a bag and head round to Rob's, and therefore bring the old git rampaging upstairs, but—

The stairs seemed impossibly long, but Eli knew it was true the minute he reached the landing. He'd left his bedroom door open. It was now firmly shut.

Eli grinned, stuffing his phone back into his pocket and taking a deep breath before opening the door.

The room was pitch black. The curtains had been drawn, and as Eli shut the door with a snap behind him, he struggled to pick anything out but the dim form of his bed under the window. He brushed his feet carefully across the carpet, and licked his lips.

"Rob?" he whispered.

He *knew* someone was here. He could *feel* eyes on him, could sense another presence in the room even as he could see and hear nothing. He took another step—and gasped, scrabbling instinctively at the powerful arm, as a hand clamped over his throat and another trapped his elbows to his sides.

"Evening."

Rob's voice was a deep, hoarse whisper in his ear; the rasp of his stubble against Eli's ear brought him out in goose bumps. He squirmed, arching, and Rob's hand tightened around his mouth.

"Ssh." The sound was nearly a purr. "Don't want Mummy and Daddy to hear you, do you?"

Eli stilled, both hands clasping Rob's elbow. Slowly, he shook his head.

"Red sky in the morning and all that."

The nonsense phrase—and the colour within it—made Eli smile. "Green sky."

"Yeah?"

"Yeah."

"You going to fight me?"

Eli dug his nails into Rob's arm.

"'Cause I can make this quick and easy, Eli, or I can hold you down and hurt you. Either way, you're gonna keep quiet for me. Don't want to be disturbed."

Eli's breathing was ragged. His pulse was pounding, and he could feel Rob's erection pressing into his arse. Eli ground back against it, and a soft snarl was his reply.

"You gonna keep quiet for me?"

Eli nodded.

"Good. You know the rules. Strip."

Eli's fingers were shaking with an intense, burning arousal as he fumbled for the buttons on his jeans. *Fuck,* he loved these games, when Rob got deadly and just *pounced* like this. Rob fucked like other men breathed—in all varieties from hard and desperate to soft and barely-awake. And when he got like this, when his voice dropped so low in his throat that it barely qualified as a voice anymore...

Eli dropped his jeans and boxers in one fluid motion, and was immediately pushed towards the bed.

"Hands and knees," came the hoarse order, followed by one more command to be quiet.

And then Eli was posed, wearing nothing but his T-shirt, and Rob was almost casually knocking his knees wider and throwing him off-balance.

Then he was gone. Eli dropped his head, breathing hard, and waited. He wasn't a fool. Rob in this mood...he'd notice the *second* Eli tried to move from the ordered position. And that hoarse voice, the casual commands, the language—Eli was going to get fucked, and fucked *hard,* and the very thought of it...he was already aching for Rob to get inside him and screw him raw.

A hand seized his shoulder and he was roughly flipped onto his back. Against his own volition, Eli gasped, and his chin was promptly seized in a hard hand. Knees dropped painfully onto his shoulders, and something ripped audibly in the quiet room.

"What did I fucking *say?*"

"Keep quiet," Eli croaked, then realised his mistake.

"Shame," Rob murmured, almost softly. Definitely mocking. "And I was looking forward to having those lips around my fucking cock. Guess not."

Eli swallowed. He wanted it, too, to get to taste Rob, to feel the exact shifts of Rob's thrusts, to have those heavy hands in his hair, to hover on that edge between taking too much and not giving enough—

"I'll be quiet," he breathed. "I promise. Just let me—let me suck you."

"You want my dick in your mouth?"

"Yes."

"You want to suck me off and drink it?"

"Yes," Eli breathed shakily. Rob's knees were still planted in his shoulders, too heavy but deliciously painful, and that meant his cock was barely out of reach as it was...

The knees moved and released Eli's shoulders. "Hands on the bars."

Eli's headboard was a series of vertical bars, and he wrapped his fingers around them eagerly. The ripping sounded again, followed by the distinct tug and pull of masking tape as it was wound around his wrists—three, four, five times—until he was firmly lashed to the head of the bed and stretched out, helplessly, under the invisible weight above him.

"Oh God," Eli breathed, his chest heaving. He already wanted to squirm. This—fuck, this was right out of his fucking porn collection and every fantasy ever. He *loved* it like this, Rob literally tying him down and just taking control, ripping it away from him. Eli was burning, his heart pounding right out of his chest—he strained his head and hips up, desperate for a friction or a kiss, or that promised cock—

That same hand seized his chin in a bruising grip. Rob chuckled, very close to Eli's ear.

"You couldn't keep quiet to save your fucking life, you little shit," he sneered. "Forcing my cock down your throat's going to have to wait for a day your fucking parents aren't downstairs playing happy fucking families over the fancy desserts. Right now? It's gonna be the tap method. You got that?"

Eli nodded, and rapped his knuckles against the bars. They clinked gently.

"Good," Rob praised. "One for stop. Two for slow down. Three for permission to continue doing what I'm doing—if I ask, which I'm telling you right now I fucking won't."

"What're you gonna do?" Eli demanded breathlessly.

Rob sneered.

"Shut you up, first off. Bite your lips or lose 'em."

Eli sucked them in barely in time before the tape was roughly pressed down—and firmly, too. He flexed his jaw, got a slap for his troubles, and another two pieces added to the makeshift gag. He inhaled deeply through his nose, squirming against the bonds, and got a hand firmly wrapped around his neck.

"You fuck me around," Rob snarled, "and I'll make sure you fucking regret it."

Eli whimpered, bucking his hips. Rob growled, lips trailing down Eli's neck and chest before vanishing altogether. His knees were wrenched brutally apart and dry fingers brushed up under his arse threateningly. They vanished, and a moment later returned slick and probing, the lube cold and Rob's fingers impossibly hot and thick. He probed with finger and thumb before pushing the index in, followed too quickly by the middle.

Eli arched away from the intrusion. When he whimpered, his thigh was harshly pinched, the nails twisting in his skin, but Rob said nothing.

And it was the silence that was so maddening—all Eli could hear was his own harsh breathing, the twist and crinkle of the tape around his wrists as he squirmed. Rob was silent; it was like being finger-fucked by someone who wasn't there at all, the probing intrusion something made up in a fit of madness. Rob wasn't touching him bar the nails buried in his thigh in warning and the fingers spreading him open.

Eli rocked his hips and whined under the gag, desperate to be touched, for Rob's hands or mouth, for *something*—

He choked when Rob eased the fourth finger in, wondering

for a dizzying, terrifying moment if Rob intended to fist him. But then the hand was being withdrawn, and his knees were being forced up and even more open, and—

He jerked violently against the headboard and was soundly slapped.

"*Silence*," Rob hissed, his voice barely audible before he bucked his hips and *rammed* home.

Eli would have screamed if he could.

The entry was slick and smooth but sudden. He arched powerfully, the sudden sensation of being completely and utterly filled and *possessed*—pinioned on Rob's cock like a thing, like a mere doll or a toy, a plaything for Rob to fuck into and discard—setting off every nerve in Eli's body in an explosion of such intense pleasure that the room tipped. His fingers tightened impossibly around the bars; his legs locked around Rob's waist so hard he almost stopped the forward motion. He wanted to shout, wanted to claw at Rob's shoulders and force him even deeper, wanted to beg for more, beg for movement, beg for—

Something creaked. Rob's fingers digging into Eli's thigh stilled, and Eli fought to control his own breathing.

Another creak. And another.

There were footsteps coming up the stairs. Heavy, plodding footsteps, long legs taking the stairs two at a time in a slightly too-heavy tread.

Dad.

CHAPTER 7

ELI FROZE, EVERY muscle from fingers to toes tightening. He tightened impossibly on Rob's cock, too, the shiver in the arms bracing his thighs noticeable but silent. The footsteps were continuing up the stairs, like drums of doom, like—

Eli's eyes widened, back flexing involuntarily when Rob, quite suddenly, rolled his hips. With Eli's father *right outside on the landing*, he just rocked his hips and began to thrust as though he had never paused, that powerful cock sliding almost all the way out before being shoved back inside, raw as the first time and twice as incredible.

Rob's chest pressed down, and then lips were brushing the shell of Eli's ear as the footsteps passed the bedroom door. "He's right there," Rob breathed, his words barely a movement of breath. One of his rough-fingered hands pressed between their bodies and found Eli's need, slick and wet.

The first hint of a touch was maddening, and Eli pushed his hips desperately up into it, pulling Rob's cock deeper with the motion, so deep it ached and burned.

"Right there," Rob repeated, still thrusting, almost idly now. "Door's not locked. He could just open it and see this, see his precious son taped to the headboard and gagged, getting fucked right open by an ex-con, and worst of all, see how much his son is *leaking* for this, see how much he's begging for it even though he can't speak, see—"

The boards outside the bathroom creaked, the bathroom door closed, and Eli, with Rob's rough fingers rubbing insistently at his flesh, came so hard he smashed his chest into Rob's and nearly dislodged him but for the fierce catch of Eli's thighs and calves locked around Rob's body. He shook under Rob's weight, pinned and tied in place, and felt his own eyes roll back in his head, the dark room spinning away from sight dizzyingly, and grounded only by the soft grunt in his ear and the warmth of a heavy hand in his crotch.

He must have drifted after all, though, for the next he knew the tape was severed at his wrists and his hands were being rubbed in Rob's fingers like dough, his arms slowly lowered onto his chest. Eli sighed breathily, curling into the heat of Rob's chest and wrinkling his nose when the tape gag was gently peeled back and away.

"Alright?" Rob murmured.

Eli pressed a dry kiss into Rob's throat.

"*Yes*," he breathed fervently, and caught at Rob's wrist when he made as if to get up. "Stay."

"I need to get rid of the condom."

"No. Stay. Drop it on the floor."

A heavy hand raked through his hair, and then Rob shifted and resettled. Eli felt empty without him, void and cold, so burrowed into the heat of his chest and arms. They were both still wearing their shirts—in fact, Eli drowsily realised Rob was still nearly fully-clothed, his jeans and underwear at his thighs.

"Kit off," he mumbled, squirming with his own T-shirt.

Rob chuckled deeply, moving away for maybe ten horrific seconds before naked skin met Eli's, hot and sticky with sweat, and that emptiness began to dissipate.

"God."

"Ssh, I've got you," Rob whispered, tugging the blankets over them both and performing an octopus of a hug, until Eli was buried in hot skin and heavy muscle.

"So fuckin' forceful…"

Rob buried his nose in Eli's scalp. "Perfect opportunity, perfect prey—and you *were* perfect."

Eli hummed, tracking his hands over Rob's pectoral muscles and tracing the ink lines of the tattooed heart in the dark. He could feel Rob's real heart behind it, calming and settling, and the soft sweeps of Rob's hands over his skin, as though smoothing down ruffled feathers.

This was how the aftermath worked. Eli talked. Rob did not. That was a general rule about their respective lives, both apart and together. When Eli took control of a scene, he talked Rob out of the roughness, smoothed the jagged edges, and coated them over with loving words. Rob, by contrast, cuddled. Oh, he'd never call it that, but that's what it was. Hands that had been brutal were suddenly soft and tender; lips that had spoken cruelly were ghosting across Eli's skin, kissing the marks left by the tape and the slaps in reverent, soothing touches.

Eli fought sleep a little longer, though, resisting the pull. As his muscles recovered a little from the ordeal, he curled tighter into Rob and burrowed properly, burying his nose under Rob's jaw and sliding his arms around that powerful chest to cling. His knee found itself tucked safe between Rob's thighs, Rob's spent cock a soft weight against Eli's hip. The tighter Eli wound himself, the less cold he felt, and the less cold Rob would feel. They'd not been together long, but they had talked about their sex life in great depth, and what little Rob hadn't admitted to under Eli's probing questions, Eli had worked out for himself. Eli knew, despite Rob's hard exterior, these scenes affected Rob as deeply as they could him, whether Rob controlled them or not. He could be—and had been—shaken by some of their rougher scenes and role-plays. Things that were enjoyable at the time could leave seeds of uncertainty and doubt for later. And Eli, despite having been the recipient of Rob's hunger this time, wasn't an idiot. Doubt didn't care which of them started it, which received, and which finished it. It just cared what had happened.

And Eli knew, in Rob's case, what those doubts would be. That Eli hadn't truly consented to it, or—by contrast—wanted Rob exclusively for the sex. That their sex life was either damaging, or the only reason Eli was hanging around. Rob was a hard man not prone to angsting and emoting if he could remotely help it, but he wasn't a brick wall. So Eli nestled into the hot lines of definitely-not-brick muscles, and made his contentment as well-known as he possibly could without raising his voice and alerting his parents to Rob's presence in the house.

Because Eli's biggest concern was that Rob wasn't—yet, at least, because Eli was going to get him there if it killed the both of them—open enough to simply tell Eli he was having issues, or ask for affection or reassurance if he needed it.

So Eli curled as close as possible, daring to whisper, "Fucking incredible," in an ear when a board creaked loud enough on the landing to drown him out to all but Rob, and Eli smoothed his hands in soft, aimless patterns across overheated skin.

Slowly, Rob shifted them around and settled, twisting over until his head was planted solidly over Eli's sternum. Eli smiled sleepily, pulling his fingers in idle massage through thick, dark hair, and stared at the rising moon outside the window in exhausted, sated pleasure.

Fuck what anyone else thought. This man—this man right here, this terrifyingly complex, brilliant, sarcastic, passionate, capable man—was motherfucking perfection.

ELI WOKE ALONE.

For a moment this didn't concern him. He'd slept in the same bedroom since he was a child, so it took his brain a moment to catch up on itself and remember that he'd fallen asleep with a warm weight against his chest and arms, and cupping Rob's thigh between his knees.

The warmth was most definitely gone.

Yawning, Eli slid out of bed and rummaged for his jeans. What the hell, maybe Rob had decided to finish his little break-and-enter, aggravated-burglary game by nicking one of Eli's things and climbing back out the window, or however he'd gotten in.

The sky was a deep grey as Eli crept downstairs. The house

was silent as the grave. He leisurely wandered through the living room en route to the kitchen to rummage through the treats drawer Mum kept for Flora and steal a chocolate bar. He ached—arse, back, wrists, shoulders, thighs, hips—and he loved it. The only way it could have been better was if Rob had forgotten the stupid condom for once in his life, but Eli was still pretty damn happy with the results. Nothing beat this, the sensation of Rob still inside, the phantom ache from being filled almost too deep to take—

"Morning."

Eli stopped dead in the kitchen doorway, jaw sagging.

Then he laughed. "Make yourself at home, why don't you?"

Rob grinned sleepily. He was holding an obscenely large mug of tea in both hands, and wearing nothing but his boxers.

Eli eyed the view appreciatively and sidled right up close to drop a kiss onto one cheek.

"Morning," he whispered, and kissed the scar at the corner of Rob's mouth. "How's my burglar?"

"Sore, you kneed me in the bollocks about an hour ago."

Eli grimaced. "Shit, sorry."

Rob coughed a laugh and sipped at his tea. "Toast?"

"'Kay."

"Have that when it pops then. Not got the hang of your toaster yet."

"It's Mum's fault, she likes it all blond."

"Grim," Rob opined. His eyes were still hazy with sleep, and Eli pressed close into the heat of his nearly-naked body and nosed at his cheek affectionately.

"Lay off. Leech."

"You love it," Eli scoffed then kissed the stubble. The remark said that Rob had bounced back from the scene, though. "You're going to need to shave today unless you want Dad to think you're homeless, too."

Rob smirked.

The toast popped and Eli busied himself with it, putting in more bread for Rob and taking the blond toast that had been produced. It was a little too underdone for his liking, but Rob had taken the butter out of the fridge already, so Eli could melt the butter into the toast and enjoy it properly anyway. He enjoyed the quiet domesticity of it, Rob simply watching in comfortable silence and accepting Eli's little touches whenever they were offered.

The creak on the stairs, however, was not so welcome.

"Oh shit!" Eli hissed, suddenly hyper-aware that Rob was in his underwear, and Eli shirtless. And, judging by the sting on his neck, covered in bruises. *Shit!* "Bugger, if—"

"Relax," Rob drawled, catching the new toast when it popped. "What're they gonna do? Chuck me out for all their fucking neighbours to see in me keks?"

"Just—be *nice*," Eli pleaded as the footsteps shuffled down the hall.

"Yeah, yeah," Rob grunted, then smirked over the top of the toast. "Mornin', Lou."

Eli winced. Sure enough, Mum stood in the kitchen doorway, clutching her dressing gown around herself and staring wide-eyed at Rob like she'd never seen him in her life. Which Eli supposed was semi-true—at least Rob had been wearing *clothes* every other time.

"Mum," he squeaked. "You're up early!"

"Yes," she said slowly. "Nice to...nice to see you, Rob, dear. When...when did you get here?"

Rob shrugged. "Yesterday evening."

"Yesterday...evening?"

"Uh-huh. While you were having dinner."

Her gaze sharpened.

"*I let him in*," Eli snapped firmly. "Didn't I, Rob." And God-fucking-help him if he denied it, Eli thought viciously.

"Yeah," Rob drawled, grinning. "You did, babe."

"Right," Mum said suspiciously.

"Tea and toast?" Eli offered desperately. "We're nearly done here, then Rob's going to shower and go home."

"Tea, please." Mum's voice was flat; she hadn't moved from her position in the doorway, and was flicking her gaze between them as though calculating. Her eyes lingered on Eli's bruises and Rob's tattoos, and Eli could almost see the cogs turning.

"Shower for me, then," Rob grunted, and pulled himself away

from the counter, setting the mug down. His fingers brushed Eli's ear, and then a kiss—stale, covered in crumbs, but warm and welcome—pressed itself to Eli's mouth. "In a bit, babe."

Eli squeezed his arm before Rob pulled away, and watched him edge around Mum and disappear. The moment his heavy tread sounded on the stairs—and how exactly *had* he snuck in so silently the night before?—Mum pursed her lips.

"Eli," she said.

"I don't want to hear it."

"Dear—"

"No," Eli said firmly. "And he agreed to come to dinner. So pick a day."

CHAPTER 8

MUM PICKED A Tuesday.

Circumstance—Eli's job at a shop in the city centre, Rob's job doing...whatever it was he did, most of which Eli suspected was at least semi-illegal, and a critical incident calling Dad into overtime shifts for several days and thus delaying the dinner—meant Eli didn't see hide nor hair of Rob for nearly ten days, either personally or for the stupid meal. It was the longest time without him in six months.

I miss you :(Eli complained on the ninth day.

In true Rob fashion, the reply was *I salute you* and a photo of his erect cock.

Wanker, Eli had sent him sulkily, but received no reply.

The only positive side to Rob not being around was the lack of...well, talking about Rob. The atmosphere in the house noticeably improved, despite Dad working overtime and Mum being stressed because of it. Eli was always more comfortable when Dad wasn't around anyway—he wasn't *bad,* and Eli *did* love his father at the end of the day, but Dad was difficult. He didn't get Eli at all, and when Dad didn't understand something, he poked and prodded and niggled at it. And that picking away hurt, even when Dad didn't mean it to. Mum—and Rob, when Eli thought about it—

was more the type to simply accept she didn't understand something and keep quiet about it.

Still, Eli wouldn't have traded the better atmosphere for Rob.

So when Mum decided dinner would be on Tuesday—more than two weeks after the last time Eli had set eyes on his own bloody boyfriend, he sent the order immediately.

Tuesday. 7pm. You will be here on time and presentable. Understood?
Presentibl???
Nice jeans and a button-up.
I dont own a buttonup!
BUY ONE.

He got a scowling selfie for that, but didn't care.

Play nice = reward play. Fuck me around and I WILL punish you. Don't push me.

There was no reply to that at all.

In fact, Eli heard nothing until Tuesday itself. He'd come home from work to find Mum fussing over which tablecloth to use, told her that Rob would regard any tablecloth as fancy, and received the message.

From Danny.

Yo eli its danny is ur diner thing w/ rob n ur folks 2nite?

Eli crushed a bad feeling as Mum asked, "Who's that, dear?"

"Rob's brother," Eli mumbled.

"Like him, I suppose?" Dad asked acidly.

Eli ignored him. *Yes why??*

its off m8 he just got niked lol!

Eli ground his teeth against the surge of irritation. For God's *sake*! The *one* night of the week—hell, the one night of the last *fortnight* that he'd needed Rob to stay out of trouble and he bloody well went and got himself arrested!

ARE YOU KIDDING ME?!

Nope just seen it. Soz m8 beta luk next time?

Wtf did he get nicked for?!

Local just got raided 4 drugs n u no rob he sounded off. called this big guy a pigfucker.

Eli groaned. Fucking brilliant. Just fucking *brilliant*, not only did he do that but he was down the pub an *hour* before he was meant to be coming over to meet Mum and Dad, and—

"What's the matter, dear?" Mum asked, shaking out a tablecloth.

"Dinner's off," Eli said shortly. "Rob can't come."

"Can't come? Why?" Mum asked.

Dad, leaning against the oven, curled his lip.

"Something came up," Eli mumbled.

"Really," Dad said. "This wouldn't be anything to do with the, ah, planned raids across Parson Cross, would it?"

Eli scowled. "Fine. He got arrested. Is that what you want to hear?"

"I want to hear you come to your senses," Dad said coldly.

"Right," Eli said, clenching his fists. Then he unclenched them and turned on his heel.

"Eli…" Mum called.

He kept walking, out into the hall and up the stairs, and heard his mother snap, "Samuel, *must* you antagonise him?"

Antagonise. Yeah, well. Eli called it patronising, frankly. He wasn't a child. He'd made his decision—*Rob* was his decision— and he was done waiting for Dad to actually treat him like an adult and respect his choices. Eli *knew* he'd led a charmed life for the most part, he'd never had to struggle like Rob, but he'd had his own problems and he'd come out the other side. Some people like Eli—*loads* of people like Eli—fucked themselves up for life, or took years and years to become happy, normal people. Eli *was* happy and he *was* normal, and he was strong enough upstairs to know that. Why the hell couldn't Dad respect that, when even *Rob* could respect that?

He threw a bag on the bed and started stuffing it with clothes. He texted Danny asking if the man was at home yet or not and raided the bathroom for his razor. Eli's facial hair was slow and patchy, but it was starting to come through a bit too much for his liking.

Footsteps creaked; a shadow fell in the doorway.

"I don't want to hear it," Eli snapped, shoving the razor into his bag and opening his desk drawers for some pens. Rob wasn't going to be home until morning; might as well take something to fill the time.

"Eli." His father's voice was deep and steady, and Eli hated it irrationally for a minute. "I don't like clashing with you over this every time, but—"

"Then don't."

"I don't like seeing one of my children walk blind into a bad idea."

Eli slammed the drawer and turned on his father furiously. "And maybe it's not a bad fucking idea! Maybe it's the best idea I ever had—newsflash, Dad, going after a guy who respects you and supports you no matter what, that's not a bad idea! Rob is not some fucking monster—and frankly he's supported me better in the last six months with my shit than you have in twenty-one fucking years!"

Dad's face—wavered. For a split second his mouth twisted and his brows crumpled, and a flash of intense guilt stabbed Eli in the gut. He turned back to his bag, pushing the feeling away. What right did Dad have to make him feel guilty? Dad hadn't tolerated Eli's strangeness at best. He'd done nothing to help; he'd refused to even discuss it for years until Eli decided to take things into his own hands.

But when Rob had found out…he'd just shrugged and said, "It's kinda fuckin' weird, but hey, fuck it, s'your life, en't it?"

"I'm not your *child* anymore, Dad," Eli said bitterly, zipping the bag shut and slinging it over his shoulder.

Dad's voice was suddenly quiet. "Your children are *always* your children, Eli. No matter how old—or who—they become. One day you'll understand that."

Eli crushed the hot twist of guilt and pushed past his father onto the landing. "I fucking doubt it."

Danny had replied. *Home in 15. u comin? im getin pizza, rob gave me his card 2 get a round in rite b4 the ol bill showed!!*

"I'm going to Rob's," Eli called. He slammed the front door behind him to the sound of bitter silence.

WHILE PERHAPS IT would have been odd if Eli had been dating Danny and he'd come to the flat with just Rob here, it didn't feel strange as it was. Although the brothers looked similar, that subtle shift in features—and although Eli would never tell Rob for fear of over-inflating his ego, the difference in eye colour—allowed Danny to adopt the perpetually cheery idiocy that made him so easy to be around. He was not, and would never be, the intense, brooding hulk that his older brother was. Although Danny was dangerous in his own right, with a vicious sadism to the way he'd attack a perceived enemy that Rob, who simply cracked skulls and moved on, lacked—despite that danger, Danny in a good mood was an uplifting man to be around.

So it didn't feel strange to throw his bag into Rob's bedroom, ask Danny to order a pepperoni pizza with double cheese for him, and head for the shower. Even showering to the sound of Danny's rock music in the living room, complete with off-key screeching masquerading as singing, didn't feel strange.

It just felt…homey.

Eli eyed the tiles, and wondered when Rob's casual offer of him moving in if he went to college had become a serious option. It'd be nice living here, he reckoned—if he could persuade Rob to give up the weed dealing permanently, because Eli didn't fancy the cops pawing through his stuff every time Rob or Danny got caught with more than a single spliff in their pockets.

He stayed in the shower until the doorbell heralded the arrival of the pizza, before wandering back to Rob's room to fish his pyjama bottoms out of his bag. His hair was still too wet for the shirt, so he tucked it into his waistband and wandered towards the smell of food.

Without thinking—for the minute he stepped over threshold, Danny looked up at him, a look of confusion washed across those familiar-but-not features and he said, "Mate, kind of scars are *those*?"

Dread pooled, cold and wet, in Eli's stomach. *Fuck!* Of course Danny would notice—they were still clear, only eighteen months old, and the placement and mirror images they made of each other were so fucking unusual he'd have been *bound* to notice, just like Rob had noticed, and—

"I," Eli said, and hastily shoved his T-shirt over his head.

"Seriously, what happened? You get stabbed or something?

I've never seen slices like that!" Danny exclaimed. He was still staring at Eli's chest like he could see through the cotton.

"It's nothing," Eli tried, and made for his pizza box.

"Oh, fuck no," Danny said, jabbing a finger in Eli's direction, though he didn't move from his chair. "Who did it?"

Eli stiffened. "Danny, it's *nothing.*"

"Ain't fucking nothing, some fucker's carved you up! What, you got a psycho ex or something? You tell Rob who did it so he can sort it out, or am I gonna have to push shit?"

"There's nothing to push, and it's none of your busin—"

"Course it's my fucking business," Danny sneered. "You're family. So either you up and tell me, or I haul Rob's arse into this. Trust me, Eli, we'll find the fuck out, and then—"

"A *surgeon* did it," Eli blurted out, without meaning to. His face flooded with heat, and he decided to sit down before his knees could give out.

"You what?" Danny said stupidly after a minute.

"It was…it was surgery."

"What kind of surgery does *that?*"

Eli swallowed and closed his eyes. "Chest—chest reconstruction," he said after a minute, and took a deep breath. Danny would…Danny would be alright. Rob would *make* Danny be alright with it.

Only Rob wasn't here, so…Eli wasn't *afraid* of Danny, exactly, but—he could say things, here and now, without Rob there to hear them and tell him to shut his face before Rob did it for him. And—

"Chest what now? What, like rebuilding? What d'you need your chest rebuilding for, you in some car accident or something?"

"No," Eli croaked. "To—to remove my breasts."

"To—*what?*"

"I'm transgender."

Silence. Or rather, Danny said nothing—the music played on obliviously, and the people in the flat below were having a row. Eli stared at the pizza box, stomach churning, and waited.

"You're—what, you was a girl?"

"Yes," Eli said quietly.

"What, like—boobs, cunt, shave your legs, *girl* girl?"

"Well, *yeah.*"

"That fucking bastard!" Danny exploded.

Eli jumped violently, eyes flying from the box to Danny's face, which was twisted in comical fury.

"Rob! That fucking shit! I said right, when you first hooked up with him, I said you were a bit of a girly-looking bugger and he just about pissed himself, he found it fucking *hilarious* but he wouldn't tell me why, the piece of *shit!*"

"Er—"

"So what, you're Ellie?"

"I *was* Sarah. I changed my name when I was eighteen."

"Fuck me, that's young. So have you got a prick? And how do you fuck Rob, 'cause mate, I've *seen* him walking funny, I know you're up to *summat.*"

Eli flushed hotly. "They're called toys and that's all I'm saying," he replied primly.

"D'you got a pussy, then?"

Eli groaned. "I—yes. I am still...*physically* female."

"How does that work then, 'cause no offence and you know, you look and sound like a dude an' all, but Rob's a pouf. Like...he's a man's man. I mean, he's always been a hard fucker, but everybody knew he couldn't give two shits about girls since he was, like...eight."

Eli grimaced. "We, um...he doesn't..."

"Fuck you in the cunt?"

"Oh, God. Yes." *God*, he hated Danny sometimes.

"So he fucks you up the arse?"

"Danny! Seriously?"

"I'm just curious!"

"It's your brother's sex life, you shouldn't be!"

Danny pulled a face. "*Ew*," he said pointedly, then grinned widely. "Never thought our Rob would get within ten feet of a pussy, though, I'm kinda weird proud of him. He never left the girls-got-cooties stage."

"Yeah, well, I'm not a girl."

"You just said—"

"Having...female *parts* doesn't make me female," Eli said stiffly. "If I cut your dick off, you'll still be male."

Danny shrugged. "I guess."

"Anyway, I'm—I'm not finished yet. I can't afford the last surgery yet."

"What, no NHS?"

Eli scowled. "The NHS think I'm too fucking young and keep referring me back to psychiatrists."

"Well, you *do* hafta be nuts to wanna get rid of a sweet pair o' tits," Danny said agreeably.

Eli rolled his eyes.

"So what about your voice? Never heard a bird like you."

"I have testosterone injections," Eli said, gingerly lifting a slice of pizza from the box and watching Danny out of the corner of his eye. The incredulity was...kind of nice, actually. Eli was still getting used to people thinking he was a man and not having to ask. Before the chest surgery, he'd never really passed.

And the fact Danny wasn't moving, just gnawing on his pizza and staring, that was good, too. The questions were good. Danny didn't ask questions. He was like Rob—hit first, ask questions never. Asking questions, for Danny, was like donning a rainbow T-shirt and marching in the next pride parade. It was reassuring.

Thing was, Eli had never lived in a bubble. His parents were nice and all, but they'd been shocked when he'd come out. He'd never had *understanding,* just...support because of other things. His family didn't support him because they were pro-transgender people, they supported him because he was one of them. Rob didn't *understand*—and how could he? He was the epitome of a man one hundred percent comfortable in his own skin—but he supported Eli anyway out of love.

Eli didn't expect Danny to understand. This—these incredulous questions and the wary side-eye—was plenty enough for Eli.

"Does that make Rob bi, then?"

Eli swallowed. "Er."

"I mean, he's fucking someone with a pussy."

"Up the arse, as you so elegantly put it."

"Yeah, but he's sexually attracted to a girl, then, f'you wanna get specific."

"I'm not a girl," Eli said coolly. "I dress like a man, I sound like a man, for the most part I look like one. I have chest hair and everything…"

"Yeah, but, you have a cunt," Danny insisted.

"That doesn't make me a *girl*," Eli insisted right back. "Look—Rob thought I was a man the first time we…did anything—"

"Uh, *how?*"

"I blew him, Jesus!"

Danny nearly snorted his beer up his nose.

"But anyway, he thought I was a man that first time. And when I told him, he just…shrugged and said I felt enough like a guy to him. I don't—I don't have sex like a woman. So yeah, Rob's still gay. He's still not sexually attracted to women, he's just…attracted right now to a guy without everything there yet."

Danny grinned. "S'one way of putting it, I guess."

Eli shrugged, toying with the pizza.

"Look, man, I'm not trying to be a dick," Danny said earnestly, leaning forward and propping his elbows on his knees. "It's just…Rob's…he's the only person who ever gave two shits about me, y'know? Mam were shit, Dad were shittier, the Scottish lot…they care, right, but they're far away and end of the day, they didn't take us in when Mam got banged up. And the only time—we all knew, always, Rob were queer. Dad used to try and beat it out of him, s'what made Rob such an aggressive fucker, but we all knew. But th'only time I ever saw Rob proper…light up, like, proper *like* someone before, it were kinda like you. This kid way outta his league, this pretty, clever, confident kid with all this fucking opportunity and talent and crap, and—that kind of guy, that kind of guy just looks at Rob like a fun bit of rough. So yeah, I wasn't too pleased about you. He's fucking crazy about you, you've proper turned his head, right, and I figured you were gonna just fuck him and go."

Eli stared.

"But I guess you look like you're sticking around."

"Yeah," Eli breathed.

"And that's cool. I like you well enough. You can handle that berk anyhow, s'a rare skill. But I'm warning you, yeah, I'm fucking *telling* you—" Danny jabbed his beer bottle in Eli's direction like it were a weapon. "I'm telling you, you fuck him around, you fuck him over? I'll shave your fucking face off with a paring knife. It'll go same way as your tits. Got it?"

Eli laughed. The heavy tension lifted; the weight to his shoulders eased. Danny, jagged around the edges just as much as his older brother, wasn't going to have a problem with this. Or in fact anything, because—

"I have no intention of fucking him over."

CHAPTER 9

ELI WAS WOKEN by the bedroom door opening too loudly and too abruptly.

"F'k off!" he moaned in its direction before remembering that he wasn't in his own room, and the intruder was probably the man he was after in the first place.

So he sat up, rubbing sleep out of his eyes, and scowled at the towering shadow on the threshold.

"Either get the fuck in here," he snarled, "and shut that fucking door. Or fuck off."

Rob snorted and shut the door behind him. The chilly waft of air was cut off, and Eli dragged the duvet up to his shoulders as Rob shed his clothes and opened a drawer to rummage for fresh ones. The sky outside was grim, the window so wet with rain it could have been underwater, and as a result Rob was barely more than a silhouette in the gloom. Eli sighed, and switched the bedside lamp on.

"Oh Jesus," he said.

Half of Rob's face was damp and pale. The other half was bruised a vicious purple, deepening to a pure black around the eye socket. The eye in question looked more ethereal than ever.

"What happened?"

Rob shrugged. "Didn't fancy getting fucking nicked, did I?"

Eli sighed through his nose, and straightened his legs out. "What happened?" he repeated.

"Pigs raided the local, didn't they?"

"So you had drugs on you?"

"No."

"Rob."

"Didn't," Rob insisted. "Already had a smoke, hadn't I? But they wanted to search me, an' I didn't fancy it. That fucker Cadman was there, that tall berk who's a fucking pla—"

"Yes, thank you, I know your opinion of Cadman," Eli said waspishly. "But really, Rob? The *one* day this week I *needed* you not to be—"

"I know!"

Rob's voice was a near shout, and Eli clicked his teeth shut angrily.

"I fucking know, alright. I know I shouldn't have and I know I cocked up and whatever, Eli, we can fucking fight however you fuckin' want, but not *now*, alright? I'm fucking wiped, I'm freezing, Danny ain't answering his phone so I've fucking walked from the fucking custody suite in the city centre, think my wallet's still in the pub and I had a hundred in there I won't be seeing again, and—I just want to get me head down for a few hours, yeah?"

Eli swallowed. "Are you on bail?"

"Eli."

"*Are you on bail?*" he insisted.

"No," Rob snapped. "No, I'm fuckin' not. Happy? I got a ticket for being pissed and mouthy."

Eli ground his teeth, and got out of the bed. The tired feeling was gone. He was torn between reaching out to hug Rob, and reaching out to punch him in the other eye. "I'm going for a shower," he snapped, and seized Rob's towel off the radiator before marching out. Rob groaned, but when Eli slammed the bathroom door, it wasn't reopened.

If there was such a thing as having an angry shower, Eli had one. He turned the water up as hot as it would go, and scrubbed until his skin felt raw. He was angry at Rob for being arrested, at

Dad for being such a dick about it, and at himself for being so angry in the first place. He hadn't even waited for Rob to give him the whole story, and Eli *hated* being painted like the nagging wife, but...but *God,* nobody just randomly got nicked that many times. Rob *could* be a dick to police, he *did* overreact to them, and Eli knew better than anyone that most officers were decent guys, guys Rob would probably get along with if he just met them playing rugby or down the local like he met other people. But the minute Rob saw the uniform, he turned into a massive bell-end, and it drove Eli mad.

But then, Dad had been a dick, too, Eli reflected as he tilted his head back under the spray. And he'd bring it up if this stupid dinner ever actually happened. He'd needle and niggle until Rob exploded, and it would all go to shit, and—

The door banged. "Oi! Faggot! Or short faggot! Whichever faggot!"

"Piss off, Danny!"

"Short faggot, then." Eli could almost *hear* the grin in Danny's voice. "Hurry the fuck up, and leave some of the hot water, shit-for-brains. I got work in, like...half an hour!"

"You'll have to fucking stink, then!" Eli shouted back, but turned off the water and stepped out anyway.

"I'll be fucking late and get fucking fired and it'll be your fucking fault, now get the fuck—"

Eli jerked the door open.

"—out," Danny finished, and beamed. "Did I hear big and brutish get back?"

Eli snorted. "Yeah," he said shortly.

"Alright, misery, you could look fuckin' happy about it, didn't end up in the slammer proper, did he?" Danny jeered, then slithered past Eli in a weirdly sneaky move and slammed the bathroom door. "If this shower's cold, I'll bugger you with the hose!"

"And you call us the queers?" Eli shouted back, hitching his towel higher around himself.

Without another choice, Eli mentally steeled himself and opened Rob's bedroom door again, only to find the man himself obliviously asleep.

Eli's anger died down to a smouldering ember rather than the fire it had been at the sight of him. Rob had curled into the warm spot Eli had left behind, lying on his front with his arms under his chest, head twisted to the side so the bruises faced the ceiling, safe from squashing. The duvet had been wound around him to create a man-burrito, and he was clearly deeply asleep.

Eli bit his lip, and hesitated.

Rob rarely looked...well, anything other than a wall of bad attitude and scowls, but at that moment, he looked just a little bit vulnerable. His skin was a greyish colour under the bruising, and he usually didn't sleep through people shouting right outside his door. He must have been knackered. Eli felt himself softening in spite of the fury that still lurked under the surface, like a shark in still waters.

He dried and dressed quietly, rummaging in his overnight bag for comfortable jeans and his sketchbook, and carefully slid onto the mattress, laying a hand on Rob's shoulder, and tugging gently. Even asleep, Rob knew the gesture, and soon shifted over, sliding a heavy arm across Eli's thighs and burying his head into the soft space where Eli's stomach met his hips. Rob's breath was hot and even, the tiniest rumble audible under the exhalations, and Eli stroked that dark hair for a moment before flipping open the sketchbook and finding himself a blank page.

He would explode in a bit. When Rob didn't look so wrung-out, and Eli wouldn't feel so guilty.

ROB WAS AWAKE by the time Eli returned with lunch.

He'd slept for nearly four hours while Eli sat and drew. When he'd begun to mumble and stir, Eli had slipped free and went into the kitchen to cobble together something that looked like lunch. It was only egg on toast, but it was food, and it gave him something to do with his hands.

"I'm still pissed, you know," he told Rob when he re-entered the bedroom with the tray. "Sit up."

"Wha'?" Rob asked blearily.

"At you."

"Oh." A jaw-cracking yawn, and Rob finally sat up. "Why?"

Eli stared. "Are you kidding me, Rob? Really?" He slammed the tray down into Rob's lap. "Why? You got arrested! An hour before you were supposed to meet my parents to help me convince them you're not a total psychopath!"

Rob blinked at the tea and toast. Then mutinously muttered, "Yeah, well, getting nicked was more fuckin' fun."

"What?"

"Fucking come off it, Eli." Rob's words were harsh, but his voice was tired. "I could have fucking dinner with your fucking parents every night of the fucking week for the next fucking year, be on my best fucking behaviour and dress up really fucking nice, and they'd *still* think I was the cousin of the fucking Yorkshire Ripper!"

"Do you know a word other than fucking?"

"Tell me I'm wrong."

Eli paused.

"Tell me."

"I—I have to *try*, Rob, and last night you—"

"Right, yeah, you have to fucking try—why the hell am I the one proving shit, Eli? Your old man—hell, your old lady, too—they work for the same cunts who've nicked me for being out after dark, the same fuckers who think they have the right to tell me where I can live, the bastards who live hand-in-fucking-glove with the social, and God knows at least the police have the fucking decency to *label* themselves as thugs and idiots! Least they've got the fucking common decency to make sure you *know* what they are!"

"Oh, for God's sake, I am not listening to this!" Eli raged. "Don't you dare call my dad a thug, Rob—don't you *dare*!"

"Why, you think he managed to get all the way up there without giving someone a shoeing once in a fucking while?"

"If you're shitty to the police—if you're shitty to people there to *protect* us, then maybe you deserve a good shoeing!"

"Protect you from what?"

"From people like—!"

Eli stopped himself, and barely in time, but by the expression on Rob's face, he'd known what Eli was about to say anyway.

"Yeah," he said quietly. "From people like me."

His face looked haggard, grey circles ground in under his eyes. He stared almost blindly at the sheets, picking at them and shaking his head.

"Your old man is never gonna see anything but the record, Eli," he said harshly. "And why should I have to put myself through it? Through having those stuck-up fucks pick and pull at me like they have the first fucking clue what it's like, like they actually *believe* they'd have turned out any different. They think they're fucking better'n me, Eli, and they've got no fucking idea what it's like to actually struggle."

"Oh, don't try the fucking pity angle with me," Eli hissed furiously. "Lots of people struggle, Rob! It doesn't mean they end up in prison for three years, dealing drugs and getting into fights with anyone who so much as looks at them funny!"

"And what would you fucking know!"

"I'm not stupid!" Eli shouted. "Maybe when you were twelve, thirteen—shitting hell, Rob, maybe even later, after your mum went away, maybe you had an excuse then, but you're in your twenties! You pay rent and bills, you—mostly—have a job! You're a fucking adult, why is it so fucking hard to act like one? The minute you hear the word police, the minute you see a fucking car, it's like you turn into this angry kid pissing on everything in reach to mark his fucking territory! I get it, your childhood sucked and the social and the police did fuck all to help you, but grow the fuck up already!"

Rob smashed his arm through the tray, flinging it and its contents at the wall. "You have no fucking clue—!" he bellowed.

"Neither do you!" Eli screamed. He was standing over the bed, hands shaking at his sides. He wanted—with a desperate, burning fury—to pick up that flung tray and smack Rob around the head with it. "Don't you fucking tell me to understand, Rob! I grew up with fucking police, I grew up with parents whose idea of what a good kid was is rigid as fuck! I grew up the freak of the fucking family because I wasn't a perfect, sweet, innocent little *girl*! Do you have any fucking clue how *hard* it is to tell your copper dad and your forensic scientist mum that you're trans! That you're not actually straight despite your massive crush on the custody sergeant because inside you're a bloke! Do you know what they thought, Rob, do you? They thought somebody had been fucking touching me up! They were convinced I was mentally out of my fucking mind and about to run off and become a druggie—I grew *up* with police, Rob, so don't fucking tell me I don't understand what it's like to have them looking over your shoulder all the time! But you know what, at least I fucking understand you can't call them all bastards and cunts, at least I fucking realise a uniform doesn't make people identical! It's about fucking time you learned the same!"

There was a muscle fluttering in Rob's jaw; when he rose from the bed, the temperature in the room seemed to drop. And yet Eli was too angry to care, too fed up at being pulled from pillar to post like this, too sick of being stuck between the man for whom the police were everything, and the man for whom the police were the *cause* of everything.

"I'm sorry you grew up in a shitty way, I'm sorry that the police and the social let you down, but for fuck's sake, Rob, you didn't even live in Sheffield as a kid. Dad has *always* worked for the police *here*. Not in Leeds, not in Scotland, *here*. He's nothing to do with whoever fucked up and let you and your family down, let your mam and dad get away with how they dragged you all up. I get it, and I'm sorry it happened, but you have *got* to stop taking it out on every copper that walks past you!"

Rob's lip curled. "Right—and you've got to stop fucking pretending they're all saints in stab vests. You ever *been* nicked, Eli? Who am I fucking kidding, 'course you fucking haven't—well, it ain't all respect and reciting the arrest when the fucking chief inspector's son's not around to hear 'em. You even looking at my face? Yeah, Constable fucking Cadman smashed my face into the fucking bar before I ever touched him—and *trust* me, Eli, for that cunt? I'd go back inside for that spineless motherf—"

"You go back inside, and it's over," Eli snarled. "I'm no fucking prison wife, Rob—you go back to prison, and I'm gone."

Rob's jaw clenched.

"I am fucking done with this," Eli spat. "I am done with this anger and aggression just because my dad is a copper. He's a dick-head, I will grant you, there's days I would back you right up to the fucking *judge* to clock my dad, but that is *nothing* to do with his job. His job is to *protect* people, you got me? Including me. He's over-protective, he can be a real bastard about you and your history, but for fuck's sake, Rob, you have to at least give him the chance to know you before you write him off!"

"Yeah," Rob growled, "just like he is with me, right?"

"One of you has to be the adult here."

"And why the fuck does it have to be me, huh, Eli? If he's allowed to fucking judge me without having said more than five words to my face in his cocksucking little life, why the fuck can't I do the same?"

"Because somewhere in there—you know, between the whole you accepting me for who I am, and the bit where you offered to support me through art college—I got the idea you were a better man than that."

The silence that fell was ice-cold. There was frost on the in-sides of the windows; the hairs on Eli's arms were all on end. Rob's face was a storm, those pale eyes churning like a hurricane viewed from above.

And then he turned away.

"Go."

"Excuse me?"

"Get the fuck out of my flat before I do something I'll fucking regret!" Rob didn't say it; he *roared* it at a volume that made the glass in the window-panes shiver.

Eli jumped a mile and found himself at the bedroom door be-fore quite realising he'd moved.

"Fine," he said, and hated himself for the way his voice shook. "When you've got your head out of your arse, give me a ring. I won't be back until you do."

He slammed his way out of the flat, storming past Danny's wide-eyed expression in the living room doorway, and was halfway down the stairs before realising that, somewhere in the row, he'd started to cry.

CHAPTER 10

IT WAS A long day at work.

Eli fumed for the first half, and lounged listless and depressed against the counter for the other half. He worked in a little shop in the city centre three days a week for shit pay, selling cigarettes and *The Daily Mail* to old, vaguely-racist guys with Jack Russell terriers. It wasn't the type of job that kept your mind off fighting with your boyfriend.

And Eli hated fighting with Rob. It happened a fair bit—they were both volatile, quick to anger, and slow to back down—but it didn't mean Eli liked it. He'd known what Rob was like after that very first date, when Rob had nearly choked on his pint when Eli had told him what his parents did for a living. It wasn't like Eli was *surprised* by it.

He was just…he didn't *mind* much, not normally, because Rob was his own man with his own life, and Eli knew he wasn't really a bad person. What kind of stacked, heavily tattooed guy with a history of petty violence and theft found out their boyfriend was transgender and *stayed*, after all? He *knew* what kind of a man Rob was, but…

But he just wished Rob would curb the urge to get into fights when it was going to cock up things for Eli. Dad wouldn't let this go for *months*, and Eli hated sitting in the middle of the constant arguing. It wasn't fair of Dad to rag on Rob all the time, but it wasn't fair of Rob to hand him the ammunition either.

Bored and listless, the end of shift still came too soon. Eli had kept his phone switched off, worried he'd be dragged into a texting row with Jenny or Rob, but he turned it back on as he headed out the door and into the quietening city. It was half past five and a weekday, so the streets were quiet. Eli decided, rather than ring Jenny for a lift once she got out of work, to get the bus home.

Only to have a hand clamp down on his shoulder, and a cheery voice yell, "Alright, gay-boy!" in his ear.

He cracked a wan smile. "Hey, Danny."

"Wow, yeah, there's a fuckin' happy face," Danny said, and whistled. "You still pissed at Rob?"

"I don't want to talk about Rob," Eli said stiffly. "And you can tell him—"

"Ain't 'ere for 'im," Danny drawled. "Been down the gold shop."

Eli grimaced. "Don't tell me!"

"Alright, *alright*," Danny said, laughing. "You off home? C'mon, I'll give you a ride. Need to see a bloke about an 'orse in Dore anyway."

"Danny, seriously, *don't* tell me what you're up to. You *know* I'd have to tell Dad if he asked if either of you were out burgling."

"Ain't burgling," Danny said cryptically, but offered another one of those toothy grins, steering Eli down past John Lewis towards the multi-storey car park. "And our Rob ain't done a burglary in months, mate, I don't reckon he remembers 'ow."

Eli seriously doubted that.

"Actually, speaking of Rob—"

"Danny."

"—he *were* being a twat, gettin' caught t'other day, I clipped him round the ear with the stereo remote for you after you left."

Eli gave him a tired smile. "Thanks," he said finally. "I don't like being angry with him, but...thanks."

"He is sorry. Sorta. He didn't mean to get nicked."

"He was still getting wankered in a shitty pub an hour before meeting my mum and dad for dinner."

"Yeah, well, so'd I. Need more'n a bit of Dutch courage to cope with sitting in the same room as your old man and not punch him in the fat gob. I've met him, he's nicked me, back when he was a normal inspector, but bet he don't remember."

Eli blinked. "He...he mustn't. He's never brought it up."

"See, we remember them, and they don't 'member shit about us," Danny said amiably.

The car park was dark and dank, but Danny's car was warm. It was a battered Ford Focus, the only functioning things being the wheels and the heating, but it had a certain, er...charm. Even if—Eli winced as Danny reversed haphazardly out of the parking space—the gears had progressed beyond sticky and into 'non-functional' territory.

"It's just," Eli said as they joined the traffic, "the *one* night I needed him not to be nicked, the *one* night I needed him to behave himself—"

Danny laughed. "Yeah, 'cause Rob behaves."

"He does if he wants," Eli said sourly. "And he obviously didn't want."

"He didn't want to go," Danny admitted. "Told me, said it was just the one thing for you and if you asked again he'd say no. Said how he doesn't get why you need him to do it at all."

"Because I know you guys never had a decent family, but I do," Eli retorted. "And I don't want to fall out with them permanently over Rob."

"So dump him."

Danny's voice was harsh and cold. The cheery face had closed down, the smile gone.

"No."

Eli heard his own voice cooling, too, and swallowed.

"No?"

"No," he repeated. "I'm not choosing my dad's ideals over Rob. End of, it's not happening. But I'm sick of not being able to say I'm going out to Rob's without them getting all up in my face, and I know—you know—Rob isn't the devil they're making him out to be. I want to fucking show them that, and then Rob goes and confirms everything they think by being arrested."

"So who comes first? Him or them?"

Eli snorted. "I came over, didn't I?"

Danny was silent.

"Danny, I'm not saying I want him to change, or I'm always going to side with them. My dad can be a real cunt, I'll be the first to say it, but I'm sick of the constant battle. I won't be torn in two by them either. And I know if Rob can win my mum over, then she'll make my dad shut the fuck up every now and then."

"*I'll* win—"

"If you make a 'your mum' joke, Danny, I swear to God I will punch you," Eli threatened.

Danny cackled.

"With your piss-weak girly ha—*ow*, fucker!"

"Told you," Eli said grimly, retracting his hand. He rolled back his head against the rest as they passed out of the city proper and approached the windier, wider roads of Totley and Dore. "I dunno, Danny, I need to cool off tonight. I'll come and see Rob tomorrow maybe and talk it out with him proper then."

"Yeah," Danny said. "Tomorrow."

Eli side-eyed him, but Danny just shrugged.

"Heather Lea Avenue, isn't it?" he asked, rather than clarify anything, and Eli huffed.

"Yeah," he said sourly. "God, you're worse than Rob sometimes. At least if I scowl at him long enough he explains himself."

"Yeah, but I use complete sentences," Danny said, swinging the car up onto the grass, half-blocking Eli's driveway. "Piss off, you bellend. And if you don't pop round tomorrow and see to the grumpy fucker in my flat, I'll kick him out to come to you, fair warning."

"Yeah, yeah. Thanks for the lift."

"Sod off," Danny said, a practically affectionate goodbye from him.

Eli found himself a little bit cheered up as he got out of the car. It had started to drizzle feebly, but he let himself in slowly and quietly anyway, not wanting to have another barney with Dad about storming out the previous day, or talk about why Rob hadn't come to dinner.

Then he ruined his plans by nearly tripping on the box in the hall.

"The fuck?" he grumbled, picking it up. It was fairly large, reasonably heavy, and the items inside shifted. His name was on the label, so he shrugged and took it into the living room. Mum was in—a cup of tea in a flowery mug was cooling on the coffee table—but nowhere to be seen. So Eli settled down and tore the box open.

His anger instantly melted.

Presents. In bubble wrap rather than wrapping paper, and no explanation beyond a post-it floating loose instead with *sorry* scrawled in Rob's messy handwriting, but presents all the same. And not stupid presents, like flowers and chocolate and all that other shit. *Good* presents.

Eli faithfully kept an Amazon wish-list for Rob to use when it came to birthdays and Christmas—because Eli hated getting presents he didn't want, it just generated useless clutter—but he'd have to clean it out now. Rob had to have blown a decent couple of hundred quid on the contents of the box. Eli carefully peeled all the bubble wrap away and laid out the gifts on the sofa as gently as newborn children.

First and foremost was the new lens for his camera. Eli was an amateur photographer, always going out into the Peak District to get photos of the landscape. He'd dragged Rob out enough times to catch Stanage Edge at sunrise, or birds at Burbage. But he lacked a good powerful zoom, and had been pining after this lens for months. And now it was here, cool and heavy in his hands, and Eli just...

Even if he couldn't have been angry after that, the new camera bag—with the waterproof lining and the hundred little pockets for his kit—would have rubbed the rest of it away, a perfect replacement for the battered old one he'd inherited from his granddad. It even had spare straps for his camera tucked into the front pocket, and a tiny padlock to secure the main pocket shut.

"Oh, Rob, this isn't playing fair," Eli murmured when he found the third gift—a new collapsible tripod. He fumbled for his phone. In leaning over to grab it from his abandoned jacket, though, he caught sight of a folded piece of paper in the bottom of the box, and stooped to retrieve it.

It was a booklet, roughly stapled together. When Eli flipped through it, he found lots of handwritten notes. IOUs. *1 ticket 4 me 2 drive u out to the peaks for 1 of ur photoshoot things* and *1 ticket 4 camping 1 night at stanage* and the like.

Eli's heart shivered. Rob hated nature. He wasn't big on camping, and photography bored him—usually he dropped Eli off and went to the nearest pub to play on his phone until Eli texted asking to be picked up again. A whole booklet of tickets to get him out into the wilderness...

Eli sighed and retrieved his phone. *Thank you for the box,* he sent, and started to put everything back into it to take upstairs.

"Eli! When did you get home, dear?"

"About ten minutes ago," Eli mumbled.

"Oh, you found your parcel then. What is it?" Mum asked, settling herself in her armchair with a plate of chocolate digestives.

"Presents," Eli said. "From Rob."

Mum's face didn't so much as twitch.

"We had a row this morning, he must have already had them or gone right out to buy them after I left."

"What are they?"

"Photography gear. Look, he got me that lens I've been wanting ages. And a bunch of tickets to drag him out on my shoots."

A smile played around the edges of Mum's mouth, promptly hidden by her cold mug of tea. "He doesn't like going?"

"No," Eli admitted as his phone buzzed. "He's not a nature person."

Mum hummed. On that, Dad and Rob would probably get along. Dad didn't like things like hiking and camping either, thought they were primitive and pointless. "It's a long walk," he always said, "and unnecessarily complicating the act of having dinner and going to bed. Honestly, we invented houses for a reason." Maybe Eli ought to take Rob and his dad camping, let their mutual disgust at the act nullify their disgust for each other?

"What did you argue about?"

Eli shrugged.

"Eli..."

"About him getting nicked, what do you think," he said harshly. His phone buzzed again and he fumbled for it. "I don't want to talk about it, Mum, you'll only have a go."

She actually looked hurt at that.

Eli huffed.

"You *do*."

"I *don't*," she protested. "I just wor—"

"You don't trust me to actually make my own decisions," Eli said ruthlessly, unlocking the phone. "You and Dad—Dad's worse, but you do it, too—you still look at me and see Sarah."

Mum paused.

Eli opened the texts. The first was actually from Danny, going *u better appreciate that fucking box coz i had to drive rob all over for that shit!!!* The second was from Rob, a single *x* in probably the most contrite and affectionate text Eli had ever received from him.

"Eli," Mum whispered, "we've tried to support you in your transitioning, but…but it *has* been difficult. We *do* still see you as…as Sarah, sometimes. You were always so upset, so *vulnerable*, when you were younger that…that it's difficult sometimes for me and your father to recognise you're not so…delicate."

Eli ground his teeth. "I wasn't delicate," he said sharply, "and I'm not your daughter. If I was your son—if I had been born a boy, if I'd been a boy from the very beginning—you'd have warned me once about Rob and left it at that. You wouldn't be trying to protect me all the time."

Mum's face tightened, but—tellingly—she said nothing.

Eli huffed and closed the box, sending Rob another text. *Want to meet up later?*

The reply was instantaneous. *Depends r u still mad?*

Not as much anymore :)

The pause was longer this time, and Eli hefted the box into his arms and carried it upstairs. Mum made no move to follow, and Eli had no interest in her doing so. He started to put his gifts away, already mentally planning his next trip out into the Peaks, and pushing away Mum's little confession.

Eli *knew* it was fucking hard, for God's sake. He was the one who'd *done* it. There were still things he found himself not doing because 'girls don't do that.' He still hated using public toilets, not because he felt scared or ashamed going into the gents', but because it just felt plain strange. He still used the lemon and lime shower gel from Tesco, even though it was marketed for women, because he preferred the smell. He *knew* the lines weren't as solid as people made out, but Mum and Dad...

There was a difference, Eli thought, between still seeing him as their daughter and still treating him that way. He suspected they'd always see him as a girl, like parents always still saw you as a child, right?—but to *treat* him like that, after all this time and effort and money and surgery...

That was the part that grated on him. *That* was the part that he hated. Patronising him and trying to control his choices because he was just their poor, delicate, confused little Sarah...

Im free 2nite if u wanna try that diner w/ ur folks?

Eli blinked at the phone. *Sure?* he asked, biting his lip. Rob really *was* trying to get back in his good books if he was offering—Eli wasn't stupid enough to think one argument had *actually* changed the way Rob felt about his parents—and Eli didn't want to exploit that, but...but it was also the best chance he had of Rob actually behaving himself.

Yeah. Its wot u want n best get it over with.

Eli headed halfway down the stairs and leaned over the banisters like he was a teenager again to yell, "Mum!"

"Yes?"

"What's for dinner?"

"Your father said something about Italian."

"Is it a full sit-down?"

"I'm not sure if Jenny's coming over. Why?"

Eli chewed on his lip, then thought, *To hell with it.* "Rob says he's free to come over tonight."

The armchair creaked, and Mum appeared in the living room doorway, peering up at him anxiously. "Is that a good idea?"

Eli shrugged. "Might as well get it over with?"

Mum nodded slowly. "Alright. Alright, I'll ring your father...tell him to come at seven, that'll give us a bit of time, and..."

She wandered into the kitchen, muttering to herself, and Eli headed back upstairs. *Come at 7. It's Italian food. Bring a bottle of whiskey or something for Dad,* he added, deciding to give Rob all the help he could get.

K.

I'm sorry about blowing up, but you were being a dick.

Yeah i no x

And thank you again for the presents :) I think you maaay be forgiven.

Rob was either still annoyed, or worried about annoying Eli, because there was no reply to that, where usually there would be flirting or outright sexting, but Eli didn't mind. One dinner. An hour and a half, tops, and then they could escape and Eli could reward Rob for behaving himself, or—

And if you fuck around this time, I'll punish you. HARD.

Either way, it was beyond fucking time to do this.

CHAPTER II

"OH MY GOD," Eli said when he opened the door.

"Fuck off."

The response was all Rob. The man wasn't.

"You look...um...different."

"Fuck. Off," Rob repeated clearly, and Eli laughed.

"Oh God, you poor thing..."

"You told me to!"

Rob could not have looked more uncomfortable had he tried. There was nothing inherently *wrong* in what he wore—a simple pale blue button up shirt and some dark, well-fitted jeans—but...he looked neat. Even his stubble looked tidy for once, and it wasn't a look that really suited the Rob that Eli knew and loved.

"Well," Eli said, looping his arms around Rob's shoulders and kissing him softly in compensation, "it'll only be for a couple of hours, and then we can go back to your flat. And what I said the first time we tried to do this stands."

"Oh?"

"Fuck me around and I'll punish you," Eli said, then bit Rob's earlobe. "But behave yourself..."

Rob smiled against his face, then let go. Eli stepped back and took his hand to lead him into the house., beaming when Rob took off his boots without prompting, and was even wearing matching socks. Eli kissed him in the hall before taking the offered bottle of whiskey and propelling him into the living room with a hand in the small of his back.

For a brief second, an awkward silence flooded in. Dad was in the kitchen—Mum had ordered him to cook, saying she didn't trust him not to start a row before the starter—but Mum and Jenny were in the living room, with Eli's four-year-old niece playing with her dolls on the coffee table. All three stared unabashedly at Rob; Rob shifted on his feet, and Eli bit his lip at the strained quiet.

"Oh," Jenny said.

"Um," Eli said, swallowing. Jenny had never actually met Rob face-to-face, and judging by the critical look on her face, she wasn't enjoying the experience. "Rob, this is Jenny, my sister. Jen—"

"You're *tall*!"

The outburst came from Flora. She promptly abandoned her dolls and rocketed to Rob's knees, little hands clutching at the denim of his jeans. Flora was tiny even for a four-year-old, a little lump of fair hair and big brown eyes. She looked comically small beside Rob.

"You're a tree," she said decidedly.

"That's Flora," Eli said. "My niece."

Rob coughed. "Er."

"Mummy, he's a *tree*!" Flora insisted gleefully, then swung back to Rob, beaming. "Can I climb you?"

"Er."

"Flora, leave our guest alone," Mum admonished.

"But, Gammar, he's a tree!" Flora wailed, like this was the most important fact in the entire universe. "Can I climb you?" she implored again, clasping her hands in front of her face. "Please? *Please?*"

"Um, I suppose so," Rob said carefully. Flora beamed, then instantly scowled again.

"Well, you have to get down *here*, then!"

Rob shot Eli a dark look, but then rolled his eyes and dropped to his knees. Flora squealed in delight, clapping her chubby hands, before roughly seizing Rob's shirt and scrambling up his chest and shoulder in a graceless motion that, had she or Rob been average height, would have earned him a kick in the groin.

"Now stand up!" Flora commanded once she was in place on Rob's shoulders. He warily stood up, one hand clamped around her ankle where her leg trailed down over his chest.

She cackled in demonic happiness. "Gammar! Gammar, Mummy, look, I climbed the tree!"

"Flora, he's not a tree, don't be rude," Jenny snapped. "I'm— I'm sorry, Rob, she's a bit—"

"But *Mummy*, I climbed it!"

"No you didn't," Rob said.

Eli jumped at the interruption. He had been fully prepared for Rob to pretend he was deaf and dumb for the entire meal, or only speak when absolutely, strictly required. He certainly hadn't expected Rob to play along with Flora's insanity.

"I helped you. Real trees don't help."

Flora scowled at the back of his head. "Nuh-huh, I did it by myself!"

"Nah," Rob said. "You couldn't climb a real tree."

The argument was brief and brutal, and Eli caught his mother smiling behind her hand. Jenny seemed torn between horror at Flora's behaviour, and delight at Rob not flipping his shit. It was the one thing the family did agree on—a man couldn't be blamed for going berserk after five minutes in Flora's divine company.

Eventually, Rob planted Flora back on the floor and folded his arms over his chest while she dug her hands into his belt and attempted to climb him without assistance. Jenny laughed properly then, visibly warming to him, and Rob cracked a very faint smile.

"Well, I'd say sit down, but I guess you're stuck," Eli said. "Want a drink?"

"Er."

"I'll get you a Grolsch," Eli offered—at least that came in a glass bottle and not a can—and slipped out into the kitchen. Dad was slaving over the oven, pans bubbling on the hob, and Eli ignored him. Best not to provoke things.

When he returned with a couple of bottles of Grolsch, Flora had her feet precariously in Rob's belt and her hands were scrabbling for a good hold on his shirt. Jenny was asking Rob about what he did for a living.

"This and that," was his diplomatic response. "Security, building sites, you know. Manual labour type stuff."

"It's the ink and muscles that do it," Eli said, delivering the bottle with a kiss on the cheek.

Flora scowled at him and called him icky for it.

"Jenny, why is the monster here anyway?"

"Babysitter cancelled," she said, waving a hand. "Rob, I don't suppose you or your brother babysit?"

"How old is she?"

"Four."

"Not if you want her to live to see five."

Jenny choked on her tea.

Eli sniggered. "Rob's incapable of looking after a house plant, never mind a child."

Flora chose that exact moment to fall off Rob's chest. He wordlessly caught her and set her on her feet.

"He seems to manage quite well," Mum said mildly.

"Told you you're a tree!" Flora informed him bossily before flouncing back to her dolls.

"Trees don't catch!" Rob threw after her as Eli took his hand and tugged him down onto the sofa. For a split second, Rob's knees parted and he shifted as though about to perform his habitual, that-man-can't-have-a-functioning-spine lounge, but caught Eli's eye and corrected his posture hastily.

"So, Rob," Mum said in a cool tone. "How did you and Eli meet?"

Eli froze, bottle halfway to his lips.

Rob gave him a sideways glance and said, "Pub."

Pub. Yeah. A gay pub, in the city centre, with loud music and tiny, dirty toilets useful for couples to barricade themselves into the cubicles and get a few drunk orgasms out of the way.

"Oh, which one?"

"Er," Rob said. "Can't remember really."

"It was my birthday," Eli jumped in hastily. "We met on that bar crawl. We, um, we danced a bit and Rob gave me his number."

Rob gave him another sideways glance, but thankfully his face remained completely neutral.

"Yes," Mum said slowly. "Very...nice."

"That's how most people meet now, Mum," Eli said. "I thought he was attractive so I danced with him and got his number. I'm guessing Rob felt the same."

"Whatever helps you sleep at night, sweetheart," Rob drawled, and Eli hit his thigh. Jenny giggled though, so it wasn't all a bad remark.

"So is Eli your first...boyfriend, then, Rob?" Mum asked, still in that cool, calculating tone. It was her interview-room tone, Dad had once called it, and it had always brought Eli out in a cold sweat when she'd turned it on him as a teenager.

"No."

"No?"

"Yeah. No," Rob repeated in a slightly challenging tone.

Eli pinched him.

"Ow! What? You're not."

"You could *elaborate*," Eli suggested.

A look of confusion washed over Rob's face.

"Explain."

"What's to explain?" Rob asked. "You're not my first boyfriend. Second."

"So you've been in monogamous relationships before? You have a history?" Mum interrupted.

Rob's eyes narrowed, and the bottle—raised to his lips— dropped slowly. "Yes," he said, even more slowly.

"Mum."

"I'm just asking, dear."

Rob leaned forward, propping his elbows on his knees, and stared at Mum through those focused, calculating eyes. The intense stare made Eli shiver with totally inappropriate desire, the way those pale eyes just bored into her, like they were stripping back the layers and exposing her very bones and soul.

God, he wanted to fuck Rob when he wore that expression. Eli took a hasty swig of his drink to cool his burning face.

"I had a boyfriend when I was nineteen," Rob said in a quiet, almost dangerous tone. "Michael. We were together about a year."

"What happened?"

"He didn't want to do long-distance when I went to prison," Rob said bluntly.

Mum's mouth tightened. Jenny paused in stirring her tea, glancing at Eli.

"And what did Michael think of your…conviction?"

Rob smiled toothily. "Not much, he grew weed in his attic."

Something banged in the kitchen and Dad yelled that dinner was ready. Mum sat very still for the longest time, her gaze locked with Rob's, and Eli threw a desperate look at Jenny.

"Flora," Jenny said loudly, "why don't you show Gammar which bit of cake you'd like for dessert, eh?"

The hurricane was unleashed on Mum, and as the women left the living room, Eli leaned close to brush his lips over Rob's ear. "You're getting the belt for that," he whispered.

"What? Why?"

"You know why," Eli said, wrapping his teeth around Rob's earlobe in warning. "Don't fuck me around, Rob."

Rob's answer was a deep grunt before he tugged himself free and kissed Eli's neck, mouth open and hungry.

"No marks," Eli hissed, pushing him off, but dropping a quick kiss on the corner of his lip in recompense. "But you're doing well with Jenny. Just stop rising to Mum, okay?"

Rob rolled his eyes, but nodded.

The kitchen—because Dad was a good but haphazard cook— was chaotic enough that Eli managed to get them to their seats without further incident, presenting Dad quietly with Rob's gift and planting himself between Rob and his father's seat at the head of the table in case of any worse incidents. Mum had set the table out with the best silver, a pastel pink tablecloth under shiny china plates, and a messy starter of…er…something in a something sauce already laid out.

"Dig in, everyone," Dad said, dropping himself into his seat.

He took up his fork, however, and immediately jabbed it in Rob's direction. "Shame you couldn't make it last time."

Rob raised his eyebrows. "Yeah. Shame. Sorry about the lack of notice."

His voice was steely. Eli pressed his heel warningly down onto Rob's toes.

"What was the charge, in the end?"

"Dad, stop it," Eli said firmly before Rob could reply. "Let's talk about something else. Rob, why don't—"

"No, Eli, I'd like to hear this," Dad interrupted. "Come on, Hawkes. What was the charge?"

"Drunk and disorderly," Rob said eventually. "They dropped the assault PC one."

"And you think that conduct was acceptable, do you?"

"With all due respect, *sir*," Rob said, managing to make 'sir' sound like 'fucking cunt' with the least effort possible, "have you ever *met* PC Cadman?"

"I can't say I know the officer in question, but—"

"He's the kind of man," Rob said carefully, "that sweet little old ladies would want to assault. I only spat at him. He ought to be grateful nobody in the building took his f—took his block off."

"Spitting at a man in uniform—"

"Stop it!" Eli snapped. "Dad, *stop it*. I didn't bring Rob here so you could interrogate him, I brought him here so you could meet him properly and see the man *I* see."

"I see a man who thinks spitting at policemen is acceptable, Eli," Dad said coldly.

"And I see a man who is offering to support me through art college because I have a talent, even though he hates art," Eli retorted hotly.

There was a ringing silence, aside from Flora obliviously and gleefully scraping her fork against her plate. Whatever the something in something sauce was, it was enjoyable to a four-year-old's palate.

"Are you going to go?" Jenny asked quietly.

"Go where?" Eli asked.

"Back to art college?"

"Maybe." He shrugged, toying with his own food. "Rob's offered to support me financially—"

"We can do that, Eli," Mum interrupted.

"—and let me stay at his flat," Eli continued loudly. "And I'm seriously thinking about it, it's a nice flat with a hot guy in it." Out of the corner of his eye, he saw Rob crack a smile. "Shame about the hobo in the second bedroom."

"He's not a hobo, it's like having a really big, really loud dog," Rob said.

Eli laughed.

"Oh, please, a dog would shed less, I swear I found one of those dreads in the shower last time I was there—"

"Excuse me, who are we discussing?" Mum interrupted primly.

"Rob's brother, Danny."

"Oh," Mum said. "You have a brother." She already knew that, Eli thought bitterly, but then Mum was a pro at 'polite' questions.

"Got a whole bunch of siblings," Rob said, a little roughly but in a calmer tone than before. "Five older sisters and a younger brother."

"That's a…large family."

Rob shrugged.

"Do you see them often?"

"Brother lives with me. Haven't seen any of the girls since I was fourteen."

"Fourteen?" Dad probed.

Eli sighed through his nose. Rob, though, didn't seem to have any such concerns.

"Since I went into care."

Jenny made a faint sound and put her hand over her mouth.

"Mummy," Flora asked, "what's care?"

"It's where kids go who haven't got nowhere else to go," Rob said.

"Like when?"

"I went to care when my parents left," Rob said in an unusually soft tone. "I didn't have any other family so we went into care, me and my younger brother. That's when the government look after you."

Eli slipped his hand under the table and squeezed Rob's thigh. Flora made an 'oh' of understanding and went back to stabbing her starter.

"Your parents went away?" Mum asked. Eli could almost hear the quote marks.

"Dad left. Years earlier. Then Mum went to prison."

"Naturally."

Dad's voice was cold.

Rob's head snapped round. "What's that supposed to mean?"

"Merely that children very often follow in their parents' footsteps," Dad said coolly. "Jenny and Eli have had their ups and downs but have turned out reasonably well, due to their stable background. You, on the other hand…"

"My father might've beat me for bein' a pouf, but at least he didn't bury his head in the sand and pretend he wasn't hearing what his kids were tellin' him," Rob said harshly.

The silence, this time, was absolute. Eli's heart hurt it was beating so hard, and Jenny had frozen with her fork halfway to her mouth. Mum was simply…still. Even Flora paused, the sudden tension in the room making her tiny face furrow in distress.

"Excuse me." Dad's voice was made of pure *cold*. Frost formed on the kitchen surfaces.

"You heard me," Rob replied, his tone the fire to Dad's ice. "Eli's told me the lot, how he tried to tell you for years what he was and you ignored it completely, refused to even discuss it, until he was sixteen and went to the doctor on his own to start sorting it out. You forced him to grow up fucking traumatised because you couldn't bear to open your goddamn mind and think for half a second about what was any good for your own kid—hell, my old man was a shit but at least he was a straight-up shit and didn't hide behind bullcrap like you."

"Rob!" Eli shouted, appalled.

"What's fucking traumatised?" Flora asked innocently.

"Oh my God," said Mum.

"I will not be spoken to like that in my own house by a common criminal!" Dad bellowed.

Eli saw red.

"He's more honest than you are!" he yelled, surging to his feet. "Rob's *tried*, Dad, he really has, he used to call you all sorts when we got together but he's tried—for *me*—and you won't do the same! You've judged him before you've even met him!"

"And this is supposed to enamour me! To a crook, to a lying—"

"*He's telling the truth!*" Eli roared.

A deadly silence rang in its wake.

"What," Dad said.

"He's telling the truth," Eli repeated softly. "You never once let me talk to you about it, none of it. You said it was silly and I needed to grow up. You said it was just a daft phase. You never once supported me, even after the doctor referred me to the clinic, even after the clinic helped me figure things out, even after I changed my name. The psychiatrist asked you again and again to come with me and talk to him, just one session, and you always said you were too busy. And you know what, Rob's right. You might not have hit me, but it *hurt*. You still look at me like I'm your daughter, you *do*."

"Eli…"

"Why don't you just call me Sarah and be done with it, that's who you're still seeing," Eli demanded bitterly, then swallowed against the lump in his throat. "I told Rob on our third date. Our third date, *this* guy, I told him. I was shitting myself, Dad, I was terrified, and he just turned round and went *bloody hell, that's a turn-up for the books*. That was *it*. In one sentence he supported me more than you *ever* have."

"Mummy, is Uncle Eli a girl?" Flora asked, tugging on Jenny's sleeve.

Eli scrubbed his wrist across his eyes.

"Rob, c'mon."

"Eli, for goodness' sake, Rob can go home and we can talk about this—" Mum attempted.

"No," Eli said. "You don't get to gut him and humiliate him at dinner then kick him out to talk to me. We're going. Rob. *C'mon.*"

Rob rose from his chair without a word, nodding to Jenny and wiggling his fingers at Flora in a funny wave before tucking an arm around Eli's hips and steering them towards the front door.

"Eli, this is silly!" Mum cried.

A chair scraped; Eli swore softly, and Rob tapped his hip with two fingers.

"Take me home," Eli whispered.

"'Kay."

"Mum, leave it!" Eli shouted as she followed them into the hall. "I'm done, I'm done trying to make peace because you never fucking listen anyway."

"Look, your father's—"

"You're just as bad, harping on at Rob about how we met and if he cheated on his ex-boyfriend!" Eli snapped.

Rob held out his coat, and Eli batted it away.

"We're going. We're fucking going!"

"He is going!" Dad's thunderous boom rattled off the words, and he came storming into the hall, shouldering past Mum and jabbing his finger at Rob. "He is going, you are staying right here, and we are through with this—this—"

"This *what?*"

"I will not have my son under the thumb of some drug-dealing scumbag and his halfwit psychotic brother!" Dad roared.

Rob stilled.

"You will only end up hurt and I'll be damned if I see the likes of Hawkes and his addict excuse for a brother—"

"No!"

Eli lunged.

But Rob lunged faster, his inked fist slamming into Dad's eye with a sickening crunch.

CHAPTER 12

ELI PACED THE living room, and Rob lounged in the kitchen doorway.

For the longest time after they'd got home, there'd been silence. Then Eli had begun to swear—at his parents, at his sister, at Rob, at everyone. He didn't know who he was angriest at, and the hurt was bubbling under the rage, too, the memory of a whole childhood of being told he was just going through a phase and it was all in his mind, surging from wherever he'd buried it in the back of his head.

Finally, though, he dropped onto the sofa, and kicked the coffee table.

"You're a shit," he told Rob.

Rob said nothing.

"I told you—I fucking *told* you—not to piss them off, not to rise to it, to fucking *behave,* and you think punching my dad in the face is behaving?"

"He was being a cunt to you. To Danny."

"I don't fucking care, Rob, you weren't to be a cunt back!" Eli shouted.

Rob fell silent again.

"Oh my God," Eli groaned, raking both hands through his hair. "You fucking disobeyed me. I told you—I told you in a *scene*—to behave yourself, and you didn't."

"He was—"

"I don't fucking care! Dad can be an ornery old git but it didn't give you the excuse to rise to it!" Eli shouted.

Rob nodded, twisted, and vanished into the hall.

"Fuck's sake," Eli grumbled. He didn't need this, too. A row with his parents *and* a row with Rob—it was too much. He was sick of this shit, sick of neither Rob nor his dad trying in the *slightest* to make peace with each other, and—

The belt landed in his lap, a heavy coil of black leather, and Eli sat back. He stroked it with one finger as Rob came around to kneel in front of him, hands clasped on Eli's knees.

"What's this?"

"I disobeyed you."

"You think you deserve this?"

"I disobeyed you," Rob repeated flatly.

"Yeah, and you also get off on punishment," Eli retorted. "You think you fucking deserve it?"

"I think you need it."

Eli pursed his lips. To punish Rob for what he'd done, to force him to take Eli's rules seriously when it came to his father—Eli's fingers itched. He *did* need it. He did...but he was also very, very angry, and knew all too well that belting Rob when he was angry...

"Go for a run."

Rob tilted his head.

"Go for a run," Eli said. "A long one. Then come back. Shower, and clean yourself properly. And then we'll see how I'm going to punish you because right now, Rob, I am so fucking angry with you that I will seriously hurt you."

Rob didn't say a word. He simply nodded.

"Go on, fuck off," Eli said harshly.

Rob kissed the linen over Eli's knee and fucked off.

❖

ROB WAS GONE for an hour and a half, and it was an hour and a half that Eli sorely needed.

Left to his own devices in the flat, his anger had started to cool. At his core, he'd not really expected the dinner to go well in the first place, and when he sat back and scrutinised it properly, it had actually—from Rob's side—gone better than Eli had hoped. He'd nearly won Jenny over, and little Flora loved him, as much as the tiny psycho loved anyone. And if Jenny and Eli agreed on anything, it was that the way Dad had treated Eli growing up hadn't been fair.

So, really, it boiled down to the clash between Mum and Dad, and Rob. Which was what Eli had expected.

Putting himself in Rob's shoes, he found that the evening didn't much change. Rob had, in the end, spoken out in Eli's defence, not really his own. Yes, he'd attacked, but Dad had been attacking Rob from day one, and at least Rob's attack was a challenge to Dad on how *he'd* treated Eli—which was the whole reason Mum and Dad hated him, their belief that *Rob* was mistreating Eli, and—

Eli's head hurt.

He supposed, when he drilled right down into the heart of the dinner, that he couldn't blame Rob for snapping, all the little digs at his lifestyle and his family. To call Rob bound to take after his mother was a low blow, especially as Eli knew Rob hated his mother. And yes, Rob's conduct had been unacceptable—especially after Eli's orders—but...well, it was understandable, if not excusable.

So by the time the door popped open, and a set of keys hit the wall, Eli had cooled off. Mostly.

"Shower," he called, without turning his head. When he heard nothing, he added a stern: "*Now.* Don't make it worse for yourself."

Footsteps padded away, and Eli drained his glass of juice before switching the TV off. This would be in Rob's room; he would not tolerate this lesson being interrupted.

Eli set up the room while Rob started his shower, and checked the first aid kit in the kitchen cupboard just in case. He'd restocked it after last time—not, ironically, a scene, but Rob falling off the bed and bashing his forehead open on the side table—but with

Danny around, the thing could get depleted in a week, easy. Guy was an idiot.

Once everything was set up, Eli let himself into the bathroom.

Rob's shower was just an over-the-bath job, and Eli jerked the curtain back roughly before retreating to sit on the closed toilet lid. His arousal burned low and fierce, the sight of Rob's naked body under the spray tempered by the cool mantle of control that was settling on Eli's shoulders.

"You were out of line at dinner," he said calmly.

Rob pushed back his wet hair and peered at him from under the water.

"You disobeyed an instruction I gave you in a scene—a scene you agreed to. You embarrassed me, you angered me, and you ruined the attempt I made at making peace between you and my father."

Rob dropped his gaze, but said nothing.

"I'm going to punish you," Eli continued, "but that's not all I'm going to do. You *did* speak out in my defence. You *did* make the effort with Jenny. And my parents were both out of line themselves in picking at you like they did. Any man would have gotten angry, and I accept that. And I will recognise where you did good, too."

A muscle in Rob's jaw fluttered.

Eli narrowed his eyes.

"I will tell you my plans for you tonight. I will hurt you, but not beyond your limits. And I will reward you at the end, for the things you did right. If you take your punishment properly, that'll be the end of it. If you don't, I'll punish you more. You got it?"

This was the part that gave Eli control—the formal speech, the way Rob would quiet and listen to his tone, the one he'd adopted from his mother when she was scolding people. It let Eli distance himself from his thoughts and anger, let him apply calm and rationality to his hands and actions. It stopped him from overstepping the mark, or really hurting Rob, because this was the dangerous ground, the areas in which Eli's kinks and games were more extreme than Rob's play.

And Eli had learned early that this laying out of plans was the best way to draw Rob in. He didn't react well to surprises at the best of times, and in the middle of punishment even less. And angry as Eli was, determined as he was to punish Rob for being such a shit at dinner, he never wanted to *really* cause any damage.

"You're going to finish your shower and dry off, then go to your room. You won't put any clothes on. You will kneel by the bed, facing it, and put your arms over the mattress. I will tie them there—"

"Close?"

Eli forgave the interruption, but gave Rob a warning look. "Your arms will be pulled straight, and apart. There'll be no ability to move."

Rob nodded, and the sudden stillness eased. He returned to washing his hair, although those eerily pale eyes remained on Eli's face.

"I'm going to beat you," Eli said calmly. "Five strikes for everything you did that angered me. You won't move or cry out. You won't speak unless I tell you to—the only exception is to use a safeword. You'll get hard, I know you, but you will not try to rub yourself on anything and you won't come. When the beating is over, I'll make you come, and on my terms. Understood?"

Rob blinked; water cascaded over his eyelashes. "What will you use?"

"For the ties or the beating?"

"The beating."

"Whatever I like," Eli said coldly.

Rob's jaw clenched again.

"You've got an objection?"

"I—yes."

"Tough," Eli snapped. "If you hadn't have stepped out of line, I wouldn't be doing this at all."

Rob's lip tightened, and he shook his head. "If you use the cord, I'll safeword."

The cord was a short length of a former washing line, thick and heavy and made of metal wire in a blue rubber casing. It delivered a heavy blow, but was a bit unwieldy and too clumsy for Eli's taste. He used it more for restraint than beating—but he narrowed his eyes anyway. This wasn't the time for Rob to call the shots, unless...

"Why."

Rob shook his head.

"*Why*, Rob."

Rob visibly swallowed. "I can't. Not that, not for punishment. I'll safeword."

Eli softened. He knew not to screw with the limits of a man who had been beaten for real in the past. He rose from the toilet to step up onto the edge of the bath, cup Rob's wet face in one hand, and kiss him lightly.

"Alright, no washing line cord," he said quietly, catching Rob's eye and holding the contact firmly. "I'm doing this to teach you a lesson, Rob. It's not about hurting you, it's about you realising your behaviour wasn't on tonight. Okay? I'm not trying to humiliate you or abuse you. And I'm not being a dick, okay? You also did some things perfect tonight, and I'll reward you for those, too."

Rob nudged his face into Eli's and kissed his jaw, soft and lingering. "Yeah." His voice was a deep rasp, and it calmed Eli. He would have to tread carefully, but it could be done.

"Finish up and go to the bedroom," he said quietly, then turned on his heel and left. He retreated to the kitchen to get a couple of glasses of water and several deep breaths, calming himself and centring his mind. He couldn't do this angry. If he did it angry, he'd be no better than Rob's shit of a father—and it wasn't about hurting him. It was about getting him to break that aggressive arsehole cycle of behaviour he had going. About making him learn how to not rise to it whenever someone pissed him off.

And after, if Rob proved himself, it would be about rewarding him, too. Because Eli wasn't blind to *why* Rob had snapped.

He heard the bedroom door click shut, and counted slowly to thirty to give Rob the chance to get settled. It was always initially a struggle to get Rob to let go of his own control, and this wouldn't work if Eli had to force him to do that as well.

"Five for five," Eli told himself quietly, then rolled his shoulders and straightened his spine. "Alright."

The walk to the bedroom door was the longest of Eli's life, but the sight beyond it washed away all his reservations. Rob was completely naked, kneeling by the side of the bed, arms laid out across it and head bowed to expose the nape of his neck. His breathing was deep and even, his powerful shoulders shifting with every inhalation, the tattoos shivering and swimming in ripples across his bare skin.

Eli swallowed against a suddenly dry throat, and locked the door.

He said nothing as he set up, opening the bottom drawers and finding the long chain and cuffs. The chain was taut once he'd wound it around the radiator and padlocked it to the cuffs, and he made sure Rob couldn't pull his arms back once he'd been cuffed in. Those massive biceps were stretched flat; his shoulders were tight with the strain

Eli kissed the skin between his shoulder blades then stepped behind him and tugged sharply on his hair.

"I'm going to blindfold you," he said calmly, "and you will only speak when spoken to, or to safeword. Understood?"

"Yes, sir."

The honorific—so rarely given, even in a scene—caused Eli's skin to prickle, a pulse beginning to make itself known in his groin. He kissed Rob's ear as he slid the blindfold into place and knotted it tightly, then stepped back. The picture of Rob naked and immobilised, his cock already rising half-hard from a dark crop of wiry hair, was still incomplete. Eli rubbed his thumb over his bottom lip. He knew what he *wanted*, but...

He shrugged, and rummaged in the drawer. He rarely used the plugs, as he preferred strap-ons and the lack of a thrust action frustrated the hell out of Rob, but the sensation of them, forcing you open and keeping you totally filled, was itself quite immobilising. It was a vulnerable thing, and it was just what Eli was looking for.

So he dropped it on the bedspread with a packet of tissues, and began to warm the lube in his hands.

"One day," he said, almost conversationally, "I am going to get it through to you that it's not acceptable to get aggressive every time someone says something you don't like. One day, you are going to grasp that there's a time and a place to be an arsehole, and at family dinners in front of four-year-olds isn't it."

Rob twitched, knees shifting further apart, when Eli pressed the first finger inside. His head turned to the side, as though trying to look at Eli through the blindfold, but he said nothing.

"I can excuse *why* you lost your temper this time," Eli continued blithely, working the second finger in before Rob was really ready for it. Let him feel the sting. "Coming to my defence, I can excuse that. I can even appreciate it. But I told you specifically to behave and *not* lose your temper."

"I—"

"That's another five strikes," Eli interrupted.

Rob's jaw clicked shut.

"Five for six now, Rob. You break another rule, and I will have to use a heavier belt."

Silence.

Eli nodded, and pushed the third finger in, stretching his hand only briefly before Rob clenched down and forced him to stop. He waited patiently, rubbing circles into Rob's hip with his other hand. He had all the time in the world for this—it would, after all, be Rob begging for it to stop by the end.

He didn't stretch Rob as much as he normally would. He wiped his hands off with the tissues before slicking up the plug and—rather than easing it in—pushed it with enough force that Rob grunted and rose up on his knees with a harsh noise deep in his chest. Eli braced his hip with one hand and kept pushing with the other, until the plug was firmly seated and Rob was breathing heavily through his nose, harsh pants loud against the sheets.

"If that comes out," Eli said quietly, "I'll put it back. And every time I have to, it will hurt more. Understood?"

"Y-yes, sir."

"Good," Eli said, and kissed the tight skin of Rob's shoulder. His tattoos were heaving as he breathed, and Eli waited there, lips pressed to hot skin, until the shivering began to calm.

Then he stood, and reached for the belt that Rob had offered earlier.

It had been, once, a perfectly standard man's leather belt: black, heavy, and clearly designed to hold up jeans and combats. It was old but sturdy, the buckle a bright gold. It was their standard weapon of choice when Eli felt the need to punish Rob's misbehaviour, and the one Rob was least likely to reject—but Eli had modified it. He didn't like drawing blood or leaving permanent damage. That, to Eli, crossed the line into abuse, so he'd wound several layers of tape around the buckle to lock the prong into the main frame. It couldn't cut or rip the skin, but was still harder than the leather strap itself and, therefore, more effective.

Eli curled his fingers around the end, and felt cool, raw power flooding up his arm in a cold rush of adrenaline.

"I'm going to strike you five times for every one thing you did wrong," he said quietly. "I will tell you what you did, punish you, and then we will move on and it will be forgiven. Understood?"

"Yes, sir."

"Colour?"

"Green."

Eli nodded, and ran the leather through his fingers. "First, for hitting my dad."

He raised his arm, and slammed it down. The buckle made a sound like a dull slap as it struck Rob's shoulder, a red mark blooming instantly. Rob grunted and rocked into the bed, forehead pressed into the mattress, but Eli gave him no time to recover from the blow, lifting his arm again, and again, and again.

The blows were rapid and hard, Eli's muscles burning with the force of it, his blood humming with wild, hot anticipation. His heart was hammering in his chest, and he felt invincible, powerful, and almost like the sensation of it was too large for his own body.

On the fifth blow, he stepped back, and coiled the belt in his hands like a whip. Rob was breathing harshly, but not wheezing. Five marks gleamed on his white skin, a pale pink and ready to form welts.

"Secondly, for swearing at my family. Being angry is no excuse to use that kind of language towards them, especially not in front of my niece."

The chain rattled, the radiator groaning at the first blow. Eli brought down the belt harder in response, and heard the distinct sound of Rob biting back a curse. He was rocking up into every one lightly, knees wide and toes curling when the strike hit.

"Thirdly," Eli said, a little breathlessly. When he glanced down, Rob was completely hard, his cock flushed so dark it looked painful. "Thirdly, for being rude to my mother. Don't think I didn't notice you trying to wind her up when she asked about your dating history. You should have answered her politely and calmly, and with no fucking cheek. Understood?"

"Yes, sir."

Rob's voice was shaky. Eli struck to cut off the title, causing Rob to groan loudly over the 'r.' There was a light sheen of sweat on his back, his skin gleaming. Eli had to pause to grind his own hand into his crotch and breathe through the urge to drop the belt and punish Rob by biting him all over instead. God, he wanted to sink his teeth into Rob's shoulder, wanted to drive Rob mad when he couldn't touch himself by twisting the plug but refusing to touch his cock, wanted to—

"Amber."

It was like a bucket of cold water over the head; Eli froze, hand still raised for the next strike, then dropped it. He braced his arms on the bed, bending over Rob and kissing the nape of the man's neck, waiting for either the instruction to continue, or the axe to fall.

Up close, the layer of sweat was thicker than Eli liked, and he mentally scratched off the fifth and sixth punishments. Rob wouldn't last another fifteen blows, not the way his breathing was going and the reddening of his wrists in the metal.

"Talk to me," he said.

Rob shook his head, almost burrowing his face into the sheets.Eli flicked the back of his neck.

"Talk to me," he repeated. "Help me help you. It's not an option."

"Just…a bit…intense," Rob mumbled eventually.

Eli stroked his hair.

"You want to stop?"

"No. Just pause."

Rob was still very hard. Eli kept a hand on his shoulder and waited, unsure of which way Rob was leaning, uncertain if he was struggling with the pain, the arousal, or the vulnerability. So Eli waited until Rob's chest began to slow.

"Green."

"Sure?"

"Yes. Green."

"Okay," Eli said, stepping back. "Four out of five is enough, so we'll move on to the fourth and fifth problems. The way you spoke to my father was *completely* unacceptable. You could have spoken calmly and rationally to him. But you chose to be aggressive, when I specifically told you to behave, and when we've already fought about the way you and my father butt heads all the time. I was *furious* with you about that. So for that, you deserve *ten* strikes."

Rob's throat worked.

"You disagree with me?"

"No, sir."

"You agree you were out of line?"

"Yes, sir."

"You understand that you made me feel angry and embarrassed by your behaviour?"

"Yes, sir."

"Are you sorry for it?"

Rob paused.

"Answer me."

"No, sir."

"No?"

Silence.

"Explain."

"I won't lie to you. I don't feel sorry for what I said to him. But I am sorry it upset you."

Eli pursed his lips. "Right," he said. "Eleven strikes."

Rob breathed out, and turned his face into the mattress again. "Green."

Eli hit him. It was the hardest blow yet. Rob let out a noise between his teeth like a scalded cat. The second, Eli saw him clench down around the plug. The third, his feet twisted under him and he nearly squirmed, the agitation obvious. The fourth and fifth—in quick succession—he began to shout, and the seventh he let out a noise dangerously close to a sob. Then the eighth—

"I'm—!"

He shifted as he opened his mouth, and the belt struck hard on one of the previous welts. The flash of blood was like a floodlight. Eli stopped dead, his mind screeching to a halt, Rob's transgression of speaking forgotten.

"That's enough," Eli said, dropping the belt onto the bed. "That's enough. You've been punished enough. Now let me reward you."

Rob pushed back into him when Eli slid down to the floor and pressed kisses to the damaged skin. The broken welt was bleeding sluggishly against his mouth, and he murmured reassurances as Rob shook in his arms, the chain and cuffs rattling with the force of it.

"Let me take care of you," Eli breathed softly, rubbing open hands over Rob's hips and encouraging the way he thrust up into them. "You came to my defence, you were angry for the way I've been treated, and I will never, ever punish you for that. You weren't angry for *you*, you were angry for *me*, and I love you for that, I love the way you're so fiercely protective of the people you care for…"

He kept his voice low and soothing as he grasped the base of the plug and twisted it, pressing it up deliberately into Rob's prostate, wrapping the fingers of his other hand around that steel-hard cock. It was scalding hot to the touch, slick with precum. Rob's chest shuddered like he was sobbing silently, his back arching and his arms straining against the chain with desperation.

"Please," he begged.

Eli ignored the breach of the silence rule.

"God, please, Eli, please—"

Eli pushed his hips flush against Rob's and rocked, rolling them up in light thrusts. He slid his left hand high to press the palm lightly against Rob's throat and pin the man to Eli's movements. Squeezing that painfully hard erection in his right hand, Eli jerked Rob with rough, firm strokes designed for raw pleasure, not teasing.

Rob came so hard his breathing stuttered and momentarily stopped entirely. Tears were running down his face, and Eli held him tightly through the shakes until his cock softened and the sound of grinding teeth faded.

"Ssh, savage," he whispered, stroking every inch of skin he could reach. "Ssh, you're alright, I've got you, I've got you, and I won't let go, always got you…"

Rob moved sluggishly, weakly, allowing Eli to manhandle him gently against the side of the bed again to unlock the chain and rub the circulation back into his arms. The cuffs hit the floor with a clunk; the bedsheets were ripped back and the exhausted body near-poured into the bed before Eli removed the blindfold. He was intent on holding that near-delirious gaze the moment it appeared, and cupped that usually stern and powerful face in both hands to litter the skin with kisses.

"Beautiful," he whispered to Rob's glazed, exhausted look. "You're so good, you did so well for me, and you're not perfect but you're trying so hard for me, and I'm so *proud* of you for trying, and proud of you for the way you stuck up for me even if you shouldn't have done…"

He talked and soothed, pulled the blankets high and smoothed back sweaty hair, until something sparked in the back of Rob's eyes again and he closed around Eli like a trap, burrowing his face into Eli's neck and inhaling so deeply it pulled at Eli's skin.

"Mine," Eli whispered, recognising the clingy behaviour for the need for reassurance that it really was. "All mine, you're all mine, and I'm never gonna let go of this, never gonna let go of you…"

He whispered until the shakes and the quiet gave way to exhaustion-heavy limbs and the slack breathing of sleep. Then— because, after all, Rob had had to pause the scene, and Eli was fiercely wary of accidentally letting doubt leak in after a punishment—he stayed right where he was, against his instincts to clean up the room and have a shower.

Instead, he wound his arms around Rob's neck, burying his hands in thick, dark hair to scratch soothingly at Rob's scalp, and closed his eyes to drift. The adrenaline was leaking away, leaving him tired and—

Peaceful.

The frustration and the anger, the sensation of being caught between a rock and a hard place was gone. And in its wake only peace remained.

CHAPTER 13

ELI WAS WOKEN by the usual annoyance at Rob's flat—the sun poking him in the eyes from the firmly east-facing bedroom window. Not to mention there'd been a light dusting of snow overnight, so the outside world was *blinding*.

Eli grumbled and rolled over, burrowing into the wall of muscle and heat formerly at his back. Rob was out for the count when Eli blinked sleepily at his face, but the stern line of his brows wasn't relaxed, and when Eli slid an arm around under Rob's shoulder with the intention of pulling him closer for a cuddle, the skin of his back felt hot to the touch.

Rob's grimace deepened.

It brushed the tired cobwebs from Eli's mind, and he sat up, peeling the sheets back carefully. They were army green, but did nothing to disguise the rusty stains. Eli winced. Sure enough, when he slid free and coaxed Rob over onto his front a little further, that highest welt had split open again.

"Oh," he whispered, and pressed a kiss into Rob's hair. "Okay. Okay. Let me take care of it."

Rob didn't so much as mumble, and Eli slipped from the room to the bathroom. The flat was silent, Danny's bedroom door wide open and Eli's shoes lonely and forlorn on the mat by the door. At least there was that.

Eli turned on the bath taps before heading to the kitchen and fetching the first aid kit. This was typically for bar fights and Danny's chronic inability to get within thirty feet of an oven without burning various parts of his body. (Eli did *not* want to know how he'd needed burn cream you could apply to the genitals, but it had happened at least once.) But a first aid kit was a first aid kit, and Eli had no intention of leaving any scars. Sex-induced scars were *not* sexy.

He dropped the kit off in the bathroom before returning to the bedroom to ferret out towels and Rob's 'lazy clothes'—a soft grey T-shirt so worn it felt more silk than cotton, and baggy pyjama bottoms that were so long even on Rob that the sight of his bare feet poking out from the ends always made Eli feel tender and warm. And tenderness was called for, when Eli had overstepped the mark enough to leave blood.

"Rob, baby," he whispered, bending over the bed and kissing Rob's hair. The pet name—so usually for Eli, not for Rob—slipped free, and maybe it was the unusualness of that which roused the sleeping dragon. "C'mon, babe," Eli murmured when a blurry grey eye cracked open. "Bath time."

"Bath?" Rob croaked. His voice was hoarse and raspy.

Eli kissed his ear, a spark of arousal stirring in his crotch even as the need to tend to Rob's back tempered any true interest.

"Mhmm. Your shoulder's split open, baby, I need to look after it."

Rob grumbled, trying to turn his face back into the pillow, but Eli forced a hand under his cheek and cupped his jaw in both hands.

"No," he said, injecting a little firmness into his tone. "One of the marks has split open from last night. That's scene damage, Rob. From *my* scene. It's my responsibility, and I need you to get in the bath."

Rob's gaze was still fuzzy, but the mumble less drowsy. He pushed himself up from the mattress on one powerful arm, shoulder rolling and flexing. The groan and hiss told Eli all he needed to know, and he kissed Rob's temple gently.

"See? Now let me take care of it, seeing as how I put it there."

Rob coughed out a short laugh, and caught Eli's hand on his

shoulder, kissing the knuckles lightly.

"Worth it," he mumbled, then yawned and finally rose. He was still completely naked from the night before, a faint line across his stomach muscles showing where Eli had driven him into the side of the bed. "Okay. Bath. I think I need a piss first."

"Oh, please, I've seen you vomit all down your own front," Eli said cattily, steering Rob towards the bathroom.

Eli set up the towels and clothes on the heated rail as Rob took the promised piss, and locked the door in case of Danny demonstrating his knack for wandering into things he shouldn't be wandering into.

The minute the toilet flushed, Eli wrenched off the taps, and beckoned Rob to the water.

"In you get. Toes to the taps. I'm going to sit on the ledge behind you and see to your back."

Rob yawned widely, jaw cracking, then—without preamble or flinching at the heat of the water—stepped into the bath. The water surged up that god-like physique, his tattoos seeming to ripple under the surface as he sank into the warmth, and the guttural groan spoke of abused muscles, not just skin.

"Good," Eli praised, kissing the top of Rob's head. When that face pressed up, Eli dropped fleeting kisses to cheeks, chin, and mouth, too. "Show me your wrists."

"They're fine."

"Show me, baby." Eli kept his tone soft and affectionate, but left no room.

Rob, Eli had been quick to realise, could be reluctant to ask for any reassurance, even though his face betrayed him when Eli was affectionate after playing. The first few more intense games they'd played, Rob would relax so *suddenly* after the first signs of raw affection from Eli, whether or not Eli had been controlling the scene.

Eli wasn't sure what it was—a need for love, maybe, or a need for hard evidence that what had happened had been wanted and enjoyed, or even that it hadn't changed how Eli felt? He knew when Rob carried out his more physically forceful games, he needed rapid reassurance afterwards that Eli had enjoyed it, but the need for reassurance seemed to extend beyond that. It often didn't take much—sleepy kisses during cleaning up, or being encouraged to sleep wrapped around Eli like a trap usually did it. It boiled down to the same thing: after a scene, any scene, no matter which of them had been dominating, Rob seemed to need displays of tenderness and love.

And seeing the raised welts on Rob's back, and the stiffness of the man's movements, Eli wasn't ashamed to admit he needed to provide them, too. The games were sometimes intended to hurt, yes, but not *only* to hurt.

So although he kept his voice soft, there was no room for negotiation. And Rob, sleepy as he was, knew it, for his wet wrists were dutifully presented, hands palm up, for inspection. There was a little reddening, but that was to be expected from those cuffs. Eli squeezed them both gently, watching Rob's face carefully, but there was no response, so he kissed the thin skin on the inside of each and returned those large hands to the water.

His stomach was in a similar state—standard, light reddening, with no bruising or swelling. Eli bent low over the water to kiss the tattooed heart on Rob's chest before rising, offering a light, open-mouthed kiss, and stepping back.

"Right," he said. "Sit forward and let me behind you."

He put his feet in the hot water, sinking his legs to the upper shins, and sat the first aid kit by his hip on the little ledge. Rob tipped his head back, banging his skull lightly against Eli's chest. Eli laughed, petting Rob's damp hair and kissing the line where it met his forehead.

"Hello," he crooned softly, scratching his blunt nails into the scalp. Rob's eyes slid closed, and his chest rumbled in a distinctly satisfied noise. "Sleepy?"

"Mm."

"You want to go back to bed after?"

"Yeah."

"Okay," Eli breathed, kissing the top of his ear. "I'll have to set you up on the sofa while I change the sheets, though. And I'm pretty sure you still have some tins of pea and ham soup, you want one of those?"

"You're trying to spoil me," Rob mumbled hoarsely.

"I'm looking after you," Eli corrected, kissing the other ear, still massaging Rob's scalp. He could see the tension in Rob's shoulders easing between the heat and the attention, and was loathe to disturb it, even for the first aid kit. "I know I got a bit too rough with you last night, and you were so exhausted I didn't have the heart to force you to stay awake any longer for this, but now I have to see to your back."

"S'not that bad…"

"*Your* opinion doesn't count for this," Eli murmured, raking both hands through Rob's hair in a combing motion before dropping them to his neck and starting to massage that instead, shifting his fingers in powerful, probing motions. There were knots at the very base of Rob's skull, Eli could almost *see* them. "I've broken the skin, which is *not* what that belt is meant to be able to do, so now I'm going to fix it, and I'm going to break the buckle off so it's just the leather strap. I don't like blood play."

"Not a huge fan myself…"

Eli paused, licking his lips. "Did it…hurt more? That last blow?"

Rob yawned. "A bit? I didn't know it bled."

"Was it too much?"

"No," Rob said, his tone so matter-of-fact that Eli relaxed. "I was maybe three, four strikes away from safewording the belt, but not the whole scene."

"And…and you *would* have safeworded—"

"Yes."

The reply was firm, and Eli kissed the crown of Rob's head, his gut easing. He hadn't gone too far then. Rob did use the words—had done before, undoubtedly would again—but the anxiety had still been there, lurking under the surface.

"Good," Eli whispered into his hair, then squeezed the very tops of his shoulders. "No beatings for at least a month. I'm not having that scar, I'm not having any more damage until it's *completely* healed."

"No punishments, then?"

"No, I'm just going to have to get inventive," Eli murmured

into one ear, sliding his arms around Rob's neck and upper chest in a loose hug, careful not to touch the welts. "Anyway, I much prefer playing with you than punishing you. I only punish you when you've been *really* awful."

Rob nudged his head back against Eli's neck. "I'm sorry."

"Ssh, I know," Eli whispered, rocking him very lightly. A wet hand rose out of the water to clutch at his wrist. "I know you are. And you also did good things yesterday evening. You're not a bad guy, you're just passionate and let your mouth run away with you. And I love that about you when it's not being aimed at my dad over the dinner table."

Rob was quiet, and Eli tugged his hair lightly to pull his face back for a kiss.

"I love you," he whispered against Rob's mouth. "You are everything I want and need. You are so, so good for me. You could sound off at my dad in the worst, most foul-mouthed rant in the world, and make me so fucking angry with you, and I would *still* love you more than anyone I've ever known."

Rob twisted in the bath, water nearly sloshing out and onto the floor, and clasped Eli's knee before leaning up to kiss him. It was not Rob's usual type of kiss—it was soft, a damp clasp of parted lips and brush of shy tongues, seeking…something. Eli responded in kind, cupping Rob's cheek in one hand and trying to convey, in the gentlest and tenderest of touches, every ounce of sheer, dizzying love he felt for this man.

"You are," Eli breathed, "the most wonderful, understanding, supportive, mind-bendingly attractive, incredible man I have *ever* known. You look like something right out of a men's fitness magazine, or some film about the guys you *shouldn't* fall in love with, and you let me—*me*—in under all that show and attitude to see who you *really* are. And that's the guy I love. Not the one my dad sees, not the one that keeps getting himself nicked because he doesn't know when to shut up, but the one who loans me socks when my feet are cold, the one who plays these games with me and trusts me not to take it too far, the one who'll call me a fucking pussy even as he's buying me Cokes in the pub because I'm feeling too queasy for any alcohol…"

Rob's arms slid around his waist, drenching his boxers, and Eli was suddenly dragged bodily down into the water with a surprised yelp. He laughed breathlessly, catching at Rob's shoulders, and was kissed fiercely for his troubles, water surging and crashing around his chest.

"Rob!" he gasped, pushing at the immoveable chest. "I need to see to your back!"

He was caught by wide, white eyes in an expression Eli had never seen before—completely smashed open, Rob's very heart laid out right there on his face, the near-devoted look in his eyes silencing Eli's protests in his throat.

"I need this more," Rob croaked.

And…and how was Eli supposed to say no to that? How was he meant to—?

He curled his fingers into hair curling from the steam, and swallowed.

"Alright," he whispered. "Just for a minute."

He succumbed to whatever had seized Rob, opening up to the ensuing kiss, relaxing into gripping hands, and deciding to give him this five minutes before getting the aftercare back on track.

Or maybe ten.

THE SHEETS WERE changed, Eli had had his own shower, the soup was heating on the stove, and he re-packed his bag for their Christmas trip away.

In short, Eli was done, and if Rob was still asleep, he was shortly to be bored.

Peering into the living room, he found the TV on, albeit quietly, and a change in position from the long lump under the fleece blanket on the sofa. One arm was hanging straight out, wrist up and underarm exposed in an oddly vulnerable pose. The remote was caught in the fingers of the other hand, resting over Rob's waist. He was half-turned onto his side, a cushion Eli had stuffed behind his arse, keeping him from rolling onto his back entirely and gluing his T-shirt to the salve Eli had rubbed onto the welts.

"Rob?" he called gently.

A grunt.

Eli beamed and slipped from the doorway to kneel in front of the sofa and stroke the exposed bicep reverently.

"Hey," he said when white-grey eyes stared back at him with a lot more awareness than they had earlier in the morning. Eli smiled. "You want some soup?"

Rob wrinkled his nose.

"You're eating something. You're totally shattered, and a long car ride later isn't going to help. I already texted Danny saying he's going to be driving so wherever he's gone, he better not be drunk."

Rob smirked, then yawned. "He's at his girlfriend's."

"He—what? Sorry, *your* Danny has a girlfriend?"

"No, she's a bird with low standards and a coke habit that agreed to fuck him twice 'cause he gave her weed. But two fucks with the same person is a relationship in Danny's world," Rob explained coarsely, his voice very throaty.

Eli tugged down the fleece a little to kiss said throat.

"Mm. S'nice."

"Good," Eli said, deciding to ignore Danny and his, um, tastes. "How's your back?"

"S'alright. Not stiff anymore. That salve stuff's working." A yawn split his face again, showing off his fillings. Eli laughed.

"Oh, shut up."

"Bless," Eli teased, then buried his nose in Rob's hair and inhaled. "Mm. You smell of sleep."

"So come and fucking hug me, then."

Eli heard the actual desire for a hug under the rough demand, but shook his head. "After you eat," he said. "There's soup. You're having some. Your option is what to have with it."

"What kind of soup?"

"Pea and ham, like I promised."

"There's croutons in the cupboard above the microwave," Rob mumbled.

"Okay."

Eli hadn't reached the door before he heard the sofa creak, and he rolled his eyes before heading back into the kitchen and rummaging in the cupboard. Sure enough, just as he opened the box of croutons, heavy arms slid around his waist and he had two hundred pounds of tired man stuck to his spine.

"Hello," he murmured softly, squeezing Rob's wrist before returning to his task. The marks from the cuffs had faded.

"For the record," Rob mumbled, "you aren't getting to belt me again for a good couple of months, and only on weekends. I'm *exhausted*."

"I'm not surprised," Eli said. "You were really wrung out last night."

Rob hummed, nose buried in Eli's neck. "You're hard work."

Eli chuckled. "You love it, though."

"I do." The raw honesty in Rob's voice was surprising.

Eli paused. Rob's grip loosened, and then Eli was being turned and pressed up against the counter, Rob's nose now at the front of Eli's throat, his lips roaming in soft, closed kisses.

"I don't want some fucking wilting violet or some such shit. You're fucking hot when you explode, it's like playing with fire, being with you, and it's fucking incredible. I don't have to hold myself in check or watch what I'm fucking saying, 'cause if you don't like it, you'll make me pay for it, and if you do like it, I get the fuck of my life—"

"Romantic," Eli teased, and got his neck nipped for his efforts.

"I'm not...I'm shit with words—"

"You're not shit," Eli said firmly, sensing the lingering crack in Rob's armour from the night before.

"Shut up, I am, not the point. I generally...you know, usually I figure that you're smart, you know how I...how I feel. But I...I do..."

Eli blinked, cupping Rob's neck and winding his fingers into the hair at the nape of it gently. "Rob?" he prompted softly when Rob trailed off.

Those white-grey eyes caught his again and Rob huffed, frustration clearly written in the lines of his face.

"Love you," he said finally, and promptly flushed hotly.

The smile that wrenched itself onto Eli's face was totally out of his own control, and he had to force it away in order to kiss Rob properly. And it was supposed to be a soft kiss, an affirming kiss, but it turned into a gleeful smacker. Eli hung there still for several moments afterwards, pressing his forehead to Rob's to drink in that beautiful, flushing face, and smelling the soup burning without caring.

Eventually, he said the only words he could, the only words he knew how. And he said them with his entire heart evaporating out of his body through his voice, his entire *being* straining towards Rob, knowing he would be heard, captured, and kept safe for good.

"I know," Eli whispered, and closed his eyes.

CHAPTER 14

THEY SET OFF that evening.

Rob had lounged around the flat for most of the day in his comfy clothes, and had only begun to pack after Eli had forced him to have another shower, check the welts, and eat lunch. The tired pleasure hadn't really left, though, and where normally after-care had a short window before Rob started to protest, Eli was allowed to indulge that day. And he enjoyed it.

Danny had reappeared at lunchtime, buggered off again at three, and then returned at five with an eight pack of ginger beer and a big grin—although thankfully absent the stench of weed this time.

"Who's driving first leg?" he asked.

"You," Eli said, before Rob could so much as open his mouth. "Pack the car; I need to kidnap Rob for one last thing."

"Dirty fuckers," Danny complained, but did as told.

Rob, similarly placid, allowed Eli to tug him into the bathroom by the wrist and push up his T-shirt to examine his back.

"Sore?"

"Feels fine."

The broken welt had scabbed properly this time, and the T-shirt was blood-free, but the skin was still a little too warm for

Eli's liking. He re-applied the salve, kissed the spot right between Rob's shoulder blades, and rolled the T-shirt back down. "It *looks* a bit better," he said, "but I still want to check when we get to your aunt's. I don't want it scarring, or an infection."

"Stop *fussing*," Rob said, catching Eli's chin in finger and thumb to kiss him sharply.

"Shut up. It's scene damage, I will fuss all I like until it heals," Eli retorted, but smiled into the kiss. He couldn't deny how much better he felt. How much more at peace with everything he was— the dinner hurdle had been jumped, and all his impotent anger had been released. Rob's current placid submission was welcome, too, his acceptance of Eli's affection and bossing warm balms to Eli's still slightly anxious mind. "Are there any good places at your aunt's to play?"

"Exhibitionist."

"Yes." Eli didn't bother denying it. The thrill and danger of maybe being caught, it was a *huge* turn-on, and Rob exploited it all the time.

"Lots of woodland around the village. Church cemetery if you're feeling really nasty. Or round the back of the police station, but they've probably closed it now."

"You sound very practised."

"Had a lot of practice," Rob said, and smirked. "Fuck all else to do but have a shag in the arse end of nowhere."

"Really?"

"Well, fuck all else to do, but never fucked there. Only gay in the village and all that."

Eli laughed, kissed the corner of his mouth, and unlocked the door. He fetched the last two of the bags, giving Rob a stern look, and followed Danny down the stairs to the car. They were taking Rob's Suzuki—Danny's Ford Focus wasn't up to a trip even to Leeds, never mind the wilds of Scotland—but Danny had already adjusted everything to his liking.

"If you cock up the seat," Rob said grimly, "I will fucking murder you."

"Driver does the deed, shotgun shuts his spewer," Danny sang merrily.

To Eli's surprise—and Danny's, judging by his expression—Rob got in the back seat and sprawled out as much as possible, apparently intending to doze.

By the time they reached the ring road, the brotherly bickering had tapered off; by the time they reached the M1, Eli glanced over his shoulder and saw Rob fast asleep, head dropped against the window and legs sprawled across the spare seat in a graceless slump.

"The fuck did you *do,* mate, he's wiped," Danny commented as they hit a pleasantly fast cruising speed.

The Suzuki's suspension was terrible, but Eli found it sort of entertaining. And sort of impressive, how Rob could sleep through the bumps and shudders.

"We had fun," Eli said in an innocent tone.

Danny guffawed.

"You shagged him out, you mean."

"Couldn't possibly comment."

"Yeah, whatever. S'always the quiet ones, en't it? Sicko."

Eli smiled and ignored him. It was already dark, the motorway a long collection of lights and sounds. He rummaged in his back for his sketchpad, a reading light to clip to the binding, and a pencil. Long car journeys as a little kid to seaside holidays with his family meant the movement of the car did nothing to disturb him, and he slowly began to sketch abstract ideas onto the paper, sweeps of graphite in response to the rush and fade of engines passing them, nicks and jagged punctures when Danny hummed or changed lanes. When he switched the radio on low, Eli began to draw the music itself, the style changing with every song and DJ comment.

Time bled away in the dark, and Eli felt perfectly content.

THEY STOPPED JUST shy of the Scottish border for petrol and Pepsi. Rob stirred when the engine clicked off, and Eli had to get out to allow him to escape and stretch his legs. While Danny filled up the tank, Eli perched in the passenger seat, drew Rob in by the belt to stand between his legs, and kissed his stomach through the cotton of his T-shirt.

"Good nap?"

"Ah, s'pose," Rob mumbled and yawned. He scratched at his stubble and half-smiled when Eli kissed him again. "You bored yet?"

"Been drawing," Eli said. "Danny's surprisingly quiet when he drives."

"Doesn't like motorways," Rob said. "Keeps his focus. Oi, twat! I'll take over."

"Good, fucking layabout."

"Piss off." Rob dragged out the 'f' and sounded so thoroughly idle and pleased that Eli smiled and stood up on the edge of the car to wind his arms around Rob's neck and kiss him properly. "Mm, hello."

"Hello," Eli murmured.

Danny loped off to pay, and Eli took the private moment to press his nose to Rob's cheek and inhale the soft smell of sleep. He felt thoroughly content—and if possible, more so the further they got from Sheffield, home and conflict.

"Does this mean you're gonna be a bit lively tonight?"

"You objecting?" Eli murmured.

"Maybe."

"Maybe?"

"Depends," Rob said. "Cousins are exhausting, 'specially Shawna."

Eli smiled, staying close—the air was cold but Rob's hold was warm—until Danny returned with the receipt and the Pepsi. He scrambled gracelessly into the back. Eli re-settled with the full intention of drawing again, but not before leaning over to kiss Rob on the cheek and smile at the startled look he received.

"Stop being sappy!" Danny objected.

Rob's response was to jack the seat back to hit Danny's knees. "Ow! Fucker!"

"Shut the fuck up?" Rob suggested, starting up and cruising back out of the services with practised ease. He almost lounged as he drove, and Eli decided to sketch his hands, lax but powerful on the steering wheel, instead of the radio music.

"Nah," Danny said. "Oi, Eli, you got cousins?"

"Some," Eli said. "Dad's side. Don't see them much."

"These are Mam's side," Danny said, "and they're fucking mental. Make us look like fucking pussies, mate—"

"You *are* a fucking pussy," Rob interjected.

"Fuck off. Anyway, our cousins are fucking nuts. You're gonna die. If Shawna don't strangle you, Stella will."

"I won't die," Eli said loftily. "Rob'll protect me."

Rob snorted.

"Dead guys don't fuck, Rob. Think about that."

Rob and Danny both coughed an identical, surprised laugh.

"True," Rob admitted, putting his foot down and surging past a couple of lorries. "And not like there's anyone else to fuck up there. Lonely fucking place."

"Middle of nowhere?" Eli guessed, still sketching lightly.

"Mm."

"It *is* fucking lonely," Danny said. "Aunt Stella moved up there with her old man—Bill then, not this new bloke—to grow cannabis and shit where the old bill—ha, see what I did there?—wouldn't find 'em, only there's no fucker to sell to so it didn't go too well. Then Bill bought it and she married this cokehead from Donny."

"Ex-cokehead," Rob said casually. "Got banged up one too many times and jacked it in. They're alright now, cleaner'n we are."

Eli rolled his eyes. "If I find weed in our bags—"

"Who's this 'our' shit?" Danny jeered.

"I ain't got any," Rob protested. "Don't need to be stoned with fucking Shawna around, she'll paint me bollocks or something."

"Those bollocks," Eli said tartly, "belong to me. *I* might paint them." Danny cackled disturbingly. "Nobody else gets *near* them. Got it?"

"Jesus fuck, I have a wife."

Eli wanted to hit him, but figured hitting the driver of a vehicle doing ninety on the motorway wasn't the best idea. So he stuck his nose in the air and said, "Don't make me punish you again."

"Whoa, whoa," Danny cried. "Baby brother in the back!"

"Fuck off, Danny, like you're not a fucking perv."

"Don't wanna know about *you*!"

"Sofa, hookers. Weren't *my* hookers."

"They were women and it was all vanilla, cheers!"

"That you even know that word says you're a perv," Rob returned in a lazy drawl. "Stop spreading your lies, you shit, and Eli, shut up before I pull in at the next services and take ten minutes in the gents."

"Ten minutes, lucky fucking Eli…"

"Fucking indeed."

Eli smirked at the sketchpad and turned to a new page. Out of the bickering and the banter, he drew a bird in flight, wings spread to full extent, talons outstretched towards him to attack. He fuzzed the corners of the feathers, darkening the wingspan, then homed in on the eyes.

"Aaaaand he's gone. The art-trap."

The eyes, Eli decided, would be not yellow like normal hawks, but a grey-white. The talons would be gold, and the feathers everything from white down by the body to the blackest feathers at the very wingtips. It wouldn't be large—size, after all, wasn't the danger with hawks, it was the feral rage and the knife-like talons—but it would be intricate, perfectly detailed in every way, and it would…

It would be committed to skin. Not Rob's skin, where most of Eli's good designs were intended to go, but Eli's *own* skin.

He turned onto a new page as the brothers began to argue heatedly about whether to listen to the football highlights or Heart FM, and began to perfect the idea.

ELI HADN'T KNOWN what to expect, but a ramshackle cottage on the outskirts of a tiny village nestled in the bottom corner of the Highlands wasn't it. The village was miserable grey stone brooding under a miserable black sky; the cottage roof was sagging in the middle like Rob's most ferocious scowl, and weeds were battering the garden wall in an affronted wind. The lights shining out of the cottage did nothing to help the bitter exterior, and—quite frankly—it all looked intensely fucking depressing.

"It's very…Scottish," he said finally as they got out, the wind immediately ripping at his hair.

Rob laughed.

"It's not. They're not, anyhow. Foreigners, s'what the locals think. Aunt Stella's from London—her first hubby was a Scot but he dealt down there for years before they came up here and he bought it."

"He died?"

"Yeah, a grand's worth of junk in an hour'll do that to a man."

"Fuck!"

"Aye. New bloke—I say new, been about, like, a decade and a fucking half—Mike, he's a Donny lad, poor fucker. Better'n Bill, anyhow."

"So they're En—"

The cottage door flew open, and a whirlwind of skinny blonde woman hurled herself bodily at Danny with a war-cry that, after the fact, Eli translated as, "Cocksuckers!"

"Alright, Shawna!"

Shawna was a wiry woman of maybe twenty-five or thirty with waist-length blonde hair that looked like she'd been dragged along behind a lorry for a hundred miles or so. It was *everywhere*, a tangled mess that more closely resembled a bird's nest than a woman's hair. But the resemblance, even with the colouring difference, was clear—her beam was Danny's toothy idiocy, and her eyes were the same eerie white-grey as Rob's.

"Who the fuck is this fucker?" she cheered, and caught Eli in a stranglehold of a hug.

Eli coughed, and slapped her on the back.

"So you're the Sheffy lad, then, you're our Rob's Eli, are you? Get inside, fucktards, it's motherfucking freezing!"

Inside was the opposite of the grim outside: low-ceilinged, with exposed dark beams and warped wooden flooring. They were taken straight into a living room flickering in the warm glow of an open fire, and stuffed to the gills with odds-and-ends, rugs and afghans, squashy mismatched chairs and battered old furniture. This, Eli liked, and he offered Shawna a smile as she shoved him into the depths of a ludicrously soft sofa.

"Mam! *Mam*, ye divvy, Rob 'n' Danny are 'ere wi' Rob's slag!"

"Shawna, you watch your fucking mouth!" came the roared reply from somewhere upstairs.

Rob sniggered, dropping down beside Eli.

Shawna shrieked back and vanished.

"You'll get used to 'em," Rob said casually.

"So Shawna's your cousin?"

"Yeah. Shawna is Stella and Bill's kid, so're Connor and Stu. You won't meet Stu, he's not out yet. Dunno if Connor's about."

"Out?"

"Slammer," Danny said, rummaging in a cabinet. Bottles clinked.

"Kayla is Stella and Mike's kid, and then Tony is Mike's kid from his first bird, but I dunno if Tony's with us for Christmas or with his mam."

Eli grimaced. "I think I need a diagram."

Danny laughed. "You'll only see Shawna and Kayla, probably. Maybe Connor if he shows his ugly mug. Here, Rob, reckon Kayla's still got the bairn?"

"The what?" Eli demanded.

"Ignore the twat, he tries to go native whenever we get here," Rob said, casually giving his brother a boot in the arse.

A short wrestling match ensued. Eli dived off the sofa and retreated to another armchair, watching contentedly. Rob's sudden ease was sweet; he was more relaxed than Eli had ever seen him, outside of sex or a lot of booze. Eli was already enjoying his decision to come, and the unexpected effect of seeing a Rob he wasn't quite sure he knew yet.

Then a whirlwind of even messier blonde hair—albeit shorter and clearly dyed—descended and seized Rob in another one of those painful hugs.

"You little fuckers, you didn't ring or nuffink!" the woman shrieked.

"Heya, Aunt Stell."

"Don't you 'heya' me, you little arse-mongerer!" she bellowed, then whirled on Danny. "And you! You, you troublesome little cunt, ge' your arse over 'ere!"

She was indeed from London: her voice was nothing less than the harsh scream of a Cockney fishwife. Eli had to forcibly stop his face from contorting at the sound of it. But on the other hand, it was…weirdly nice to see Rob being corralled and hugged by his aunt. It was nice to see that his entire world hadn't been purely Danny.

"Who's this then?"

And so Aunt Stella descended, two claw-like hands slamming down on Eli's shoulders and shaking him briefly.

"Too fucking skinny," she snarled, even though she was smaller and skinnier than Eli by a long shot. "What d'you fucking do with him, Rob, lock him in the closet? What's your name then? Eh, you deaf?"

"Wi' you bawling at him, probably."

"Shut your fucking mouth, you little gobshite, you ain't too old for a smackin'!"

"Think you'll find I fucking am!"

"Gerrover 'ere and try your luck, then!"

"Eli."

Her attention zeroed back in on him. She wasn't a pretty woman, her face weather-beaten and worn, her body thin in the way that spoke of too many cigarettes, too much energy, and too little decent food. Her eyes were the same eerie shade as Rob's and Shawna's, but her eyebrows were dark instead of the bright blonde of her hair, which stuck up all over the place like the same bird that had attacked Shawna's had been at Stella, too.

And yet—rather like when faced with the stern figure that was Rob, and the slightly mad druggie that was his younger brother—Eli liked her.

"I'm Eli," he repeated.

"So it's you that's turned our Rob's head," she said, and looked him up and down obviously. "Can see why, definitely your type, ain't 'e, Rob?"

"Shurrup, Auntie."

"Oh shut your face," she scoffed, and let go of Eli. "Kitchen, lot of you. You tell me what's going on—an' Danny if I catch you with a spliff near th'baby, there'll be fucking hell to pay, you little shitbag!"

The kitchen was even cosier, a table taking up nearly all of the free space. Shawna was sitting on a counter with a bottle of Grolsch in hand; pots and pans were bubbling on a stove, the smell of stew thick and heavy in the air. There was another fire in the corner— smaller, but belting out the heat like nobody's business. A skinny girl in that awkward, gangly phase of puberty that lined her up to be maybe fourteen years old looked like she was doing schoolwork at the table. She was far darker than the rest of the family, with large dark eyes and long black hair in red-beaded braids. Danny cheered and pounced on her with a yell of, "Kayla-babes!"

"Get that down your neck, you skinny fucker," Stella ordered, banging a bowl of stew down on the table and shoving Eli into a chair.

Rob laughed and took the one next to him, draping an arm across the back so Rob was almost, but not quite, hugging him.

"Careful, Auntie, you'll scare him to death."

"Needs to 'arden the fuck up then," she said briskly.

"He's proper, is Eli."

"Do you some fucking good, then. We're expecting you to be on the inside again by now, what happened there?"

Rob shrugged. "Haven't done owt worth prison for, have I?"

"And you fucking better not either," Eli grumbled, tasting the stew. Stella crowed with laughter; Shawna's giggle was like a shriek.

"I *like* him!" Shawna called.

The stew was very rich and beefy, but also *incredible,* and Eli attacked it with vigour, hungry after the long car journey. He kept an eye on Shawna, wary, and an eye on Rob, admiring. The easy smile was something Eli had considered rare, but now he thought maybe he saw Rob too often with the weight of the world on those broad shoulders, with life and worries dogging at him when here— home—Rob was...

Perfect.

CHAPTER 15

ELI WOKE IN an awkward position: naked but for his boxers, tucked under Rob's even more naked form, and totally unable to take advantage and play. Because apparently the cottage didn't have enough room for many visitors, and so they were sharing the spare room with Danny. And Eli was an exhibitionist, but getting off to the sound of Danny's snores wasn't actually part of that.

Sighing, Eli kissed Rob's neck, and pushed at his side. "C'mon, savage, let go."

The coaxing did nothing but close the trap further, Rob winding himself around Eli's torso and hips like a touch-starved octopus. Eli laughed in spite of his semi-urge need to pee.

"Nooo, savage, I need to get up," he whispered. Rob's voice rasped something inaudible into Eli's skin, his stubble scratchy and unyielding. Eli shivered, want prickling under his skin in a wash of heat. "Rob. *Off.*"

The commanding tone was a little more successful, Rob swearing at him as he let go, and Eli pulled the duvet high over that prone form to shield him from the cold. And it *was* cold, the bare floorboards freezing against his toes. He stole Rob's T-shirt from the floor, and tiptoed across the landing into the bathroom to avoid putting more of his skin on the floor than was strictly required.

Peeing was an enormous relief, and Eli rolled his head back in pleasure. It was the little things, like getting to pee when you had to, and wearing a soft cotton shirt smelling entirely of your boyfriend. Eli buried his nose in the fabric and inhaled—and smiled when he heard the distinctive creak of Rob's footsteps, first in the bedroom, and then on the landing.

Then he went downstairs, and Eli frowned. No bathroom invasion? Seriously? How fucking rude was *that*? It was Christmas Day!

It wasn't really on, Eli decided as he dried his hands and zipped back into the bedroom to find pyjama bottoms, so he'd hunt Rob down and issue a correction. Poor idiot clearly hadn't had many Christmases with a boyfriend. The *first* thing couples should do on Christmas Day—well, childless ones, anyway—was fuck, in Eli's opinion.

He sneaked downstairs in pursuit, still on tiptoes, nose still buried in the protective warmth of Rob's T-shirt, and followed the sound of voices in the kitchen. He paused in the doorway, uncertain, then barrelled ahead, tucking himself under Rob's arm and kissing his cheek like he was meant to be there.

Stella chortled. "'E's a twink, then, your boyfriend?" she asked Rob, who mumbled something incomprehensible and tucked his cheek against Eli's hair. "Fucking useless, you are. 'Ere, Eli, 'e still always this useless first thing in the morning?"

"Usually," Eli agreed amiably, tucking both arms around Rob's bare chest. He got something more approaching a hug, and allowed himself to be mollified. "He's not usually up this early, either."

"S'your fault, y'moved," Rob yawned.

"So your Danny told me summat a bit interestin' last night, 'bout your Eli," Stella said. She was making up a baby bottle, but giving Eli a sideways grin that looked almost like a leer. "Gotta say I didn't buy it, but our Danny's a shockin' liar, and he kept at it…"

A chill began to prickle up Eli's arms. Suddenly, he didn't feel hungry, for sex or for food. He just felt cold and sick.

"I…what…what did he…?"

"Said you was a tranny," Stella said.

Rob's snort was immediate and derisive.

"Trans, daft cow, not tranny."

"Don't you call me a daft cow, you twat," she retorted, tossing the milk bottle cap at him. "Anyway, s'what your Danny said. You don't sound much like a bird to me, mind, and tha' stubble…"

"That's what T does, Stel, even for a bird." Rob's voice was a deep and easy roll, his arm still heavy and secure around Eli's ribs, and yet all Eli could do was stare and swallow against the urge to vomit.

Fuck-fuck-*fuck*, he'd never…fucking *Danny*, he'd kill him! He'd kill him, how *could* he, he couldn't just go around telling all and sundry, that was how…that was how people got turned against you, that was how trans-bashing happened, that was—

"Oi, chill out, Eli, Jesus," Stella barked, then laughed. "Gone a right funny colour, you have—'ere, Rob, sit him down…"

Eli clung instead and shook his head. "M'fine," he croaked.

Rob's hand was suddenly rubbing warm, soothing circles against his side.

"'Ere, love, no fucker 'ere cares," Stella said briskly. "Got bigger things to worry about, ain't I? I was just curious, like, didn't look much like no girl to me, and our Rob's gay as a fucking Thai ladyboy, ain't he, so I—"

"I've had surgery," Eli whispered. "I'm…I'm saving for the final one at the minute."

"Expensive, is it?"

"Yeah, the NHS wouldn't do it. I'm seven hundred and forty-two pounds short, still."

"*Fuck*, love, that's a lotta cash!"

"I…I take hormones to make my voice deeper and…and the hair and stuff, I…sorry. Sorry, I'm not used to…people knowing."

"Or accepting, eh?"

"No," he admitted.

"Like I said, bigger fuckin' fish to fry," Stella said. "Me late 'ubby's still in debt to a bunch of London junkies, me current one's wanking hisself to death in fucking Wakefield prison, the cunt, and me youngest 'as made me a grandma before me oldest's worked out what a fucking cock is e'en for! If our Rob wants to get hisself up wi' th'likes o' you, I don't give two shits. 'Ere, Rob, make yourself fucking useful and give our Angel this, eh?"

Rob grunted and took the proffered bottle. He yawned enormously again and tugged Eli by the hand towards the door.

Eli was dragged into the thankfully warmer living room, where the beginnings of a fire had been lit in the grate. A baby was lying on a mat in the middle of the sofa, kicking its legs and making grabby hands and gurgly noises at a very unimpressed ginger cat sitting on the arm of the chair.

"Piss off, moggy," Rob said, making a fist at the cat.

It regarded him imperiously, then seemed to think better of it and skulked out of the room, leaving Eli to sink down onto the sofa and clutch a cushion into his lap.

"Alright?" Rob asked.

"Mm. Wasn't expecting that."

"Nosy bunch, they all are," Rob said genially, lifting the baby with surprisingly practised hands. "Here, this is Angel, Kayla's littl'un. Four months old. Not met her before, have I, muppet?"

"Don't call her a muppet!"

Rob chortled, cradling Angel along his forearm. She gurgled and grabbed for the bottle, latching on and beginning to noisily suckle. She was a blot of ink against his fair skin and tattoos, with huge dark eyes and wiry dark curls. She was, even Eli had to admit, a bit cute.

"You're good with her," Eli murmured, relaxing in the heat and the loud baby. "Don't you want kids?"

"Nah, be a shit dad," Rob said genially. "I like 'em well enough when it's just once in a while, like, but they're fucking annoying little cunts most of the time. Midgets that suck up money and time and don't give you fuck all in return."

Eli began to laugh.

"It's true and you fuckin' know it. Better off spending the cash on a cat, least the cat keeps the vermin under control. Then when it gets old and useless, you can take it to the vet and kill it, no problem. Can't kill kids when they're gobshites."

Eli curled up on himself and the cushion, his anxiety washed away by Rob's coarse ease, and he laughed until his stomach hurt from the description. "You're *awful*," he managed when Rob abandoned the empty bottle and lifted the baby onto his shoulder, his massive hand dwarfing her back.

"I'm serious," Rob said. "If my dog puked, drooled and shat on everything, I'd kill him. Better off dead than like that. But when a baby does it, it's somehow fucking acceptable. It's minging, that's what it bloody well is."

Eli's laugh softened into a grin, and he dropped his head onto the arm of the sofa to watch as Rob burped the baby, his actions thankfully a lot softer than his words. Then Rob lowered her back to the rug on the floor and tweaked her socked feet.

"You're a midget," Rob told her seriously. "You're absolutely tiny. You make Kayla look like a fat-arse baby and she was smaller than the fuckin' family cat."

Angel squealed gleefully and kicked at Rob's hands.

"No *way*! She did not, that's balls," Rob scoffed, as though she'd told him a mortifying secret about Kayla.

Eli started laughing again, and got up to rummage through the coats on the back of the living room door to find his own. And more importantly, his phone in the pocket.

"Smile," he said, starting to film Rob with the baby.

Rob rolled his eyes.

"See that?" he asked Angel, still tweaking her feet. He kept shaking them between finger and thumb to make her giggle and shriek. "He's abusing me. He knows I'm only nice first thing in the morning, and he wants to bloody well record it." She clapped her pudgy hands, beaming, and Rob huffed. "You're not meant to side with him! You're my cousin, Jesus, doesn't that count for something?"

Eli sank back onto the sofa, beaming but keeping determinedly quiet as Rob talked to the baby, slowly switching from tweaking her feet to playing pat-a-cake with her tiny hands—which took her a while to get used to—and eventually picking up the entire rug with her in it and swinging it like an interactive hammock. She *loved* that, squealing the place down until Kayla came to take her back and kick Rob in the shins for waking her up.

Eli stopped filming before Rob could start swearing and ruin the video, and sent it to Jenny with instructions to show Mum and Dad.

And frankly, if Dad could *still* see a thug in that video, then Eli was giving the fuck up already.

ROB WAS UP to something. Eli twigged when he refused to hand over Eli's presents in front of the rest of his family that morning, despite pretty much sticking his tongue down Eli's throat and groping him pretty obscenely in thanks for the T-shirt Eli had bought him. And the knowledge was doubled-up by Rob ducking out of helping cook by saying, "Gotta give Eli his present, don't I?"

Eli was expecting a fuck, frankly, but not to be told to put his boots and coat on and led out into the snow.

"Even *I'm* not up for a shag out here," he said, his breath misting in the air and his lungs stalling for a moment. It was bitterly cold, a looming grey sky promising more snow, and Rob's Suzuki buried to the bonnet.

"That's not your present," Rob said, taking Eli's gloved hand in his. "C'mon. Let's wander away a bit, or Shawna'll be eavesdropping."

Sure enough, a voice screeched, "I fucking won't!" Rob snorted.

"Bugger off, you bitch!" he bellowed over his shoulder, dragging Eli out into the narrow lane and turning away from the village. "Why'd you film me and Angel earlier, anyway?"

"Sent it to Jenny. You were being cute, it's the evidence I need," Eli said loftily, and reached up on his toes to kiss Rob's cheekbone. "And you were sleepy-happy instead of your usual grumpy self so I kept a copy for me, too."

"Piss off," Rob said, but it was half-hearted and Eli wasn't convinced the blush was entirely the cold.

"Actually, I wanted to talk, too," Eli murmured.

Rob groaned.

"No, it's a good talk. I'm giving up on getting you and my dad to get along. I've offered the evidence you're not a total prick, he's met you properly, and now it's up to him to start treating me like an adult who's made his own choice. Okay? And I'm sorry. About that row we had before you agreed to come, and about getting angry with you about it. I was being unfair on you, and I'm sorry for that. So no more dinners—"

"Thank fuck."

"—with Dad. You *did* win Jenny over a bit, and I reckon Mum'll like you given enough time, so I *might* try the odd pub lunch with them. But not Dad. Okay?"

Rob grumbled, but nodded. His gaze looked a little distant, and he seemed vaguely pre-occupied.

"Rob? You okay?"

"Yeah," he said. "Here. Just...here, here'll do."

At the bottom of the lane, where it turned into a single-track out into the farms and fields, the snow up to their knees, Rob stopped them and leaned against a fencepost, rummaging in his jacket pockets.

Eli stuffed his hands in his pockets and eyed him suspiciously, wondering what weird and wonderful present couldn't be handed over in front of Rob's extended family.

"If this is some...I don't know, BDSM exhibition or something..."

Rob grunted and smirked. "Nah." Two envelopes were produced, and one handed over. "Here's part one."

"A card?" Eli asked sceptically, turning it over. It was definitely a card. He took off his gloves with a sigh.

"Just open it."

"A card doesn't cut it."

"*Open* it, you fucking twat," Rob huffed.

Eli laughed, digging his nail into the paper and tearing the envelope open. It was a standard Christmas card, very Rob-like with some elves mooning Santa. Eli chuckled and shook his head as he flipped it open—and nearly lost the piece of paper folded inside.

"What's this?"

"Your first present."

Eli unfolded it curiously, and scanned the spaced-out, type-writer-esque font. It wasn't long. Just a printout, with Rob's name and...NHS number...

"Is this—oh my God," Eli said, his stomach clenching tightly in hot, eager anticipation. "Your test results."

"Final one."

Eli dropped the card and paper right in the snow and flung his arms around Rob's neck, pulling his face in for a hot-yet-frozen kiss. Their lips smashed together and Rob's were pushed right open for Eli's tongue, the contact so fierce their teeth nearly met. Rob's smile twisted the edges of it until Eli had to pull away and smack his arm.

"*Arse*," he hissed. "Oh my fucking God, I get to feel you proper now? You're not going to insist on condoms anymore, right? They're fucking shit and—"

"Not anymore," Rob agreed in that deep, raspy voice that just fucking *did* things to Eli's gut, and—

"You're going to take me inside, right now, and we're going to lock ourselves in your room and you're going to fuck me like it's the first time all over again, you're going to get right inside me so I can proper feel you, all the way…"

"Whoa, whoa, whoa. Part two of your present first."

"After," Eli said, and wound a hand into Rob's jacket to haul at him.

Rob didn't move.

"Now," he said, and handed over the second envelope.

Eli rolled his eyes and tore it open eagerly. Fuck the second present, he was already shivering with the need to get Rob inside him. No sheath, no horrible cold latex, just *them*. He'd wanted it from that very first blowjob, had railed against the stupidity of Rob refusing to fuck him without a condom but being okay with blowjobs…

He opened the card, and the cheque stared back at him, Rob's spidery handwriting spelling it out. *Seven hundred and forty-two pounds.* The arousal stopped short, stunned. Eli found his voice missing entirely when he tried to speak.

"Eli?"

Rob's hand was suddenly heavy on Eli's elbow.

"It's…I thought…"

"Seven hundred and forty-two pounds," Eli croaked feebly.

Rob shifted on his feet. "Well. Yeah. You told Stella this mor—"

"You...you're giving me...for..."

"For your last surgery," Rob said quietly.

Eli blinked back tears, and stared up into that pale face, into paler eyes. "Why?" he breathed, voice choking on the lump in his throat. *Why?* Rob didn't understand it—he supported, but he didn't *get* it, he'd laughed at Eli's stories of learning to shave and that he still used women's shampoo because it smelled so much nicer.

Rob's face creased. "Because...you..."

"But why?" Eli breathed. "You—you don't understand this, you told me yourself. Why would you...all that *money*—"

"'Member when I said I'd never fucked a woman and you offered to let me?"

"Yeah?"

"And how you were all fine right up until I tried to touch your cunt, and then you couldn't get away from me fast enough and you said it made you feel dirty and like you were being raped? Even though you'd said I could, you'd told me it was okay right up until that minute?"

Eli swallowed. The memory—the hurt look on Rob's face, the way his own skin had crawled with somebody touching him like a girl, intending to fuck him like a girl—was a painful one. "Yeah?"

"You've never done that before. And I realised then, this is way bigger for you than, like, not liking high heels and crap, it's deeper than that, and you're...proper hurt like, by not being what you fucking wanna be. And I don't get it. I really don't. But if this surgery is gonna make you okay with yourself, not make you feel that way, then fuck yeah I'll pay for it."

One of the tears spilled over, and then Eli surged forward to hug him. Wide hands landed in the small of Eli's back and Rob's nose was cold against his neck, but Eli didn't care. He squeezed tightly, trying to convey—convey—

Fuck, just how much it fucking *meant.* Suddenly, the end was in sight—the end of all the self-hate, the end of having to wear boxers instead of briefs because briefs still made it obvious he packed and didn't actually have a dick of his own, and...and Rob was the one to give him that, the one to give him the final cash injection he needed, even when he didn't understand and had for so long compared it to not liking having long hair or being offered perfume vouchers in Tesco.

"Oh God, Rob, *thank you*," Eli breathed, shaking from the sheer shock of it all.

Rob's voice was nothing but a gentle rasp into his neck, stubble brushing against his skin and leaving sparks of pure love in its wake.

They didn't move from the gate for some time.

CHAPTER 16

ELI HELD OUT until the evening.

The emotional sledgehammer of Rob's cheque had thrown him for a loop, so for the first couple of hours after their walk, he was simply a little clingy and wanted nothing more than to be left to process it and think. But then, he also didn't want Rob to get the wrong idea and think he was upset, so Eli opted for staying wound around Rob's side, and saying nothing at all.

But once the shock died down, the searing gratitude started to rise up again—and on the heels of it, the overshadowed first part of his present. So when the evening had rolled around, the family gathered in the living room with the telly on and Danny playing with the baby in the middle of the floor and looking even goofier than Rob had that morning, Eli found himself itching to steal Rob away upstairs and...*fuck*.

To do it bareback was something Eli had been waiting for ever since they got together. Rob hadn't been the safest guy before Eli came along, and he'd had an HIV scare about six months earlier. He'd point-blank refused to fuck Eli without a condom until the twelve-month test result came back clean—even though Eli had pointed out repeatedly that HIV could be transmitted through oral sex anyway.

"Yeah," Rob had said, "but the risk is way lower. It's not happening, Eli, give it up."

Now, finally, he could get what he wanted—if he could only prise Rob subtly away from the rest of his family. Unfortunately, the melee was warm and lively, and the easy smile and lightness to Rob's usually severe face was one that Eli was loathe to disturb, and would probably struggle to do so.

In the end though, the ache—both an emotional one in Eli's heart, and a physical one in his groin—became too much. He slipped out of the living room under the pretence of getting another drink before fleeing upstairs to the spare room that had been given over to them. The door could be barricaded, he calculated, with the heavy oak furniture and the iron frame of Danny's bed. And if they were quiet, then there was no reason the rest of the family had to know—and if they did, what did Eli care anyway? So...

He stripped naked, rescuing his phone from his jeans in the process, and crawled into the bed before texting Rob. Best to be plain. *I need you. For the next hour at least. Inside me. Come upstairs xxx*

He faintly heard the beep downstairs, and the heavy tread of Rob's graceless gait escaping the living room. He seemed to pause, and then—Eli's heart swelled—the stairs began to creak in a familiar rhythm. The tread was slow, casual, and with every creak, Eli's blood got hotter. He could feel—to his faint disgust—his own body beginning to dampen the sheets under him.

The bedroom door opened, and Rob raised his eyebrows.

"You fucking slut," he drawled, closing it behind him.

Eli smiled.

"You gave me a clean result. So you can stop your excuses and let me feel that cock *properly*."

"Mm, and what's in it for me?"

"A good, slow, *thorough* fucking."

"Slow? Eurgh. Sex ain't meant to be *slow*, Eli."

"Fuck you and your wrong opinions of wrong," Eli returned loftily. "Put that dresser in front of the door. I don't want *any* interruptions."

Rob rolled his eyes but turned to do as he was told. Eli smiled, curling his bare toes under the sheets, and chewed on his lip. His heart was picking up already; he wanted to climb out of the sheets, and—

Fuck it: he climbed out of the sheets, standing right up on the mattress, and held out his arms when Rob turned back around from hefting the dresser into perfect barricading position.

"C'mere," Eli breathed.

For a moment, Rob simply stared, those near-white eyes raking Eli from his toes to his temples. Only when Eli repeated the request did Rob step forward, one hand rising to catch at Eli's fingers, and the other finding his thigh, stroking up the back to his arse and resting there, possessive and promising. His mouth was hot against Eli's belly, sucking marks into the soft skin, and browsing lower in rough sweeps of stubble and kisses until a smile was pressing against Eli's arousal, firm against the tense pulse.

"You're wet."

"I want you," Eli whispered, carding his fingers through Rob's hair.

Damp lips closed around him and sucked. Eli sighed heavily, rolling his hips into the attention, feeling his inner thighs burn with hot blood and his skin swelling under Rob's ministrations. When aroused, thanks to the testosterone, Eli's clit could reach two inches in length, and Rob wrapped his mouth around it and sucked like it was a cock. Then a hand caught behind Eli's knee and he was brought down to the bed and pushed back onto it. Rob's tongue was still lapping at him, pausing in brief moments here and there to rub coarse stubble against his thighs and hips until Eli reached over his head to fist both hands in the pillows and whine, pushing up in thrusts, desperate for proper friction.

That first pleasure was short and intense, a lightning strike with his legs caught in Rob's large hands and pinned slightly, making him literally ride Rob's jaw to get the pressure he needed to bring himself to satisfaction—and yet it *wasn't* satisfying, Eli's brain reminded him the moment it could, because it hadn't been all that Eli wanted out of the evening.

He opened his mouth to say so, and found a slack mouth pushing against his for a sloppy kiss that tasted of himself and the sharp cotton tang where his boxers had chafed a little too tight inside his jeans since Rob had given him the clean result. He sighed, pulling on Rob's shirt to try hauling him up onto the bed, and got his lip bitten for the effort.

"What d'you want?"

Rob's voice was a low rasp, gentle in a way Eli rarely heard. Eli stroked his fingers over bare biceps and squeezed.

"You," he whispered. "As deep as I can take you, with nothing between us. I just want to feel you, like…like it's the first time all over again."

Rob smiled against his cheek. "The first time was the toilets in Lion's Lair."

"The first time we fucked proper, that was a blowjob."

"And *that* was in the back seat of my car."

"Fine," Eli murmured. "Like that time you tied me to your bed and spent over an hour just *kissing* me into coming. Like that time."

Rob nodded, then his weight was gone. Eli stretched luxuriously, enjoying the way Rob paused before stripping his T-shirt off, then propped himself up on his elbows to watch the play of muscles in Rob's abdomen as the T-shirt was discarded, his belt stripped from his jeans, and—

"Let me."

Rob paused. Eli popped the button and tugged the denim down. Rob was half-hard, and Eli brushed his knuckles over the bulge in his briefs before dropping the jeans entirely and running his palms up taut thighs, narrow hips, and a flat stomach tense with muscle. He licked from the top of Rob's pubic hair to his bellybutton, just to feel the shiver.

"I could blow you first?" he whispered, looking up that long body.

Rob's laugh was quiet.

"Not all of us can have four orgasms in a row without pausing, babe."

Eli beamed. "Maybe neither of us, after my surgery."

"Maybe."

"God, I fucking love you," Eli breathed, and tugged the briefs down, too. That cock hadn't risen yet, but it had grown to maybe two thirds of its fuck-ready proportions, plenty big enough already for Eli to wrap his fingers around and squeeze gently. Rob grunted, then swore when Eli rubbed his thumb over the foreskin and began to toy gently with it. Rob was uncut, and it was a constant source of fascination to Eli, whose porn collection pretty much exclusively consisted of circumcised guys. "You want me to fuck you deep and slow?"

"Uh-huh."

"Then stop that."

Eli laughed and let go. He lay back on the sheets, locking his hands behind his head and—very deliberately—spread his legs.

"Come on, then," he whispered. "Let me feel that where it's supposed to be. The *way* it's supposed to be."

Rob's laugh was oddly gentle. He lowered himself onto the bed almost reverently, his mouth finding Eli's hip first and kissing its way up his stomach and chest, pausing at his neck to mouth at his pulse, and finally sliding into place over Eli's lips as he settled. Rob's body was hot and pleasant between Eli's legs, one forearm resting on the bed to support his weight and the other stroking up Eli's ribs as slowly as though he had never done it before, or was trying to memorise the feel of Eli's skin. Eli squirmed up into it, hooking a foot around Rob's calf and a hand around the back of his hair, pulling Rob in as though he wanted Rob to simply sink into his skin and stay there forever.

And maybe he did—the heat, the weight, the sensation of being pinned and yet protected…Eli twisted his face away, tugging on Rob's hair to push the man down again. He sighed breathily when teeth sank into his neck and Rob sucked so hard that Eli's blood warred between his crotch and his jugular. His back bucked powerfully; it was like an electric shock to the system. He hissed when Rob began to rock lightly against him, the heavy drag of his cock against Eli's perineum both sensual and maddening, his blood already pulsing uncomfortably hard.

Rob laughed when Eli forced a hand between them and began to rub himself, and sat back on his heels, bending over the side of the bed to rummage for his bag. Eli watched his cock sway lightly with the motion and abandoned his rubbing to reach for it instead, determined to make it as wet as he was.

"Oh no you don't," Rob rasped, catching Eli's wrist. "You touch me now and it's all over."

"I could get you working again."

"Not inside of half an hour *minimum,* babe."

Eli made a high whine in his throat, unashamed of the neediness of it, but then Rob was back, settling over him heavily again and biting the other side of his neck, teeth compressing until Eli could feel the bruise blossoming. Eli was digging fingernails into Rob's shoulders with harsh gasps when Rob finally released his jaw and nuzzled the crook of Eli's shoulder.

"Ready?"

"Mm."

The first touch of Rob's hand, slick and warm, was familiar. Eli rolled his hips up into it and spread his knees wider, closing his eyes to focus on the sensation. Rob's fingers were rough and callused; his nails were shorn right down, and yet the cool backs of them as he breached Eli was a delicious edge of wariness layered over the hot feeling of being prised open and laid out ready.

And for this, Eli was always ready—to feel Rob buried inside of him, so big it almost hurt and so powerful it was as paralysing as being choked by the neck. He loved both that submission, in being a warm sheath for Rob's dick, and that dominance in having control over Rob's pleasure in how the man moved, clenched, relaxed, or even merely breathed. This was *control,* even if he was the one taking it, and Eli *loved* it.

"Fuck me," he breathed, eyes still closed and clenching his arse around the insistent push as Rob added a third finger. Eli resisted, just to feel the burn, and squeezed tightly when Rob tried to flex his hand a little.

"You want slow and thorough, you better not do that around my dick," Rob warned quietly.

Eli laughed, beginning to rock his hips properly and fuck himself on Rob's hand.

"Fuck, babe. You want me to fist you?"

"No," Eli murmured, "I want you to fuck me, and I want to

feel it, so hurry up!"

"Yeah?" Rob's voice dropped into the deep, disgusting rasp that gave Eli the shivers. "Way you're doing all the work here, babe, I'd say that makes you just a little bit of a slut. Y'agree with me? Maybe I should film this, yeah, prove how you get minute a guy waves a cock at you?"

"Just yours," Eli breathed, and reached down to grab Rob's wrist. "Cock. *Now.*"

Rob laughed and hooked his hands behind Eli's knees, physically dragging his arse over Rob's lap. It was an awkward angle, but Eli hooked his legs around Rob's lower back and yanked him down by the shoulders for a hungry, off-kilter kiss that was all lips and biting teeth. One of Rob's hands gripped his shoulder, warningly hard, and then they were chest-to-chest and Rob's white eyes were the entire world.

"It's gonna be hard."

"Fuck," Eli said, "me."

Rob covered Eli's mouth with his own—and thrust.

It was a powerful jerk of his hips, and his cock rammed home. Eli screamed into Rob's mouth, feeling blood well up under his nails where he scored them deep into Rob's shoulders, his hips and thighs clenching so hard he *almost* arrested the motion. It was harder than the scene in Eli's room when Rob had broken in; it was harder, even, than the first time Eli had discovered Rob liked dirty talk. In an instant, he went from aching to be filled, to being split open by that impossibly large, insatiably hard dick, but *God*—

"Don't move. Oh my God, don't move," he panted into Rob's mouth, clutching at skin and hair and anything else he could reach. Because Eli could also feel *Rob,* feel the slick heat of his skin, feel his pulse throbbing in the thick vein on the underside, feel the smooth press of his head...Eli clenched, slow and deliberate, and felt his blood catch fire from the electric shock of skin pressing around skin—

"*Fuck.*"

"Slow. Just...slow. Oh my—oh *God,*" Eli choked, his spine shuddering as Rob's satin-smoothness *dragged* against him, the head pulling and stretching. As Rob withdrew, a hollow emptiness trailed after it…and then he pushed back in. Eli wanted to cry at the impossibly perfect sensation of being filled, fucked, owned, *possessed*…

"Jesus, babe, your *face*, fucking hell…"

"Harder. Harder, please, God, just—fuck, fuck, fuck—"

Rob's rhythm was not the brutal, almost perfunctory fuck Eli was used to; it was an idle thing, from the knees to the chest, with long strokes. The relentless push-and-pull had the bed shaking and Eli clinging, breath nothing but a shudder. Rob's teeth were an anchor in Eli's shoulder, his hands stilling Eli's shoulders so there was no escape, nowhere to go, nothing to do but be fucked open until he couldn't take it anymore, until—

"Touch me, just…just, oh God, touch me…"

For a brutal moment—there was cold. Cold and emptiness, as Rob pulled out entirely, his heat gone. Eli's mind spun before his body did. A hard grip turned him over onto his front until both of Rob's hands were under him, one cupping his groin with a callused heel grinding into his slick wetness, and the other bracing his chest.

Rob's breath was hot against Eli's ear, his teeth worrying the earlobe, and his voice was a growled command.

"Hands on the headboard. And brace yourself."

Eli groaned, spread his legs, and pushed his arse up against Rob's cock as even he obeyed, winding his fingers around the bars and squeezing like he wanted to squeeze around Rob.

"Please," he begged, completely lost, "please, please, please—"

The slickness and the heat was easier; the thrust was hard, but not so brutal. A lightning bolt struck his hips when Rob's cock drove Eli into his waiting hand, a rough rhythm set up flawlessly again, faster than before and completely centred on wet skin, heavy heat, on *Rob*—

Eli came so hard, shuddering and shaking, his voice wavering on a cry that was so high it was nearly another scream.

Rob grunted and stilled early for a brief second, his hand rough and jerking Eli through the storm rough and fucking perfect, his breath deep snarls in Eli's ear, and, and…Then, when Eli was weak and dizzy with it, his fingers flexing uselessly and his breath catching and loose in helpless lungs—

Rob began to thrust again.

"I can fuck you stupid," he grunted, "but end of the day, your arse is there for me. It *belongs* to me. I can fuck you right open until you're covered in it. Until you reek of sex and sweat and cum. And no fucker else gets to do this to you. Gets to see just how much you can fucking *gag* for it when you're ready—"

"Mine," Eli hissed. "Oh, God, Rob, you're mine, you're *mine!*"

Rob's thrusts dropped, then began a scattered, staccato rhythm. Wet heat flooded Eli's arse, filling him, hot and burning and so unlike anything he'd ever felt before. Arousal had never been this wet; he'd never been drenched the way this was. He squeezed the pillow in both hands and gasped his way through it, felt the way it pressed against him and began to trickle free when Rob pulled back and—

"No," Eli whispered, reaching back for him. "No, no, stay inside, stay—just…hold me, c'mere, hold me…"

Rob settled over him like a blanket. Eli clung to his arm when it slid up from his crotch to his waist. Rob's chest heaved against Eli's back, his dick softening inside, and Eli clenched around it to feel Rob's skin and cum, to feel how filthy he really was.

"Oh, God, I'm disgusting," he panted, and laughed breathlessly.

Rob smiled against his ear. Then Eli was being shifted to the side, still pinned to Rob's front, and they were curling into spoons.

"Fucking filthy."

"Fucking *yours,*" Eli breathed, burying his face in the pillow and smiling when Rob kissed his ear. "Oh God, that was…I love you. I *love* you."

Rob squeezed tightly, and his nose pressed against the top of Eli's shoulder. "V'you, too," he mumbled after a beat.

Eli squeezed Rob's forearm where it was locked around his stomach.

"Later…later, we're going to…we're gonna shower. And you're gonna clean me out proper like, and then you're…then you'll fuck me again, up against the shower wall, and…"

Rob bit his shoulder; Eli shivered and quietened.

"*Later,*" Rob rumbled. "S'all the time in the world for that."

Eli stroked the tattoos, drifted, and thought that maybe…maybe Rob was right.

CHAPTER 17

THE BREAK WAS...phenomenal.

To get away from all the friction with Eli's family was good enough on its own—but to get to see Rob truly happy, to see that tension just bleed right out of him and learn when he wasn't being sardonic or defensive or playing some game, his smile could light up his entire face with this totally beautiful, childlike *glee*...

The week in Scotland was, for Eli, a bit like falling in love all over again. Which was odd, because Eli couldn't pinpoint when he'd moved from wanting to just rip all of Rob's clothes off and fuck him stupid to actually loving him in the first place.

He didn't want to go home and leave Rob's ease and happiness behind. He didn't want to return to the constant back and forth between Rob and his dad, and yet...at the same time, Eli felt more confident in doing so. The break had set his priorities firmly in order again, cemented the feeling Rob really was as important as he suspected. It had shored up what he *thought* he knew—that Rob was a long-term thing and not leaving Eli's life anytime soon—into something that was a certainty.

They left early in the morning, and drove several hours through roadworks and a heavy rain that refused to let up. Danny snored in the backseat for most of the journey; Eli worked on his tattoo design, and hummed to the radio when Rob fiddled with the stations. They didn't stop for breakfast, but Rob promised lunch. And so it was that Eli ended up going back to their flat and curling against Rob's side on the sofa eating his way through a small pile of toast while the brothers bickered over the best way to eat a double-fried-egg-with-crispy-bacon butty. Something that Eli privately thought was disgusting.

"I suppose," he said quietly, when he'd demolished a whole loaf of bread via the toaster, "that I better go home."

"Fuck that. Stay here. I can make a run and a hutch for you, and bring you treats from the outside world every now and then."

Eli laughed; Danny jeered and called them kinky fuckers.

"Fuck off, y'twassock," Rob grumbled, and then heaved himself off the sofa. "Alright, alright. C'mon, I'll drop you off."

It had stopped raining—finally—and the roads were gleaming. The moment they were in the car, however, Eli leaned across the gearstick and handbrake to catch Rob's chin between finger and thumb and kiss him soundly.

"Thanks?"

"Twat," Eli said affectionately. "Thanks for inviting me. It was great."

"Yeah?"

"Mm." Eli kissed him again, soft and slow, mouthing gently at his bottom lip and wondering whether to bite it. "Your family, and seeing you so relaxed, and the *presents*..."

Rob's smile spoiled the kiss. Eli pressed his forehead to Rob's temple and grinned stupidly. He felt too big for his skin, dizzy with delight. He wound his fingers into the shoulders of Rob's jacket and squeezed fiercely.

"I'm going to call my specialist when I get home," he breathed, "and tell him I have the money for surgery, and move my appointment closer so we can arrange it and I can get the referral..."

"I have no fucking idea what you're talking about."

Eli only beamed harder. "I can be *finished*, Rob."

Rob huffed a hoarse laugh, and butted his head lightly against

Eli's. "Only if you go 'ome and actually make the arrangements 'n' shit. Can't help you wi' that."

"You've helped plenty," Eli whispered, still smiling uncontrollably. He surged for one last kiss before letting go. "Okay. Okay, take me home, and I'm gonna get on the phone and get everything sorted, and—you'll come with me, right, on surgery day? It'll be Leeds, probably, I always get a hotel overnight and usually I have to get Mum to come with me, but—"

"Yeah, yeah, I'll come," Rob said, putting the car in gear and peeling out of the parking bay. The roads were gleaming wet in the watery run, and the bonnet shimmered under a pattern of raindrops. "D'you wanna come out next weekend? Down t'Dempseys? There's some party on or summat, drinks are half price."

Eli laughed. "Like old times?"

Dempseys, an old and small gay bar at the bottom of the Moor shopping precinct, was where Eli had pulled Rob the second time and finally gotten his name and number. There'd been a couple of dirty alleyway fucks since, too. It wasn't the classiest club in the world, but for seedy and familiar, there were none like it.

"Maybe," Rob smirked. "You get pissed and start dancin' and it'll definitely be like old times."

"You just want a blowjob in a toilet."

"I'll have a blowjob wherever I can get it, babe," Rob drawled obnoxiously.

Eli shook his head, reaching across to squeeze his knee.

"Oi, oi, hands t'yourself when I'm driving. Perv."

"Me? You're the one who grabbed my arse and started grinding against me in Lion's first time we met."

"I was appreciating your moves."

"You were appreciating my arse."

"That, too."

Eli was laughing in earnest by the time they reached Dore. When Rob pulled up haphazardly across Dad's driveway, Eli released the seatbelt and leaned across to tangle both hands into Rob's hair and kiss him sloppily.

"You," he breathed, "are fucking insatiable and ridiculous and rude and a total arsehole and I fucking love you. I fucking *love* you. You're so fun and awful and sweet when you want to be, and—Jesus, best thing that ever happened to me was you thinking my arse looked good in those jeans."

Rob nudged his nose against Eli's and huffed. "You're turning into a fucking pansy again."

"Shut up and enjoy it."

"Pussy."

"*Rob...*"

"Shutting up."

"Good," Eli said, and bit Rob's lower lip in brief punishment. "I have work tomorrow, and the day after. But after that, I'm gonna come over and throw away every condom in your flat. Then you're going to chase Danny out of the place for, like, a whole day and pin me down on the kitchen floor and fuck me until I can't remember anything except you and your dick."

Rob groaned into Eli's mouth, deep and guttural.

Eli dropped a hand to squeeze Rob's thigh and stretch his fingers out to feel a hardness pushing at the denim.

"Dirty fucking pool."

"Something to remember me by," Eli teased, squeezing Rob's erection lightly before letting go, kissing Rob on the cheek, and getting out of the car.

"You're a fucking cunt!" Rob shouted after him.

Eli laughed, darting around the car and kissing him again through the open window, cupping his face in both hands and—quite frankly—plundering his mouth. It was a brutal kiss, made better by the fact Rob couldn't get hold of him in response. When Eli decided that breathing was a bit of a priority, he stayed close enough to bump his nose against Rob's cheek and watch, at intensely close range, those magnificent eyes flicker open.

"Love you."

"Right now? My dick loves you. I think you're a fucking bastard."

Eli grinned, pecked him on the forehead, and let go. "See you soon."

"Dickhead."

The Suzuki roared off as Eli headed up the path. The kitchen curtain distinctly twitched and he rolled his eyes before letting himself in. "I'm home!" he yelled, and—surprise, surprise—Dad materialised in the kitchen doorway.

"You're later than we expected."

Eli shrugged. "Stopped at Rob's for lunch first. It was a long trip back."

"Hm." Dad's eyes were raking him. A spark of irritation lit in the back of Eli's head—what was Dad expecting, him to return with a black eye and an arm in a cast? Should he strip off and show the lack of bruises?

…Although on reflection, that would be a bad idea. Given that Rob had left a really impressive bite-mark on Eli's inner thigh the previous night.

"Eli!" Mum. Thank God. "There you are, dear—how was your trip?"

She appeared from the living room and drew him into a brief hug before holding him at arms' length and giving him the same visual inspection that Dad had.

The irritation got stronger, but Eli blew out his cheeks and tried to stay pleasant. "It was really good."

"Have fun, did you?"

"Yes," Eli said. "Got to meet Rob's aunt and cousins. Loads of snow, too, so we had a snowball fight on Boxing Day. Danny—his brother—me and Danny ganged up on Rob so he got trounced."

Dad looked like he was biting his tongue; Mum smiled, and tugged Eli into the kitchen.

"Samuel, dear, don't just stand there, pop the kettle on," she scolded mildly, sinking into the chair opposite Eli's usual one. "I'm glad you had a good time, dear. Your aunts missed you, though, we'll have to pop up to see them again at the weekend. And your presents are on your bed, you should open them tonight. Jenny's bringing Flora over…"

Eli's heart jumped. The present! Rob's present—that would convince even Dad. "Look," he said, dumping his bag on the table and rummaging inside. The envelopes were bent and creased, but he found the cheque and slid it across the table to Mum with a beaming smile. "Look what Rob got me."

The reaction was instantaneous.

"Dear Lord!"

"Where did Hawkes get that kind of money?"

"It's for—"

"Is this for college?" Dad interrupted. He was holding the cheque between finger and thumb as though it were a dead rat. "Did he give you this to go to college?"

"He—"

"Eli, I have said time and again that if you want to go to art college, your mother and I will support you and pay the fees—I certainly do not want you taking money from a criminal!"

"Dad! He's not a fucking criminal!"

"Language! And yes he is, Eli! When was the last time he was earning steady money—where on *earth* could he have gotten this amount of money legally?"

"I—it doesn't matter where it came from, it's for—"

"This is criminal proceeds, Eli, there's no question about it—it's probably drug money, at the very least, and I will not have my son accepting money from a drug dealer to go to college!"

"He's not a druggie! For God's sake, he's done something really nice for me, it's for—"

"I will not have it!" Dad thundered. He was breathing heavily through his nose, his face bulging scarlet over his collar. He was obviously due to go on shift, dressed up to the nines in his brass and white shirt. The cheque was fluttering, Dad's hand was shaking that hard. "I will not have you accepting criminal money! That is *final!*"

"You can't fucking *stop* me accepting his money!" Eli bellowed back.

The rip of paper was louder than the detonation of the atomic bomb.

Silence.

Dad tore the cheque into eighths, and the pieces drifted to the floor. He was panting like an asthmatic rhinoceros; Mum, by contrast, was utterly still and silent, both hands over her mouth. The kettle began to whistle into the horror, and Eli—so slowly that he felt a thousand years—stood from the table.

"I will give you the money for college," Dad said coldly, "and I will not hear another word about you accepting any dirty money from Hawkes."

Eli curled his fingers into fists, clenching them until his nails bit into his skin.

"You won't give me any money to get my own flat," he whispered, his voice shaking even harder than his hands. "You won't give me anything towards my transition. When you were pushing me to go to uni, you weren't going to be paying my fees. And yet the minute—the fucking *minute*—that Rob offers to do what *you* should be doing, you fucking flip your fucking shit and rip it up!"

"Eli, you watch your language under my roof!" Dad roared.

Eli hit him.

The blow was sharp and straight, his knuckles crashing into his father's nose with a flash of red-hot pain that barrelled up his bones and burrowed into his elbow, whining and complaining at the lack of preparation for the strike. And yet it was hugely satisfying, too—flesh popped dully under his hand, his father letting out a yelp more like a scalded child than a wounded officer. The rage was intense and brutal, ripping through Eli's chest and leaving a boiling trail of hurt and sorrow.

"Fuck you. Fuck you both, just *fuck you*!"

The kitchen door slammed so hard that he heard the plaster crack. The front door bounced right out of its own frame, swinging open again behind him, and Eli didn't care. He bolted, going from a furious storm to a sprint in a matter of seconds, paying no attention to where he was going. His footsteps pounded in a rhythm—*fuck-them, fuck-them, fuck-them, fuck-them*. Eli wanted to cry, to scream, to take a crowbar and beat his father's smug, red face in until he couldn't fuck things up anymore. Until he couldn't be so fucking pious all the time then go batshit when Eli accepted support from someone who actually fucking loved him enough to offer it...

He only stopped when his knees threatened to give and his lungs were screaming. He didn't recognise the street he'd ended up on—probably down in Totley, he suspected—and fumbled in the pocket of his jeans for his phone.

I just punched my dad in the face.

His eyes were burning, the sound of the ripping paper echoing in his ears along with his own heartbeat.

Wtf?

He lost his shit and ripped up the money you gave me and said he'd pay. He called you all sorts and wouldn't even let me explain what it was for. He's such a fucking cunt!

Been sayin that 4 ages babe. its ok ill wire u the £. accept his £, n dont tell him u still have mine!!!

Eli laughed wetly, leaning on a garden wall. *Yeah?*

Yeh srsly. 2 lots of £ y u bitchin???

He scrubbed his sleeve across his eyes and exhaled heavily. Trust Rob. Sneaky, criminal-proceeds-offering Rob. Eli wasn't fucking stupid, he *knew* most of the money was probably from selling other people's stuff or dealing weed, but...but it was for his surgery! It was for something good—if Rob were the douchecanoe Dad was making out, he'd have bought a load of charlie or a flash car or something. He wouldn't buy his boyfriend's sex-change surgery!

I'm so fucking angry with him.

No shit. dad proud of u tho babe, kill the pig!

Eli laughed hoarsely, scrubbing his sleeve across his eyes.

U want me 2 come pick u up?

No, Eli replied. *I'm gonna go for a walk and clear my head. I just need some space from everything right now, he's being such a dick and I'm tired, it's crap. Can we go back to Scotland???*

U wish babe. Lemme no if u want me 2 come get u l8a then. dont let the fucker get u down!

Thanks :) Eli replied, then added a quick, *Love you xxxxx* on the end. Because he did, and fuck Dad, and maybe Rob was right and Eli should punish his father for being such a douchebag by accepting his money *and* Rob's. Eli never had much money anyway, and his parents had never put a penny towards his transition. That was why he was still living at home—he couldn't afford all that private treatment *and* a place of his own on his crappy job.

LU2 babe x

Eli pushed himself off the wall, pocketed the phone, and started to walk in a random direction, mind churning.

Maybe…

Maybe it was time to give up on his dad entirely.

CHAPTER 18

ELI DIDN'T SEE Rob at all for nearly two weeks after that.

Frankly, it was torture. Things between Eli and his parents had never been so bad, not even after Eli had lashed out and hit his father. Mum was trying to pretend nothing had happened; Dad could barely look him in the face. Something had *broken,* and Eli neither knew how to fix it, nor wanted to. But there was nowhere else to turn. He picked up as many shifts at the shop as the boss would give him. Rob had scored a few shifts over the New Year working security at a couple of the dodgier clubs in the city centre that weren't too fussed about a guy's record. As such, he simply wasn't home enough for Eli to escape, and apparently one of Danny's dealer mates from Huddersfield had come down for New Year, and Rob had actively told Eli that that guy was bad news and to steer clear.

Eli had only texts and sexts until mid-January, when he was woken on Sunday morning with two messages: the first a photo of Rob's bare erection, and the second saying, *Woke up w/ this fucker. If ur not free 2day, b free neway. unles u wanna b nicked?*

Eli laughed sleepily, sitting up and rubbing the fog from his eyes before replying, *Missed you too much for games. Give me half an hour for shower and clothes and come get me :)*

10 mins 2 shower. fuck clothes. c u in a bit, may have 2 pull over on way to mine fair warnin

Eli laughed and rolled out of bed. Rob, he knew from experience, wasn't kidding, so he slammed straight into the bathroom and didn't bother waiting for the shower to warm up before getting in. He was itching with the need to just fucking touch already. Eli didn't really like masturbating—it was a shitty imitation of the real thing, and still stirred up those old, unpleasant feelings of dysphoria if he touched himself there too much—and two weeks without Rob's hands and mouth had been trying, to say the least. Especially after *last* time—God, the last time was enough to make the water feel warmer all on its own, and spurred Eli to hurry up even more.

"Eli, dear, do you want breakfast?" Mum called from the hall as Eli dashed back to his room in his towels.

"No, ta, Rob's coming to pick me up!" he yelled, and slammed the door on her grumble. Clothes, clothes, clothes. Despite Rob's cheery assertion to fuck them, Eli somehow doubted that being naked in Rob's front passenger seat was allowed. He pulled his boxers and jeans on hastily and rummaged for a suitable T-shirt—one, effectively, that Rob would allow him to actually take off, instead of one of the stretchier ones that Rob preferred to *rip* off. Eli was seriously running out of tops.

He'd barely managed to dry off his hair enough to ruffle it up with his fingers when he heard the tell-tale growl of the Jimny out on the road, and grabbed for his phone. He threw his sketchbook and pen hastily into his bag—he had designs to try out on Rob's skin, once he'd tried out everything *else* he wanted on Rob's skin—before barrelling out of his bedroom and taking the stairs three at a time down into the hall. A horn sounded, long and loud. He laughed breathlessly even as he grabbed his keys from the bowl on the phone table, flung the door open, and sprinted down the driveway. Dad was working on his car, and gave the waiting Suzuki—haphazardly parked half on the pavement and half on the road, and with music blasting out the windows—a foul look.

"Eli, you tell that man—"

"See you later!" Eli shouted.

Rob had turned the car around at some point, so the drivers' side was closest. Eli leaned in the open window to kiss him hungrily. Rob was wearing sunglasses, the wintry sunlight blinding this morning, and he grinned around Eli's tongue.

"Get your arse in here," he said roughly, and Eli bit his bottom lip.

"Straight to yours, or somewhere else?" he breathed.

"Somewhere else," Rob said, and grinned. "Flat's too fuckin' far for the minute."

Eli bit his mouth one last time before near-jogging around the car and flinging himself into the passenger seat. Rob had it moving before Eli had even closed the door, leaving him fumbling for the seatbelt over the bumpy avenue. Then they were turning not towards the city, as Eli had expected, but out towards the Peaks.

"Seriously, Rob, a hike?"

"You fucking shitting me? A field, more like."

"A fi—oh," Eli said, and laughed. "A quick one in the back seat?"

"Who needs the back?" Rob chuckled. His grin was infectious; his hair was sticking up in an impressive bedhead that Eli wanted to fist his hands in. Rob's stubble was approaching beard level, and suddenly Eli wanted that against his thighs, to feel where rough stubble just began to turn into softer hair. He said as much, and grinned as Rob's fingers flexed on the wheel.

"So you want me to go down on you, and then what? What do I get?"

"I'm sure you'll think of something," Eli teased.

Rob groaned.

"Fucker."

Not forty seconds later, Rob pulled the Suzuki through an open gateway into a field, the high hedges shielding it from the road. The car bounced and rolled over the cold, muddy earth.

Eli laughed as Rob didn't wait for it to get thirty metres from the gateway before hauling on the handbrake and fumbling with his seatbelt.

"Get in the fucking back."

Eli laughed, and scrambled to do so. Getting in the back involved getting out and popping the front seat forward. The brief foray into the cold air was unwelcome. "Put the fucking heater on!" he hissed as he heaved himself into the back and unbuttoned his jeans. "And get your fucking mouth in here and all!"

Rob—mouth and all—crashed into the back seat like a hurricane, shoving the front passenger seat far forward enough to allow him to crouch awkwardly in the leg space and rip Eli's jeans down just over his knees and then—

"*Fuuuuck*," Eli breathed, dropping his head back and bracing his arms on the headrests. "Oh fuck, fuck, fuck—yes, right there, *just* like that…"

Rob had a mouth that could have rewritten fucking history if he'd given blowjobs to the right people. And even though Eli hadn't had his phalloplasty yet, the testosterone injections had caused his clitoris to swell when he was aroused. And just then he was so aroused he could feel it in his fucking *teeth*. Rob had plenty of flesh to rasp that rough tongue over, to blow hot air into folds, to scrape his teeth against just light enough to spark off intense, hot desire, until Eli was clamping his thighs around Rob's ears, tugging on his hair, grinding against the rasp of his beard, and swearing. Loudly.

"Oh my God, oh fuck, *fuck*—"

It was quick, dirty, and just what Eli needed; he shuddered through the orgasm with Rob sucking on him like he was dying of thirst. Eli groaned when that filthy mouth unlatched, licked a thick stripe up his belly and ribs, and large hands twisted him sideways onto the seats.

"Fuck me," Eli demanded breathlessly, trying to kick his jeans off.

Rob seized his thighs and forced them still. His mouth was red and glistening, and he grinned breathlessly.

"Can't."

Eli tore open Rob's jeans. His erection was heavy, his briefs damp with pre-cum, and Eli tore them down, too, before pulling on Rob's hips.

"Try?"

"*Can't.*"

Rob dropped like a stone onto Eli's chest, forcing his cock into the small space Eli's tangled jeans allowed between his thighs. The first thrust was stuttered, but the second powerful. Eli caught both arms around Rob's neck and clung through the movements, squeezing his thighs around Rob's dick and grinding down when the head grazed his arse.

"Oh God, fuck, get the edge off then take me home and fuck me raw—"

"I am going," Rob grunted, pressing his forehead to Eli's and closing his eyes. His biceps flexed as he braced his weight on the car seat and thrust entirely with his hips in short, brutal strokes, "to handcuff you to the fucking headboard, and fuck you so hard you're gonna need a fucking *helmet.*"

Rob lasted even less time than Eli had, a deep groan rattling out of his chest and a hot wetness flooding Eli's thighs and the car seat beneath as he finished. Eli laughed giddily, biting Rob's earlobe and sucking when he made a protesting sound.

"You forget," Eli whispered, "I can still get off again within thirty fucking seconds."

Rob laughed. A hand slid over Eli's thigh, fingers grazing his pubic hair and swollen clit. "Tell you what," Rob grunted as he began to rub and Eli arched up into his fingers, sore but definitely not yet sated, "maybe straight guys have a point sometimes."

IT WAS EVENING before Rob finally stirred and unlocked the handcuffs. Eli sighed, drawing his arms down into the warmth and letting Rob massage his wrists and hands with a pleased hum. He was sore—Rob had not been difficult to persuade about the whole fucking him raw thing—and sticky. The exhausted heat of having finally scratched a maddening two-week itch was coiled heavy in Eli's blood, and rendered him utterly fucking blissful.

"God, I needed that," he whispered.

Rob chuckled, hand warm and heavy on Eli's side.

"I was crawling out of my skin by the time you sent me that picture of your cock."

"That was after a wank, too."

"At least you *can* wank."

"True," Rob said amiably, and kissed the top of Eli's head. "Sorry about the straight guy comment."

"S'fine," Eli said lazily. "Make it up to me by feeding me."

"Give me half an hour…"

"Not *that*," Eli said, and pinched Rob's bicep.

Rob's chuckle would have been a giggle if his voice had been capable of a higher pitch.

"Proper food. I need a shower and some proper food."

"Chinese?"

"Heavier."

"A pizza each with a side of garlic bread?"

"Cheesy garlic bread. And get me some chicken wings, too."

"One day you'll tell me where you fucking put that shit," Rob grumbled, lifting an arm to release Eli when he squirmed. "'Kay. Leave the bathroom door unlocked. And it's cool, Danny's at some gig in Manchester tonight, he won't surprise us."

Eli slipped naked from the bed, his arse and thighs sticky with half-dried…well, mess. He could *feel* Rob's eyes on him, and grinned to himself as he let himself into the bathroom and turned the water on, still just a little thrilled by Rob's frankly insatiable sexual attraction to him. It wasn't something Eli had imagined ever happening when he'd started to transition. What gay guy would want to fuck someone who'd had surgery to totally make over their chest, a swollen clit instead of a penis, and a vagina?

Apparently Rob Hawkes. And Eli's sore, sticky state was the proof of it.

He sang in the shower, washing his hair with Rob's shower gel in lieu of anything decent to use, and was joined after maybe ten minutes by the man himself. Eli turned around to kiss him. Rob stood passive and allowed himself to be washed, kissing Eli's wet skin whenever it came into reach and making the odd sigh or rumble deep in his chest when Eli touched him. Rob had retreated into his silent, post-coital coma, and Eli beamed at being the cause of it.

"Love you," he whispered, stretching up on his tiptoes to card both hands through Rob's hair and begin to wash it. The reply was a lazy blink and a slow, open drag of lips on lips that vaguely resembled a kiss.

The doorbell rang before the shower was over, and Rob slipped away again. Eli sighed and shut the water off, retreating to the bedroom to rummage for clothes and his sketchpad. He 'borrowed' one of Rob's jumpers out of his drawers and a pair of socks, and shuffled back into the living room damp-haired and bundled up, surrounded in the smell of powder and *Rob*, feeling so utterly contented that the world could have ended, then and there, and Eli wouldn't have given a shit.

He gave even less of a shit when Rob, sprawled on the sofa in his briefs, pizza boxes arranged and opened on the coffee table and some shitty telly already playing, gave Eli's attire a dirty look.

"I'm going to allow you to break the rules just this once," he grumbled.

Eli laughed.

"It's just to prolong the good shower feeling," he promised, tucking himself into the middle of the sofa and seizing a slice of pizza. "I'll strip off again after we eat if you want."

"S'the rules."

Eli smiled and kissed Rob's bare shoulder. "Speaking of those rules, actually, I wanted to show you something."

"I've had my face in your fur three times in the last four hours, I think I know what it fucking looks like."

Eli laughed and hit him with the sketchbook before opening it and rifling through the pages until he found the design. "Here."

Rob took it and squinted at the paper. It was the hawk in flight—Eli had spent painstaking hours perfecting it, down to the very last feather, and now he was finally happy with it. It was ready. He even knew where it was going to go.

"Tattoo?" Rob guessed.

"Uh-huh."

"Looks good," Rob said. "Where's it gonna go?"

"Chest."

A frown rippled across Rob's face as he chewed thoughtfully on a hunk of garlic bread and handed the sketchbook back to Eli. "Haven't got room," he said. "Might fit on my back, or—"

"Oh!" Realisation dawned. "No, no! It's for me."

Rob blinked. "For *you*?"

"Uh-huh."

"Wait." A grin was blossoming. "You're finally gonna lose your ink virginity?"

Eli flushed hotly. "Oh shut up, you fucking perv."

Rob cackled.

"*Yes*, I am. I've been playing around with the design for ages and I'm finally happy with it. So…come with me? I want to go to that guy who did your magpies."

Rob had a collection of tiny magpies on his leg just above the ankle, none of them bigger than a fifty pence piece, but all of them beautifully detailed.

"Fair enough," he said, "but you're fucking mental. Start off small—that thing is gonna be a four hour job, minimum."

"Nope," Eli said. "That's why you're gonna come and hold my hand."

Rob guffawed.

"Say you'll come!"

"Alright, Jesus, I'll come watch you get tortured," Rob said.

"That money Dad gave me, to replace yours, I'm using that for this."

"He's gonna fucking murder you. Or me, it'll be my fault."

"Well, it *is* your fault. It's a hawk. Hawk, Hawkes? You know?"

Rob paused, hand hovering over the pizza box.

"What?" Eli asked.

"Isn't that…well, s'a bit like getting your boyfriend's name tattooed on you, that."

Eli shook his head. "It's not about that."

"So what is it?"

"It's…it's because even if we break up, even if we had this horrible awful break up and I spent the rest of my life thinking you were a total cunt, you're always…" Eli felt his face heating up rapidly. "You're always going to be the guy who proved to me that…that being trans isn't a death sentence for my love life, you know? That there *are* gay guys out there who aren't going to run a mile when they find out I was born a girl, that there are gay guys who are going to find me sexy and want to sleep with me, want to be with me, aren't going to...I dunno, run away screaming because I have a vagina..."

Rob sniggered. "Screaming? What the fuck do you keep in your cunt that makes guys run off screaming?"

Eli hit him with the book again and rolled his eyes. "Shut up, you know what I mean. But that's...that's you, you know? You did that for me. I nearly died of fright telling you, I was terrified you were going to...to just up and walk right out of the pub, or hit me, or something. And when you didn't mind...you know, when I got home, I locked myself in the bathroom and just cried because I didn't know how else to feel. It was...it changed *everything*, you and your no-clothes rules to make me feel better about myself, and your money for the surgery, and your...see, you're always going to be the guy that made me realise it was okay to be me. And that I could actually find someone. That Sarah isn't stopping me. And that's what this tattoo is—it's *that*, that knowledge that it's not impossible to be happy and find someone just because I'm trans."

Rob was openly staring, completely frozen in place, those grey eyes fixed on Eli's face like he was a mirage. When Eli finally shut up, Rob slowly tapped his bare thigh. "C'mere."

"Rob?"

"C'mere." Rob's voice was very hoarse.

Eli crawled over the cushions into his lap as beckoned, winding his arms around Rob's neck and shoulders, nuzzling the now-definitely-a-beard.

"You okay?"

Rob burrowed, arms closing around Eli's waist, face burying itself in Eli's bare neck, using his own chin to push aside the loose fabric. It tickled and when Eli squirmed, Rob tightened his grip.

"Rob? Everything okay?"

"You're fucking incredible."

The reply was so flat and factual Eli could almost feel it physically sink into his bones. He smiled against Rob's hair before kissing his temple.

"I'm beginning to get that," he murmured softly. "Thanks to you."

CHAPTER 19

ROB BOXED THREE times a week.

Danny said he wasn't very good—although Eli knew jack shit about boxing, so didn't understand the fine distinction between boxing and just hitting people until they fell over, which Rob was *excellent* at— but he did amateur matches now and then. Frankly Eli was all for anything that kept Rob's incredible biceps at the incredible stage.

It also meant that on Monday lunchtimes, he knew exactly where to find Rob. And on that Monday, Jenny had taken the day off, Eli had no shifts offered by the shop, and Mum was on rest days. So Eli had planned accordingly—because he was buoyed, after their lazy day together and Dad's furious outburst. If he could cut Dad out of the entire thing, would things be okay? Could Dad be led by Mum? And if he *could*, then the solution was right there, ready for the taking.

So Eli made his plans, and went to the gym.

Unfortunately, hanging around the gym foyer and watching an entire class of half-naked, sweaty men built like brick shithouses cooling down through the glass door to the main training room…Eli was rapidly forgetting said plan. Sometimes—not that he'd admit it to Rob, because the guy could get really jealous—Eli fantasised about some of the other boxers. There was one guy in particular, a tall black guy with an incredible set of dreadlocks that put Danny's to shame, that Eli had seen doing pull-ups on the wall bars once. He still broke into a sweat just *thinking* about that guy.

It made the loitering fun at least, and the only part Eli liked about not being born a man was the lack of inappropriate boners. So when Rob finally emerged, freshly showered and dressed in heavy jeans and a white T-shirt that did sweet fuck-all to hide his musculature, Eli was the picture of composure.

"Not complaining, but why are you hanging around?" Rob asked, slinging his kit bag over his shoulder. To Eli's surprise, Rob flung an arm around his shoulders and kissed him.

"Um," Eli said, a little dazed from the weight of that muscled arm and the fresh smell of deodorant. "Um, lunch?"

"What about it?"

"D'you want to get it?" Eli snarked. "I figured we could drive out to The Norfolk Arms, have a pint, get a meal…"

Rob squinted at him. "The Norfolk Arms? Fuck's that?"

"It's that nice country pub up beyond Bents Green. Right out in the Peaks, nearly. You know, where we watched the fireworks in the city on Bonfire Night, near there."

"You want to go all the way out *there* for lunch?"

"Yes?"

Rob wasn't buying any of it, Eli could tell. Eli chewed on the corner of his lip, wondering whether he could tell Rob and bribe him with sex like last time, or whether it would be better to con him even further and pay the price of a seriously fucked-off boyfriend later.

He went—to his own surprise—for honesty.

"I wanted to meet Mum and Jenny for lunch, and bring you."

Rob stiffened, and his arm was withdrawn. "Oh hell no, Eli. Not another fuckin' family dinner."

"No, listen—"

"After you and your old man had that barney about the money, and I didn't see you for two weeks you were so spitting mad about the whole thing? After *last* time? How about *fuck* no."

"*Listen.* Dad's not coming. Dad doesn't even know. It's just them and us."

"I don't give a fuck," Rob snapped. "I'm done with trying to fucking fake it for your family, Eli. They don't like me, get over it."

"*Dad* doesn't like you," Eli insisted. "Jenny did, Jenny was a little bit won over by the way you behaved with Flora. And Jenny *can* be won over proper. And I reckon you could win Mum over, too, you know, she's not as closed-minded as Dad, and—"

"And I said no," Rob said sharply. "Get it through your head, Eli, I am done putting myself through the fucking wringer to prove myself to your fucking family. If those pigs can't—"

"Don't call them that!"

"I'm done with it!" Rob snarled. "What the fuck is this, Eli? Every time things get easier and a bit better and we get a bit happier, you bring this up again! Are you gonna keep dragging me in there to see them every fucking month, every time we get past the inevitable row about *last* time they fuckin' saw me? And then start all over again? I thought you were done with this!"

"I'm done with *Dad,* I'm giving up on *Dad*—"

"Right, but you're still gonna punish me because your mam doesn't like me neither?" Rob's accent was thickening, and Eli's stomach twisted painfully. "Fucking make up your mind, Eli. Either I'm fucking good enough for you or I'm not, don't—"

"Don't you *dare* say that again!" Eli snarled, seizing a fistful of Rob's hair and shaking it roughly. "Don't you fucking dare. You are *exactly* what I fucking want, don't you *ever* question me on that."

"Yeah?" Rob's eyes were furious. "It doesn't fuckin' feel like it when you keep forcing me on your folks, trying to prove I'm something I'm not!"

Eli swallowed and backed down. He let go and stepped back, licking his lips, debating what to do. Eventually he slid his hands around Rob's neck and stretched up to kiss him lightly, lingering until they breathed together.

"I've chosen you," he whispered. "I chose you when I refused to dump you when Dad found out who you were. I chose you when I came to Scotland. I chose you when Dad tore up the Christmas present you gave me. You're what I want, Rob. And if it really comes to it, I'll walk away from my family over you...but I don't *want* that. I want to have *both*."

Rob closed his eyes, and his head dropped. Eli stroked the hair at the nape of his neck hopefully.

"I want you to be able to come to some of our family days out without my parents throwing a total fit. I want to be able to come over without getting a lecture about it. I want to be able to bring you to my Aunt Judy's wedding next year without having to threaten to not go at all if they won't let me invite you. I don't want to fight with them about it all the time. And if having lunch the odd weekend on neutral ground will let Mum and Jenny see you're not what they think you are—"

"They think I am what I fucking am, Eli."

"No they don't," Eli countered softly. "They think you're nothing more than a violent, weed-smoking criminal. They don't understand anything else about you, they don't see what I see. And I want them to get that, too. And you *can* win them over, I *know* you can. Dad's a lost cause, and I'm not putting you through trying to talk to my dad again, but you *can* win my mum and sister over. You can be downright charming when you really want, you know."

Rob's face was still twisted unhappily.

Eli's heart hurt. He hadn't reckoned on Rob being so...upset. Angry, yes, but not upset.

"If you really don't want..."

"Of course I don't fucking want to. Would you? They look at me like I'm inferior, Eli. They look at me like I'm scum. And I know I'm not exactly a fucking hero, but it's not like I'm a fucking kiddy-fiddler neither. I'm not fucking evil."

"I *know*," Eli implored desperately. "Oh shit, Rob, I'm sorry. We won't go if you feel that bad. We'll just—"

"You've obviously made your fucking plans."

"And I'll cancel them. I told you, if I really, really had to, I would walk away for you."

"Doesn't feel like it, the way you keep forcing this."

Eli's gut twisted so painfully, he actually twitched—but then Rob sighed gustily, and shook his head.

"Alright," he said. "But...fuck it, Eli, if this goes wrong today, it's the last fucking time. I'm sick of feeling like crap because of your family."

"Okay," Eli whispered, his heart aching. He squeezed Rob tightly in a hug. "I'm sorry," he breathed in his ear. "Most things just roll right off you, I didn't realise you felt that bad about it." Eli had been so busy, he realised, thinking about how he'd feel if he was forced to choose between Rob and his own family, which he'd forgotten how the constant fighting would make *Rob* feel. "If it goes wrong, then I'll give up on them."

Rob's mouth was tight and unhappy when Eli stepped back, and he kissed the corner of it gently.

"Hey," he whispered. "I'm sorry, okay? Tell you what—no matter how this goes, I'll come back to yours after and it'll be *your* evening. Whatever you want."

"What, sex-wise?"

"Or anything-else-wise," Eli promised rashly.

Rob finally cracked a tired-looking smile, and Eli kissed that, too.

"C'mon, yeah? Let's go show them you're *amazing*, and then we'll go back to yours and do whatever you want."

Rob sighed, rolled his shoulders, and nodded.

JENNY'S AUDI WAS gleaming in the pub car park, but she was sitting alone and nursing a glass of Pepsi. "Mum rang to say she got called in to provide an emergency statement for court," she babbled as she stood up to hug Eli. "She's going to be a little bit late—I think she's finally left Derby, though."

"Derby?" Rob echoed.

"Mum works for Derbyshire Police, not South Yorkshire," Eli explained. "Um—"

"I'll get a round in," Rob grunted, and sloped off towards the bar.

Jenny's eyes followed him briefly, then she turned them on Eli. "He looks..."

"He's a bit fed up," Eli admitted, sinking into his chair. "I didn't exactly approach the subject of coming to lunch in the best way and he's a bit sick of trying. And I can't blame him," he added pointedly.

"Well you can't blame us for being wary," Jenny retorted, then bit her lip. "But Mum did tell me why you and Dad have been at odds lately. About him ripping up the college money and everything. That was low, even for Dad."

Eli scowled. "Yeah, well." They hadn't spoken since. Eli had more-or-less reverted to his early teens and locked himself in his room whenever he was home, away from both of his parents. He was still furious and hurt at his father's reaction. If Rob had been available at that minute, he'd have probably just moved right out and into the flat.

"Come on, Eli, you can't stay mad forever."

"He didn't even want to hear what the money was for. He just jumped to his usual shitty conclusions and treated me like I was a fucking eleven-year-old. Just drop it, Jen," he added sharply when she opened her mouth. "I don't want to talk about Dad and his being a shit the whole time."

"Well...if it was a cheque...Rob could write you another?"

"He wired it me," Eli said shortly.

"How much?"

"Seven hundred and forty-two pounds."

Jenny shrieked and nearly spilled her drink, just as Rob returned with his and Eli's pints.

"'Sup with you?" Rob asked.

"You gave Eli seven hundred pounds?"

Rob raised his eyebrows. "Yeah, I did." He dropped into his seat and took a healthy gulp of his pint. "Not like I needed it for shit."

"It was lovely," Eli said firmly, twisting his fingers in Rob's and squeezing. "Anyway, Jenny, how are you? How's work?"

"Shit," she said shortly, and rolled her eyes at Rob. "Between you and me, I think maybe you've got the right idea, selling weed like Dad says."

"I don't sell weed anymore," Rob retorted.

"Well, it's better than a call centre," Jenny said sourly. "I ring people up asking if they have any outstanding PPI claims. I get hung up on all *day*. And it's minimum wage."

"Yeah?" Rob said. "Nice job on nicking the Audi out front, then."

"I didn't nick it!" Jenny yelped, going bright pink.

"Funny, s'what your old man would've said if I rocked up in one."

Eli squeezed his hand again, but said nothing.

"It's my ex-boyfriend's," Jenny said coldly. "He was a total douchebag who thought it'd be funny to slap me around in front of our Flora, and that's why Mum and Dad are so wary of you."

"Yeah?" Rob grunted. "Shame, that, 'cause I can't say I ever got a kick out of smacking around my partners." His voice was very hard and challenging.

Jenny narrowed her eyes.

"Never?"

Rob snorted. "Piss off, you silly cow."

She bristled.

"Me, I'm big and moronic. S'kinda it. My kid brother, that little fucknut with the dreads that ran into you and Eli out shopping before Christmas? He's the psycho. I might hit you, but Danny'll take a knife and carve up your fuckin' tits for cutting him off in traffic."

Jenny went white; Eli groaned. "Rob…"

"Maybe you and yours ought to figure out that people ain't what they fuckin' seem," Rob snapped. "An'…"

"Sorry I'm late!"

Mum arrived in a flurry of bags and flyaway hair. She'd obviously dressed in a hurry, her usually very colour-coordinated look totally mismatched, and her scarf a summer one instead of the heavy wool that was sorely needed in bitter Sheffield winters. She didn't seem, thankfully, to have heard Rob's tirade, or picked up on Jenny's pale, horrified expression, and settled herself with a flurry of apologies.

"Drink, Mrs Bell?"

To Eli's surprise, Rob's voice was suddenly cordial, and he rose from his seat already reaching for his wallet.

"Oh! Oh, er…oh go on then, just the one glass. The house red, please, just a small one." She flashed Eli a startled little smile as Rob vanished, and blew out her cheeks. "I'm sorry, both of you, absolute chaos! They called me in and I got all the way down to Clay Cross before they rang me back to tell me they'd mixed up which officer went and I wasn't needed after all, they needed Maggie Bentley! Honestly, I swear that sergeant couldn't find his oversized backside with both hands if he tried…"

Her flustered ranting filled the air until Rob returned, and when he did, Eli firmly took his hand again. He knew the signs of Rob on the defensive, and it hurt to think that just coming out to meet them put him in that mind set. This time—no matter *what* he said—Eli was determined to side with him.

"So," Mum said. "What have I missed?"

"Oh," Jenny said tightly. "Just Rob saying we've judged him too quickly and we ought to know better."

Mum looked startled.

"Jenny compared him to Greg," Eli pointed out.

"I did not *compare* him, I said that Mum and Dad are wary *because* of Greg—"

"And Greg being an arsehole doesn't mean Rob's an arsehole!" Eli protested. "Rob's right, people aren't what they seem, and—"

"Come *on*, Eli!"

"They're not," Rob interrupted harshly.

Jenny scowled.

"Eli should've taught you that."

Jenny blinked. Mum frowned.

"What do you mean?" Mum asked.

Rob levelled her with a highly unimpressed look.

"The whole being-a-bloke thing?"

Eli went scarlet.

"You…you know that Eli's…?"

"Of course I fucking know," Rob said, snorting. "I've had sex with him, you do notice when a guy's missing the meat and two veg."

Fuck scarlet. Purple.

"I…see," Mum said.

"I did tell you that Rob knew," Eli protested weakly.

"Well, yes, but…well…in all honesty, Eli, and please don't get angry, dear, I didn't quite…believe you," Mum admitted, going a little pink herself. "I mean…I thought you were just…trying to convince us that Rob had accepted it."

"Oh fucking *thanks*, Mum!" Eli snapped. "That money Rob gave me for Christmas? Before Dad went ballistic, I was *trying* to tell you it's for my last surgery. It's the last bit of money I needed!"

"Seems a bit shit," Rob said roughly, "that I have to be coughing that up when his pretty well-loaded parents can't be fucked to fork over a bit towards it."

Mum went scarlet and started spluttering. Jenny, by contrast, had gone very quiet. "I—well, I—"

"Look, I get it—you don't like me, I don't like you. But end of the day, I'm here. I'm coughing out hundreds for that surgery, I'm getting texts about you lot being crap, I'm the one who's made Eli feel like he's not some malformed weirdo because he's got a scarred chest and he packs his boxers. So it's pretty fucking rich that you lot are sitting here calling me a shit partner when you've never given two fucks about one of your own."

"We…" Mum said weakly. "We, um. We're not…Samuel and I…we weren't brought up in…in times that particularly recognised transsexual—"

"Transgender," Eli interrupted hotly.

"—individuals, and—"

"Oh, right, an' I was?" Rob said, snorting. "Fuckin' hell, Louise, my old man beat me with a washing line cord every Sunday night for three years to get rid of all the gay stinking up the place. You think I knew or cared the first thing about trannies before your Eli? Like fuck I did. But there's this weird thing where I fucking care about him, I fucking love him, so I'm gonna fucking support him. S'how it works. Even I know that."

Eli curled his toes in his converse, and suddenly—*desperately*—wanted to kiss Rob. His heart swelled and prickled with heat that was nothing to do with arousal, and everything to do with affection.

Mum was silent and staring.

Jenny pushed her glass aside, leaned right forward to peer at Rob's face, and said, "So…Eli mentioned you boxed?"

Rob eyed her back. Eli could see them both calculating, staring each other down briefly, before…

There. Rob shifted in his chair, shoulders rolling down against the backrest, spine flexing until he was sprawling, knees parting under the table until one bumped Eli's. He visibly relaxed, and Eli's heart jumped.

"Yeah," he drawled. "'M a bit crap, though."

Eli squeezed his hand and beamed as the ice—at least with Jenny—began to thaw.

CHAPTER 20

ELI WOKE ALONE in a patch of warm sunlight and the wide emptiness of Rob's messy bed. The sheets were rumpled, even the mattress cover creased under his back. He stretched luxuriously only to find Rob had, at some point in the night, stolen Eli's boxers and pyjama pants.

"Dick," he mumbled, and turned over to find the warm spot.

Only it was missing. So with a seriously disgruntled sigh, Eli got up, found his discarded T-shirt and stolen underwear, and ventured into the rest of the flat.

Or, rather, followed the smell of burnt toast.

"You're inhuman," he told Rob when he turned into the little kitchen and saw the charcoaled former-bread vanishing into Rob's mouth.

"And you're wearing clothes. One of us is fuckin' wrong here, and it ain't me," Rob drawled.

"You *stole* my clothes."

"You know the rules. Shut it 'n' strip."

Eli laughed, despite himself. Because had he failed to mention how Rob was standing there and eating that toast, entire body lounging against the fridge and showing off those muscled thighs, taut stomach, and lazily powerful biceps—all of it on show because he was entirely naked? Well, he was. And Eli was thoroughly enjoying the view, charcoaled bread notwithstanding.

"You've stripped enough for the both of us," he said, eyeing Rob from toes to temple with a wide smile.

"Rules are rules."

"Mm," Eli said, tucking his hands behind his hips and leaning back against the doorframe. "And you're a stickler for rules, aren't you, Rob Hawkes?"

Rob smirked, and brushed off his hands on his own chest. He crossed the kitchen in a slow swagger, and his long body was still warm from the bed when it pressed up against Eli's front. The kiss that he offered was slow and oddly gentle, but somehow dirty and full of intent at the same time.

"Strip," he rumbled, "or I'll do it for you."

A little thrill chased up Eli's spine. He smiled before leaning up and sinking his teeth slowly into Rob's bottom lip. A large hand smoothed up his thigh and to his arse, pushing under his boxers like they weren't even there. Eli slapped at a strong shoulder before pulling himself free.

"It's too cold to strip outside the bed," he said haughtily, and firmly turned his back. Rob's low laugh followed him back to the bedroom, where the rumpled bed and the sunlight waited. Eli stripped almost casually before climbing back onto the ruined sheets, dropping his head onto the squashed remains of the pillows, and beckoning with both hands. "C'mon," he implored. "Warm me up."

Rob's smile was almost real, a flash of teeth amongst thick stubble. Then his heavy weight and miles of rough, hot skin were pressing Eli down into the loose sheets, hands a soft counterpoint to the teeth that sank into Eli's neck and bit down, hard enough to mark and certainly intended to.

"Mm, morning," Eli whispered, closing his eyes and splaying his fingers out over Rob's back contentedly.

Every bone in Eli's body was happy here, under Rob's naked weight, miles of skin on skin and yet feeling satisfied and content rather than the urgent drive to fight and fuck. He hummed gently as Rob rubbed his jaw against Eli's shoulder, his stubble prickling and rasping, like a cat seeking affection.

They had come straight home after the pub lunch yesterday, and Eli had lavished so many kisses on Rob's skin his lips still felt swollen. There had been a need behind it, an urgency to demonstrate—and erase all doubt—of what Rob exactly was to him and just what it was like for Eli to look at him and know Rob was *his*...

Now there was no such desperation.

If anything, Eli simply drifted for the longest time, stroking his fingers over the edges of ink on Rob's skin, turning his head when Rob pressed into his neck to kiss or lick it, murmuring heavy words that Eli barely heard. He didn't need to hear them. This was exactly what Eli wanted—peace, the ability to simply lie here and *enjoy* Rob, and not feel a twinge of guilt or anger about the path they'd had to take to get here.

This was more intimate than sex, in Eli's opinion. Anyone could fuck. And Rob could fuck anyone—his patchy history before Eli, the HIV scare and the fact he couldn't put a name to half his sexual partners—said that. But Rob did not do this with just anyone, or indeed anyone else at all. Eli basked in it, in the soft affection and the idle touches and strokes that spoke of something deeper than lust and sex, something underpinning the teasing and the rough-edged passion that Rob held tightly leashed like a river ready to burst its banks. This was almost something secret, something only he knew Rob was really capable of, and Eli hoarded it greedily, protective of the treasure he'd found, and nobody else was allowed.

Eventually—because of the heat in the bed, and the naked contact, blood went where it would go. Rob began to roll his hips lightly against Eli's thigh. Eli simply wound his fingers into Rob's hair and let him. Pressing their foreheads together, Eli watched the play of pleasure across those strong features as the lazy thrusts became more rhythmic and consistent, Rob's moves slowly deepening, and then—as gently as they had begun—ceasing with a soft grunt, and a rush of wet heat. It took only a matter of minutes, and Eli simply held and watched, and felt a rush of possessive...almost ownership over this man.

"Now we really do need to sort the bed out," Eli whispered.

Rob chuckled deeply. His kiss was heavy and possessive, yet somehow also…undemanding.

"I'm serious. There's cum on my leg."

"S'been in worse places'n that…"

Eli laughed, and pushed at Rob's shoulder. "I'll sort the bed. Go and shower. Or start proper breakfast, not your shitty toast."

Rob snorted, but nipped at Eli's earlobe and heaved himself off the bed and away. The rush of cool air was unpleasant, and Eli shamelessly stole Rob's dressing gown from the back of the bedroom door before stripping down the stained bed. He was still sore from the night before, from the moment Rob had tired of the focus being all on him and had lifted Eli up against the wall and fucked him standing. It wasn't a position Eli found comfortable, but then who was going to complain about positions when they had Rob's cock up their arse and his lips around their neck?

"Clothes!" Rob shouted when Eli took the sheets to stuff them in the washing machine.

"Turn the heating up, then!" Eli bitched in return, and ducked away from Rob's wayward hand. "Not until it warms up in here, I'm serious. It's fucking cold."

"Pussy," Rob sneered before returning to rummage in the fridge. "Eggs and bacon do you?"

"S'fine," Eli said, and pulled himself up to perch on the counter. "Are you free today?"

"Gotta see a man about a horse this evening. Free 'til six, though. Something in mind?"

Eli shrugged. "Not really. Just fancied staying here with you today."

That earned him a smirk and a brief kiss before Rob started setting out pans. Eli contented himself with changing the radio channels and, once Rob had started the promised eggs and bacon, hugging him with arms draped loosely around his neck.

"You're clingy."

"It's called affectionate."

"It's called fuckin' weird, s'what it's called."

Eli laughed and kissed Rob's hair. "Shut up. I'm feeling good, alright?" His gut twinged, and he nuzzled Rob's scalp. "You were really honest with me yesterday about how unfair I've been to you, and I'm sorry, and I want to make it up to you."

Rob stilled.

"You did fine with Mum and Jenny," Eli continued in a quieter tone, petting Rob's hair and examining it to allow Rob to do his distinct, I-will-not-look-you-in-the-face-when-you're-being-mushy thing. "And I think this is going to be alright. Hence I'm being *affectionate*."

There was a beat. Then: "Clingy."

"Oh shut up!" Eli groaned, exasperated, and shoved him.

Rob cackled, seizing Eli by the thighs and hefting him bodily off the counter until Eli yelped and was dumped very unceremoniously on the tiny table against the wall.

"Cunt!"

"That'd be you, sunshine."

"Fuck off! Not anymore. Not with your cash," Eli said gleefully.

Rob rolled his eyes as the doorbell rang. "S'probably Danny. And don't sound so pleased, I googled that shit, you ain't gonna be fucking for like a month after that. I might have to play away, y'know?"

"Play away and I'll give *you* a sex change," Eli returned loftily, padding out towards the front door as the bell rang again. "Steady on, Danny, I'm com—"

The smile slid off his face as he jerked the front door open. Because neither of the visitors were Danny. In fact, they were very distinctly not Danny.

"Rob!"

There were two policemen at the door.

"What—what's—Rob!" Eli called again, after an embarrassing moment of simply stammering. He yanked the dressing gown closed, suddenly hyperaware of his scars and the fact that the gown was obviously miles too big for him, and flushed an angry red. Why the fuck were there fucking *police* knocking on Rob's door at nine in the morning?

"What?"

"Door! Now!" Eli shouted.

"Why the fuck—what do you fuckers want." Rob's tone changed instantly.

"Rob Hawkes?" one of the policemen asked.

"Yeah," Rob said, lip curling.

"You're under arrest on suspicion of burglary. You do not have to—"

Eli's stomach filled with acid. "Burglary!"

"I ain't fucking burgled nobody!" Rob snarled.

"You *burgled* someone?" Eli yelled. "I said, didn't I say, didn't I fucking *say* no—"

"I *haven't!*" Rob insisted. The policemen were both looking rather embarrassed, one of them coughing awkwardly. "I ain't burgled anybody—I fucking quit it after you threw your shit-fit when you saw that text from our Danny after we got together proper!"

Eli clenched his jaw. The policeman was still clearing his throat determinedly, but they both ignored them. "I can't believe this," Eli hissed. "I thought everything was working out, I thought everything was going fine, thought you'd maybe won over Jenny and Mum, thought if I just cut Dad out of the picture for you it'd be fine and now the fucking *police* are here?"

"Are you fuckin' deaf?" Rob bellowed. "I didn't fucking do it!"

"I'm sure that if you didn't, Mr. Hawkes, then you can give us a good explanation down at the station," one of the policemen interrupted very loudly. "But you are our main suspect at the moment, so you are under arrest. This argument with your, ah, friend will have to wait."

"Fucking go," Eli seethed, fisting his hands in the cloth of Rob's dressing gown. "And so help me fucking God, Rob, if they charge you with anything, I'm going to fucking *kill* you!"

He stormed into the bedroom before Rob could answer him, and slammed the door. He kicked it for good measure, too, then scrambled for his clothes, a red-hot rage thrumming in his blood. How could he? How *could* he? Just when Eli had managed to get things settled and sorted, just when things were turning out okay, Rob had to go and—

Eli wanted to scream.

So he waited in the bedroom until Rob's voice quietened and the front door closed. He waited even longer, until he could hear a distant car engine start and pull away.

Then he left, with an angry hurt bubbling in his gut that threatened to make him stay away for good.

"WHAT HAPPENED TO you?"

Jenny was visiting. She was wearing her jeans and T-shirt rather than the flowery, flowy things she liked to wear in public, and looked fit to burst now, the pregnancy bump having reached ridiculous proportions. Through the living room window, Eli could see Flora leading Mum on some game around the garden, despite the cold weather.

"Rob," he snapped, throwing himself onto the sofa beside her.

"Oh?" Jenny said. "I would have thought everything was going great, you were dead loved-up yesterday." She sounded a little sour, and Eli ignored the tone.

"Yeah, that was until he got fucking arrested this morning," he snarled.

"He did what?"

Eli flinched and groaned at his father's deep voice, and felt his mouth involuntarily tighten as his father wandered in from the kitchen. Shit. Eli had presumed he would be at work.

"He got arrested," Eli said coldly.

"And you're surprised?"

"Oh, God, shut up, Dad."

"Eli!"

"I don't want to hear it!" Eli retorted. "I'm angry at him but you can keep out of it."

"That man—"

"I said I don't want to hear it, are you deaf?" Eli shouted, his stomach twisting at Rob's own furious demand coming out of his mouth. He flung himself back up from the sofa, the fury itching and burning in his chest.

Dad snorted.

"You keep expecting him to change, Eli, but he won't. He's always going to be a criminal. Men like Hawkes just do not change. It's about time you realised that."

Eli shook his head, his face feeling hot. "Men like you don't either," he snarled, not quite sure what he was even getting at with the remark. He turned on his heel to storm up to his room and slam the door. Alright, so he was a little old to do it, but it was satisfying all the same.

Then he fell backwards onto the bed, stared at the ceiling, and wondered if there was even hope that Rob—weed-smoking, brawl-starting, petty offender Rob who'd been burgling since he was thirteen years old—had been telling the truth.

CHAPTER 21

ELI REMAINED IN his room until late in the evening, watching bad TV shows and generally sulking. He kept veering between hurt, angry, and guilty. He had exploded so quickly he'd never given Rob the chance to give his side of the story, and Rob *had* denied it, but then…but then, he had a history—a long one—and of course he'd deny it in front of the cops, he wasn't stupid.

In truth, Eli knew he'd jumped the gun there. He knew Rob would be angry about it. But, fuck, if Rob *had* been burgling again…

Eli didn't know what he was going to do if Rob had started burgling again. Was that how he'd gotten Eli's Christmas money? Eli could handle the weed-dealing and the nicked wallets. That wasn't, you know, invading other people's homes and spaces. Burglary…you couldn't know who lived in a house, not if you were burgling lots of houses, and the idea of Rob burgling little old ladies or single mums struggling to make ends meet and stuff, it made Eli's skin crawl. He knew it was inconsistent, but burglars were bad men in Eli's mind. People who left their wallets out on the McDonald's counter and didn't keep an eye on them, well, they deserved to have them stolen.

Eli didn't know what he was going to do if Rob was charged.

Even worse was the inability to talk to anyone else about it. Danny was as unreasonable as Rob when it came to the police. Dad was completely unreasonable about Rob, and Mum would side with Dad. And Jenny…well, Eli just didn't want to talk to Jenny about it. Not after she'd warmed a little to Rob lately. She'd totally backtrack if Eli let slip Rob was burgling again.

This was the part Eli hated most about growing up wrong. He'd been so awkward in school that he'd never managed to keep any friends, and the few people he'd been friendlier with had ditched him when he'd come out and started transitioning. He was the youngest person at the shop by about forty years, all of whom believed he was a man and would be horrified to find out he wasn't, and until Rob, he hadn't really had the confidence to go out much and make new friends. Hell, he'd only been clubbing to get plastered and forget how lonely he was.

So there was literally *nobody* to talk to, and it made Eli want to punch the walls.

The solution was—as it had been growing up when he'd had nobody to vent to, his sister was wrapped up in boys and makeup, and his parents were steadfastly ignoring that he was a boy, breasts notwithstanding—shitty TV. The Jeremy Kyle Show could make even the crappiest life look pretty sweet, and so Eli lounged, sulked, and snacked his way through an entire double packet of bourbon creams before he heard the doorbell ringing downstairs.

Incessantly.

Like someone with a big finger and a towering temper was holding it down.

Bugger.

Eli heard the study door open before he could even get off the bed, and then his father's voice. And a deep, hoarse rumble that was most definitely Rob's voice. Fuck!

Eli flung open the bedroom door and stormed downstairs in time to hear his father saying, "I want you off my property in the next—"

"*Thank* you, Dad, I'll deal with it," Eli snapped, elbowing his father. Rob's countenance was as grim as Eli felt. "C'mon," he said, jerking his head towards the kitchen. "Dad, leave us alone.

We need to talk."

"We can go out to talk," Rob snapped, giving his father a dirty look.

"We can talk now or you can fuck off," Eli returned, his temper rising fast. He was not dealing with any more of this shit. He was sick of fighting, sick of police, sick of Rob saying he'd try and then doing fuck all, sick of Dad needling and prodding all the time, sick of—

He dragged Rob into the kitchen by the wrist and slammed the door behind them to keep Dad out before pacing around the table in a fit of energy. Rob leaned against the fridge, folded his arms, and said nothing.

"So?" Eli snapped.

"So what?"

"So, when are you in fucking court?"

"I'm not," Rob retorted. "Because I didn't fucking do it. I gave them my alibi—which was that when Mrs. Miggins or who the fuck ever got burgled last night, I had my cock up your arse and the Chief Inspector's son was the witness—so stop being so fucking angry with me."

Eli's temper somehow managed to rise and fall at the same time. "You told them *what?*"

"Yeah, it was a pretty interesting interview," Rob sneered. "Your old man's gonna have a great day at work tomorrow, the ginger cunt couldn't stop sniggering."

Eli dragged both hands over his face. "I can't believe you."

"Yeah, well, frankly, I thought better of you, too."

"Excuse me?"

"Fuck off, Eli, you were just like your old bastard of a father this morning!"

"*What?*"

"Minute they said they were nicking me, you were all at me like I actually fucking did it! Didn't fucking occur to you maybe I hadn't, even when I fucking said I hadn't!"

"I didn't *want* to believe it, but—"

"Fuck off you didn't!"

"—you have a history, Rob!"

"Look me in the fucking face and tell me you think I did it."

Eli stopped pacing, and looked. Rob's face was furious, his eyes ablaze, and yet…there was something else there, too. Something more vulnerable, a little more wounded. Eli bit his lip when he found the hurt in that angry expression, and felt his temper drop…and the hot burn of guilt rise.

"Rob…"

"I didn't fucking do it, Eli."

"Okay," Eli whispered.

"I didn't fucking do it and I don't fucking expect you to be at my throat for it the minute someone suggests it—that's what your dad does, assuming I'm the scum of the earth all the time—but for you to do it…"

"I just—"

Rob finally pulled himself away from the fridge, shaking his head and tugging a hand through his hair in sharp, jerky motions. It looked painful, and Eli grimaced.

"I can't do this."

Eli jerked. "What."

"I can't fucking do this," Rob snarled. "Your family makes me feel like I'm shit on the bottom of their shoe, you keep insisting I have to get along with them when they're shits to me, too, and if you're gonna start in at me every time I get accused of something like your fucking father—"

The kitchen door banged open. "Dad, get out!" Eli bellowed furiously, but Dad jabbed a finger at Rob, completely ignoring him.

"I want you out," he snapped.

"Then fucking call your mates and kick me out!" Rob shouted.

"Dad, will you fuck off and let us—"

"Eli, I have had enough of this—it is *completely* inappropriate for a known criminal to be coming to my house and—"

"If I was *half* the fucking gang member you seem to fucking think I am, I could make a fucking *fortune* selling this address on, but I'm not a fucking cunt!" Rob's voice was so loud that the room seemed to shiver with it.

Eli shrank back against the counter for a moment, startled.

"Get the fuck out of my way then, and you won't fucking see

me again!"

"Rob!" Eli cried, jumping to catch his arm.

Rob shook him off angrily.

"Fuck off, Eli! I need a fucking break from pigs and their fucking kind!"

And then he was gone, the front door slamming so hard that the doorbell rang.

"Eli—"

"Oh, will you go *fuck* yourself!" Eli snarled bitterly, and stormed upstairs.

He had the awful, sickening feeling that Rob had just dumped him.

WHEN ROB WANTED space, he vanished off the face of the earth.

Usually, Eli didn't mind. They argued a lot—they were both hot-tempered, highly-strung and prone to exploding at the smallest things—and usually Rob stomping off to cool down was a good idea. Plus the make-up sex was fantastic.

But with the fear that he'd just been ditched, Eli didn't *want* space. He wanted to lock them both in a tiny cupboard and kiss Rob, blow him, fuck him until he forgave Eli. It *had* been a major cock-up on Eli's part, he *should* have had more faith, but this vanishing act...

For the first couple of days, it simply scared the shit out of him. He nearly missed his testosterone injection at the doctor's, he was so busy trying to track Rob down. He wasn't in any of his favoured pubs, he wasn't at his boxing club, and he wasn't at home. Danny wasn't much help, saying he was 'around' but never seeming to quite know where 'around' actually was.

It was only after Eli spent an entire shift at work spamming Rob's phone with variations on everything from *call me, we need to talk* and *I'm sorry* to *if you don't fucking call me in the next hour I am getting the cops on your arse and reporting you fucking missing! RING ME!!* that he got any kind of reply at all. And that was simply:

In leeds. stop spamin me.

No, Eli replied. *I'm sorry about not having more faith in you, I really want to talk to you properly, and I promise I'll get my shit together. We're great when it's just you and me, it's all this pressure from my family that fucks it up and I swear I will grow a pair and tell them where to go. Come on Rob, call me already.*

The one-word reply, *busy,* didn't help Eli's anxiety.

Are we over? he asked finally, exposing the raw nerve and silently praying. If Rob said anything other than no, Eli was going to go straight to the flat and attack Danny with fucking thumbscrews or something until he told Eli where *exactly* in Leeds Rob had—

No but i need sum space.

That was the beginning of the next tortuously slow three weeks. Rob was completely uncommunicative, even as Eli showered him with affectionate texts, *I miss you* several times a day, and sent pictures of what he was up to. So when, on the twentieth day of stony silence, Danny texted him to say Rob was back in town, Eli seized at the opportunity.

Is he ok?

Really fuckin moody. wat hapned???

We had a massive row and I think he's thinking about dumping me :(

LOL yeh rite

I'm serious.

Fuckin hel m8 wat?!

He got nicked for burglary and I had a go at him about it.

so? dont u do that evry time he gets bangd up?

This time was different.

Danny seemed to leave it at that, but for the next couple of days, Eli was at least drip-fed information on Rob's mood and what he was up to. Danny wasn't the reassurance kind of guy, but the odd one came in, and on the four-week mark, Rob sent him a photo of the biggest fry-up Eli had ever seen with the caption *danny is fucking up to summat…*

The longer Rob stayed quiet, though, the more Eli started to shift from guilt to anger. How was freezing him out fair? He was being actively ignored for 'space' rather than talking—or fucking—it out like they usually did. *Okay,* Eli should have had more faith but this was a really gutless way of punishing him for it. Four *weeks* of 'space,' come on. They needed to deal with it. Rob needed to man the fuck up already. Eli would beg forgiveness, and learn from it, and provide whatever reassurance Rob needed from him about how they were and where Rob came in his list of priorities. But for that, Rob had to actually fucking *talk* to him.

Eventually, after a month of silence, a month of guilt slowly festering and turning into a lingering, building anger, Eli snapped.

Are you at home? he texted on Thursday evening. When he got no reply, he sent *is Rob at home?* to Danny instead.

Danny was more forthcoming. *Yeh pretty sure. r u going over?*

Yes, Eli answered, already gathering what he'd need into his backpack. *And if you value your sanity you'll stay away tonight.*

CHAPTER 22

ROB ANSWERED THE door, barefoot and shirtless, and Eli shoved his way into the flat without a word.

"The fuck, Eli?"

Eli stormed into Rob's room, throwing his bag onto the side table and unzipping it. Rob slammed the front door with an exasperated huff and followed.

"I told you I need fucking space."

"You've had a week and I'm fucking sick of it," Eli retorted. "We're sorting this out now. Strip."

Rob sneered. "Oh right, what you gonna do? Give me a belting for getting sick of your old man? You'd have to beat half of fucking Yorkshire first."

"I don't care anymore if you argue with Dad," Eli said. "You've fucked me off with your fucking behaviour, freezing me out like that, and we're going to fucking sort it out. Now!"

"And if I fucking say no?"

"Well, it'll have to be a colour then, won't it? Because unless you fucking safeword me, Rob, I am *not* taking no for a fucking answer!"

Rob caught at Eli's arms and spun him, shaking him between both hands. "What, you just gonna fucking swan in here and beat me for your lot making me feel like shit? I don't think so, Eli! How about you give me the fucking space I asked for!"

"Because every time you have fucking space, you get stupid fucking ideas in your head like thinking I agree with my dad about you!"

Rob's flinch said it all; Eli shoved him, the element of surprise giving him an advantage, and pulled at his jeans.

"I don't think so," Rob spat, seizing Eli's wrists in both hands and squeezing. He steered Eli with them into the side of the bed, and then down onto it, eyes nearly feral with unleashed rage. "How about I work out my anger first, yeah? You've pissed me the fuck off, so maybe you ought to be the one to calm me down?"

"That's what I'm here for," Eli spat, but Rob's weight was pressing him irreversibly down into the sheets. Eli squirmed a hand free, groping for the sideboard, but Rob had bracketed Eli's chest with his knees, and there was no getting out.

"So what's my fucking stress-relief?" Rob sneered. "Tell you what, Eli, how about I hold you down and fuck you stupid and remind you just who the one is in this relationship who isn't living at home with his nice copper mummy and daddy and fucking a bit of rough because the excitement gets him off?"

"How fucking *dare* you, you son of a bitch!"

"Could even go for two rounds, show you your fucking place—how's this, one fuck up the arse and one fuck up the cunt like God fucking intended?"

Eli slapped him, the sound like a crack. Despite the fury, he also felt the raw, wet heat of lust roaring in his blood. Fucking Rob and his fucking hot-as-shit dominance—this wasn't Eli's goddamned plan!

"I'm not fucking playing games tonight, Eli," Rob sneered, bracing himself with a hand on the headboard. Eli's hand, groping on the side table, seized what he wanted. "You get the fuck out now before I take hold of you and fuck you so fucking hard that even your fucking fantasies won't—"

Eli moved like lightning, catching the headboard bar in one cuff and Rob's wrist in the other and slamming them shut. Rob swore and yanked, but the links had already caught. Eli locked them before sliding out from under Rob and stepping away from the bed.

"Eli!"

"You're staying there," Eli said sternly.

"Like fuck I am!"

Eli scoffed and dropped his boxers, rummaging in the bag for the other set of cuffs. "I have the leg restraints. I'll use them if I have to."

"No you fucking won't."

Eli frowned. "Are you going to safeword, then? Because if you don't, then I'll do whatever the fuck I feel I need to."

Rob's jaw worked, but he said nothing.

"Are you?"

After a long pause, Rob said, "No," in the most mutinous voice Eli had ever heard.

"Put your other hand on the headboard."

"No."

"*Yes.* I'm sick of this, Rob." Eli deliberately kept his voice level and calm, but steel-hard. "Whenever you're angry or hurt, you lash out. You don't talk about it, you don't explain where you're coming from, you don't tell me you're feeling bad until it's too late. And then you lash out, and you make it hurt. I was out of line in not believing you straight away. But the way you reacted was unacceptable, too. You strung me along instead of sat me down and told me what was going through your head, and I am not standing for it. So you can do as you're told and learn your lesson on its own, or I can punish you for the disobedience, too."

Rob's glare shifted slightly, and his lips tightened. After a long, *long* minute, his free hand inched towards the bars, and his fingers closed around one.

"Thank you," Eli said coldly, snapping the second set of cuffs into place before Rob could change his mind. He locked them, making sure both sets could be tugged up and down the bars, before slapping at Rob's thigh. "Lie down."

"Why."

"Because I told you to."

Rob snorted, but awkwardly did so, twisting his head to the

side, hands limp in the cuffs. Eli stripped him of his jeans and briefs quickly and with brutal efficiency, leaving him entirely naked on the sheets, and then opened the window.

"What the fuck are you—"

"If you speak again, I will gag you and use the tap method," Eli warned.

Predictably, Rob shut up. He wasn't a fan of being gagged.

"Thank you. Now stay quiet and still until I'm ready to begin."

He took his time, laying out his equipment on the side table in Rob's eyeline and picking out what he wanted. He'd brought everything, unsure of how Rob was going to receive him, but the quiet—if grumpy—submission meant he left the more brutal toys on the side. He had spoken the truth—he would punish Rob if he had to, but he would prefer not. Rob's furious reaction said that punishment, and being made to feel like he was wrong, was not what he needed.

He needed looking after and calming down all at once, and given that Rob was prickly and angry when he was upset made that a near-impossible task.

But it was one Eli was more than prepared for.

"If you kick at me, or try and get away from me, I'll tie your legs down, too," he said firmly, placing the bottle of lube in the small of Rob's back.

"You gonna fuck me?"

"What did I say about talking?"

Rob lashed out with an ankle; Eli shook out the leg restraints and caught the ankle in one heavy cuff. He tied both to the bedframe with firm, heavy movements, leaving Rob's legs spread wide and his arse completely vulnerable and exposed.

"I warned you," he said. "One more word, and I'll gag you."

Rob said nothing.

"Good," Eli said, slapping the back of one thigh lightly. He picked the blindfold up off the dresser and slid it into place, shaking Rob by the hair when he squirmed. "Stop it. I want you focusing on my voice and my touch, nothing else. There's no other way you listen to me, sometimes."

Rob's chest heaved, but he stayed quiet. Eli gave in to a tiny amount of affection and kissed his ear before retrieving the dislodged bottle. He lined up the toys he wanted, then settled between Rob's legs and slicked up the smallest plug. It was barely wider than two of his fingers, and half the length—a preparation, nothing more. Eli wasn't about to give Rob the warmth of his fingers. He didn't deserve that yet.

The cuffs creaked when Eli pushed it in, savagely quick, and Rob snarled at him again, the sound nothing more than a primal noise. Eli ignored it, thrusting the toy lightly, loosening him up despite his efforts to clench and force it still.

"What you don't understand," Eli said firmly, "is that you are mine."

Rob hissed.

"You belong to me," Eli said calmly. "I'm sorry I didn't believe you right away. It was wrong of me, and you had every right to be upset. I'm not punishing you for being upset with me about that. But the way you reacted afterwards was out of line, and I think out of a serious misunderstanding."

He exchanged the plug for a slightly bigger one, and Rob grunted as he was stretched further open.

"Why were you so angry?"

Rob turned his face into the pillow as Eli twisted the plug. Although his hips jerked, he said nothing.

"Rob. Answer me."

When Rob still said nothing, Eli sat back and delivered a heavy slap to one arse-cheek. A handprint bloomed in red instantly.

Rob swore loudly. "Fuck!"

"Answer me."

"You should have believed me."

"Yes, I should have. You're my partner and I should have trusted you. But you froze me out for a month. Why did you do that?"

He pressed his fingers lightly against the slap mark when Rob stayed quiet, and received a frustrated noise.

"Because I needed fucking space, I told you."

"Space for what?"

"Space from fucking coppers who think I'm fucking scum!"

Eli paused. Gently, he pulled out the plug and rose up on his knees. He fitted the strap-on quickly and quietly, aware Rob couldn't twist enough to see him, and smoothed it generously with lube before, very carefully, laying both hands on Rob's arse and spreading him.

"Who thinks that?"

"Your whole fucking family."

"So why did you freeze *me* out?"

Rob paused.

"Rob."

"Because you fucking believe them."

Eli closed his eyes against the sharp shard of raw pain that sliced through his chest, and pressed forward. He went slow, hands firm on Rob's hips, but relentless, refusing to let him get away. Rob buried his face in the pillow and groaned so deep Eli felt it rattle down that strong body, but he rejected the distraction and only stopped when the strap-on was buried to the base, and Eli's hips were resting against the swell of Rob's backside.

Then he dropped his weight—the shift clearly hitting Rob's sweet spot, judging by the full-body shudder—and spread himself out, a blanket of heat to defend Rob against the chill from the open window. Forcing Rob to push up, even as he turned his face away and tried to hide the crack in his armour.

"So when you're feeling bad because my family situation makes you feel bad, you get it into your head that I'm like them? That I think you're not worth it?"

It was the longest, heaviest pause that Eli had ever heard. Or not-heard, in that there was utter silence for long minutes.

Then finally: "Yes."

Eli sighed, then kissed one of the tattoos beneath his face. "You're wrong," he said simply. He rocked his hips very lightly so the toy brushed Rob's prostate again. When Rob shivered, Eli began to move in a very gentle rhythm, so small it was almost an undulation rather than a real motion.

"M'not."

"Yes you are," he said firmly. "I think you are the most incredible man that I have ever met. You are the man who has made me feel like I can be attractive. You make me feel like I can be sexy. You're the guy who has repaired my totally shattered confidence. You're the one who made up a rule banning me from wearing anything more than underwear when it's just the two of us, in order to give me that confidence. You're the one who has put up again and again with my family's completely *wrong* assessment of you, but put up with it because you love me."

Rob was straining against the cuffs, clenching around the strap-on, but Eli refused to stop. Rob needed to hear it; Eli was going to repeat it until it got into that thick skull of his.

"Your background is crap. Your history is crap. Your parents were crap. But *you* are an amazing, complicated, generous, dedicated guy. You still look out for your baby brother even now you're both adults. You protected him when you were younger. You didn't walk away from me when you found out what I used to be, even though you're gay and it would have been reasonable for you to think this wasn't an option. I am getting a hawk tattooed on my chest because of how incredibly good you have been for me, and I *love* you."

Rob shivered at the stress, goose bumps prickling across his skin. Eli pressed harder into Rob's back, stretching to kiss his neck.

"Do you believe that?" he whispered there. "That I love you?"

"Yes."

Rob's voice was very thin and faint, the rasp so strong it nearly obliterated the reply. Eli bit his lip. It didn't sound too convincing.

"I love you," he said quietly. "That's the base for everything. I *love* you. More than anything or anyone. I have cut my dad out of this for you. I will cut my whole family out for you if I have to. You are the priority for me, Rob. You have been better for me than them, and you are not what you look like. I know that, because I love you."

Rob's hands were balled into fists above the cuffs and shaking. Eli stroked his hands over Rob's skin, catching heat and tiny beads of sweat on his fingertips, and began to kiss whatever was within reach.

"I love you, and you belong to me," he whispered. "You are mine. I am never letting go of you, not for anything, because you have been the best thing to ever happen to me. And if I have to tell you that every single day, if I have to repeat it for you the way I repeat it for Dad just how utterly incredible you really are under all that swagger and sneering, then I will."

Rob coughed, twisting his face to the side. The blindfold was damp. "Fuck me," he croaked, his voice cracking in the middle. "Just—just shut up and fuck me, please, please…"

"No," Eli whispered, but he did deepen his movements into proper thrusts, beginning to tilt his hips the way Rob liked best and rock him properly against the mattress. He kept talking and kissing though, the fucking gentler than Eli had ever given, and who cared if Eli wouldn't get off on this, this topping with tenderness? It was about Rob right now, and Eli couldn't give less of a fuck about his own orgasm.

It didn't take long, Rob grinding down against the mattress and Eli whispering endearments and the little things he liked about their relationship and about Rob. When Rob snarled and shuddered his way through his release, Eli slowly withdrew, kissing down Rob's spine as he pulled out and removed the strap-on. He did, however, heat and slick up one of the larger plugs in his hands before filling Rob again, and twisting it firmly into place.

"You need reminding, tonight, just who owns you," he murmured, kissing the top of Rob's thigh as he worked, then he slid up the bed and kissed Rob on the corner of the mouth. "But you're staying here. I'm keeping you tied down tonight. You can't run away every time you're upset."

Rob nudged his face into Eli's, his breathing shaky. Eli gently removed the blindfold and kissed his eyelids. Those white-grey irises were rimmed in pink when his eyes slid open, and Eli kissed under them, too.

"Hey," he murmured, cupping Rob's face in both hands. "I love you. You're brilliant for me. You might be a mess sometimes, but you're brilliant. All I ever wanted was some peace and quiet between you and my family, never to make you feel bad."

Rob swallowed convulsively, and nodded, though his gaze slid away. Eli's heart ached.

"Look at us," he murmured. "The transman and the criminal, and *I'm* the one doing the comforting. Nothing's what it seems, eh?"

Rob cracked a tiny smile, and Eli kissed him again before uncuffing one arm and massaging the hand as he lowered it to the pillows.

"I'll get us a blanket," he murmured, "and we can curl up and cuddle for a little while, and I can really get the message through to you about being exactly what I need, yeah?"

Rob nodded again, but when Eli returned and covered him with a thick fleece blanket stolen from the sofa, he lifted his freed arm and beckoned with the fingers. Eli had to slide half under him to cuddle, but when Rob settled his weight firmly on Eli's chest and let out a bone-shattering sigh, Eli didn't dare to complain or change the arrangement.

He kissed Rob's hair, smoothed a hand down his back, and began to whisper again.

"I love you…"

CHAPTER 23

ELI CAME BACK to himself bathed in heat. Bright light was spilling over the bed, drowning his skin in warmth raw and powerful—but more welcome was the hot pass of a thumb rubbing lazy circles into the skin of his belly, dangerously low. His back was pressed into steel muscle overlaid with soft skin and hair, the rasp of stubble shifting against his neck and shoulder with every breath. The arm over his waist was heavy, the hand it controlled left purposefully low, almost cupping Eli's naked flesh. It made Eli feel completely surrounded in heat, weight, and safety.

He arched his shoulder back into that scratch, and a kiss emerged from the stubble to press itself into his neck, silent and certain. The thumb stilled, and the hand pressed a little firmer into Eli's crotch. Wet heat sank into Eli's pelvis, and he rolled his hips forward with an involuntary sigh. The rhythm caught, Eli rubbing himself on Rob's rough fingers, and feeling a hardness press itself between his thighs as Rob, slow and idle, began to follow his lead.

It was lazy and gentle, the movement more shifts than thrusts. The only sound was the rustle of sheets and the slow build of Rob's breathing from deep and tired to a grunt in the back of his throat when Eli's thighs squeezed around Rob's length and clenched hard enough to bring him to the peak. And the only mark of that was the sudden jerk of Rob's hips, flush against Eli's back-side, and the sudden dampness of the sheet over Eli's legs. Rob's fingers did not so much as twitch, maintaining their steady motion until Eli squeezed the solid wrist and pushed himself hard into them, shuddering through his own orgasm in Rob's heavy grip, shivering and twitching like something caught fast in a storm.

When he could breathe again, and his limbs began to regain feeling from the soft wave of pleasure that had crashed over him, Eli twisted in Rob's hold. He curled under that heavy arm and pressed his face into Rob's neck with a contented sigh, kissing a long scratch he'd left there last night. Rob mumbled, his voice an incoherent rasp that stirred Eli's heart if not his exhausted blood. He tucked himself closer still, sliding a leg between Rob's and bur-rowing into too-hot skin without a care for the heat of the sun at his back.

"V'you," he murmured, and Rob nudged his nose against Eli's hair.

"Move in with me."

Eli blinked.

"What?"

"Move in with me," Rob repeated. His throat was so relaxed that the words were barely forming out of pure sound, and Eli pressed his lips to that thick neck to feel them rather than hear them.

"For real?"

"Mm." The hum vibrated lightly against Eli's mouth.

Eli curled impossibly closer, wanting nothing more than to simply melt into Rob's skin, burrow right into his very being, and take up residence there.

"Why?" Eli whispered.

"S'it wi' you and why?"

Eli shrugged. "I dunno. We argue a lot…"

Rob huffed a laugh. "I'm a cock and you're a total fuckin' queen. 'Course we argue."

"But—"

"When we don't, s'great," Rob mumbled.

When Eli unburrowed enough to peek, those world-changing

eyes were closed, the usually stern face still slack and relaxed.

"I miss you when you're gone."

Something squirmed in Eli's stomach, hot and pleasant. He pressed his lips to the very corner of Rob's mouth, and breathed, "Do you?" against the skin.

"Mm."

"Like—"

"An' you should be happy."

"What? I am—"

"No." Rob was waking up a little, his voice clearing and his hands turning in to hold Eli properly. "You're not. You hate your job, you row with your folks a lot, you don't relax at home like you do when you're lounging on our sofa in your keks drawing."

Eli swallowed. "And…and living here, with you, I'd be happy?"

"Maybe."

"Maybe?"

"You'd have to quit the stupid job to get the full effect," Rob said, his eyebrows scrunching.

Eli knew the warning signs, and backed up just in time to avoid getting the world-record-setting yawn right in the face.

"S'rry."

Eli laughed quietly and kissed him anyway.

"Quit your job, move in with me, go to art college," Rob mumbled, eyes flickering once before closing again. "S'easy."

Eli bit his lip. "Is it? I mean, we'd still fight. My parents would go mental. There'd be—"

The mattress tipped, the sheets rustled, and then Rob's warm body was pressing Eli down into the bed, heavy and unmoveable, those eyes boring into his own like they were pulling his soul out of his head. Eli's breath caught, his hands stuck halfway up to touch Rob's hair, and he lay in the gaze like a mouse paralysed by the stare of a very hungry cat.

"It's easy," Rob repeated, his voice a low rasp.

Despite how he'd been woken—raw desire began to burn at Eli's stomach and crotch again.

"You got stuck after school in that crap job and living at

home. Maybe it's time to tell those fuckers at school to stop holding you back and get on with it."

Eli hardly dared to breathe, dragged into the near-white burn of Rob's eyes like he was falling to his spellbound death, surrounded by that deep, unshakeable voice.

"Sign up for art college. Move out of your parents' place—either in here, or I can help you find a place for just you—and start moving on. You're not the kid you were."

Eli swallowed.

"And if you came here, I'd like it. Some days I think you'd like it, too. An' I can support you through art college if you need it, jus' like your other stuff. Don't overthink it, Eli. Just do something, yeah? Just jump, for once."

Eli's chest shuddered as he tried to inhale, and nearly failed.

"I—" he began, then the words failed him, and he had to give Rob a wobbly smile. "You're going to have to clear out some of the bathroom cabinet for me. And the dresser. And…and this'd be my room, too, so those ugly green sheets have to go."

For a brief second Rob's face didn't so much as flicker. Then—like the sun bursting through heavy clouds, like the dash instruments lighting in the dark on a car that coughed its way to life rather than simply started—he smiled. And not just *smiled-*smiled, but beamed. He smiled the way he'd smiled in Scotland, the gleeful grin that make him suddenly look like Danny, and look as young as he really was, not the thirty his scowl and heavy posture could hint at.

Eli dragged him down by the hair for a fierce kiss, tongues and morning breath clashing almost violently under the weight of a sudden surge of raw desire and feral excitement. Something solidified with Eli's own words and Rob's happiness, as real as if he'd signed a rental contract. He suddenly itched anew with the need to touch and be touched, the need to hook Rob in the way he knew best.

He didn't say, "Okay, I'll move in," until Rob's fingers were stroking his inner thighs again. And then Rob's mouth pressed open, wet kisses down Eli's chest and waist, and Eli groaned the final word, the *in,* as Rob's tongue found the heavy pulse of his need, and *pushed...*

Eli pushed his wrist against his mouth to stifle the cry as Rob put his mouth to its best use, and thought—wildly, almost deliriously—that this was *not* going to go down well at home.

"YOU'RE *WHAT?*" DAD bellowed.

Eli rolled his eyes, thankful that his back was turned, and continued to pack the contents of his drawing desk into a box. He would have to commandeer the desk in Rob's room properly—it wasn't like Rob used it for anything other than an oversized shelf after all. The man didn't even have a laptop.

"I'm moving out," Eli repeated.

"Moving out. Moving *out*. Yes. Well. And where do you think you're going to go?" Dad blustered.

"I found a nice two-bed flat that I'll be sharing with two other guys," Eli said flippantly, and shut the box. He added it to the admittedly small-so-far pile, and dragged another empty box over to start emptying the drawers in the bedside table.

"Hawkes."

"Yep."

"You're moving in with *Hawkes*."

"His first name is *Rob*, and it's really rude of you not to use it," Eli retorted. He didn't pause or look round at his father, knowing that if he did, he'd explode. And wasn't that exactly what he'd punished Rob for doing before Christmas? "And yes, I'm moving in with him. He asked—twice now, actually—and we talked about it. So yes, I'm going to move in with Rob and get myself a better job than the one at the shop, and in September I'm going to go to art college."

"And just what are you going to do with an art degree?"

"I don't know yet," Eli said peacefully. "But I'll enjoy *doing* it, and it'll open up a lot of opportunities. And Rob's being very supportive of the idea."

"Oh yes, and how is Rob going to support you? And *why* is Rob supporting you—what are you giving him in exchange for—"

"If you finish that sentence, I will walk out of here right now, ditch all my things, and I will never fucking come back," Eli interrupted icily.

Dad—to Eli's mild surprise—actually shut up.

"It's not an *exchange,* Dad. Rob loves me. I know you find that really hard to believe, but he does. He loves me, and when you love people, you want to support them. That's all it is. There's not some sordid sex slavery shit going on, or whatever you think."

"Eli, for God's sake—"

"No," Eli interrupted again. "I'm moving out. I am moving in with Rob. End of story. He's going to come pick me up this evening and we'll get my stuff up to the flat."

"As if I'm going to allow it!"

"And you're going to stop me *how* exactly?" Eli demanded. "It would be illegal for you to even try—I'm twenty-one, and—"

"And you are walking into exactly the same scenario as Jenny did with Greg!"

"Rob is nothing like Greg."

"Rob is *exactly* like Greg, Eli. I know he's turned your head so you can't see it, but—"

"No. He's not." Eli abandoned the box and rose to his feet, folding his arms over his chest, finally turning to look his father in the eye. He pushed back the instinctive anger, and unlocked the one thing he'd never bothered to tell his vaguely transphobic father. "I know he's not, because Rob is gay."

"I'm sorry? Eli, you can't possibly think because a man's gay he's incapable of—"

"Let! Me! Finish!" Eli shouted.

His father's jaw clicked shut, a startled expression washing over his features.

"Thank you," Eli said in a clipped voice. "Rob is gay. Rob is one hundred percent gay. He has never been remotely interested in women. *Ever.* He's never had a crush on a woman, he's never experimented with girls even when he was a teenager, he's so gay he's actually incapable of telling you if a woman is pretty. It's actually a bit funny, it's like asking anyone else if…if, I don't know, a twig is pretty. It's a nonsense question to him. He's *gay*."

"Which doesn't mean—"

"Which *means*," Eli said loudly, "that I put off telling him I was transgender until about the third time he dropped a hint about wanting to have sex with me. I just blurted it out in the middle of a pub, the middle of our date, no planning, no prepared speech, and you've *seen* Rob. I expected it, too, I expected him to at *best* just walk right out on me, and at worst beat me up. I *knew* he was gay, he'd told me so, I *knew* he wouldn't want to be with someone who even *used* to be a woman."

"Where are you going with—"

"He looked at me, and said this wasn't the kind of conversation people had in the pub, and asked if I wanted to go and grab a takeaway and find a quiet park and talk about it in private but neutral ground." Not in so many words, but that had been the gist of it. "And he drove us right down to Endcliffe Park from Parson Cross because he knew it's my favourite one, and we sat by one of the little waterfalls and I told him everything. And he listened. And when I was done, he said that he really liked me, it wasn't just about whether I had a dick or not, and he had no idea what he was supposed to do when it came to the bedroom with a transgender guy but it couldn't be that different to figuring out what a new partner likes in bed anyway."

Eli paused, and his father, frowning, said nothing.

"He's—I *get* it, Dad, I do, Rob can be utterly pig-ignorant and he drinks too much and he can fix anyone's car from scratch but can't operate online banking without locking himself out or accidentally getting new credit cards, but he's a *good. Guy.* Underneath it, he really is, he's been amazing for me, amazing *with* me, and maybe you are never going to get it, but can you *please* respect my decision in this? I'm not moving into a Jenny-and-Greg situation, I'm moving in with a man who doesn't know the first thing about the gender binary but was willing to hear me out and try having this relationship anyway."

And that was the crux of it, for Eli—because nobody had ever done that before. He'd tried dating in school, going to a few youth

LGBT events in Sheffield, but had been firmly turned away by any of the gay guys there. He'd tried online dating as he got a little older, and found that messages promptly stopped the moment he mentioned it. Nobody had ever even talked about it with him, much less decided to try going out with him regardless.

"Eli...listen, I *want* to believe you, but—"

Eli snorted.

"No," Dad said earnestly, "I do. I don't want to believe you're putting yourself in that situation, but you *are*. Rob's record speaks for itself, and what you have described is *typical* of an abusive relationship—he has picked out someone who is by their very nature vulnerable, and he's exploiting that. As long as you're not under his roof, you're not under his control, so for now..."

"We met in a bar, Dad, he had no idea I wasn't a man," Eli said firmly. "He's not luring me in or whatever you think he's doing."

"And how would you know, Eli? You're too close to the situation, you're blinded by—"

"You're the blind one," Eli said stiffly. "Blinded by prejudice. You think because he's got a record that he's like that with everyone. And I can't just say something that'll make you believe me, Dad, because you *won't* believe me, you refuse to."

Eli's phone started ringing in the pocket of his jacket, abandoned on his bed. For a moment he held his father's gaze, then turned away. He felt...oddly freed. He had said his piece, and far from the anger he usually felt, he felt...fine. As though suddenly it didn't matter whether his father liked it or not.

Jen! flashed up at Eli from his phone, and he rolled his eyes. "Hey, Jenny."

"Eli!" she sounded harried. "Thank God, I can't get hold of Mum or Dad."

"Dad's here, must've left his phone in his jacket again. You okay?"

"No, my car won't start! Can you come and pick me up? I'm at work, I don't want to have to walk right down to get the bus back into town, you know what it's like round here..."

"Yeah, okay, no problem," Eli said, glancing at the clock. It was half past six, and pitch black out already. He'd told Rob to come by at seven, but…"I'll start out but Rob might be closer, do you want me to send him?"

"Um…"

"He's coming to pick me up later anyway."

"Oh, okay then. Thanks, Eli, I *owe* you, majorly!"

"See you in twenty, sis." He hung up, and levelled his father with a flat stare. "I'm going to text Rob, then go and pick Jenny up, and then we'll all come back here and Rob and I will get my stuff and be off out of your way. And Dad, seriously, if you don't stop needling at me about my relationship every time I see you? We'll be off for good."

JENNY WORKED IN Attercliffe, in a moody call centre set well back from the main road and poorly lit at the best of times. It was generally not as creepy as it looked, but things *had* been known to happen. Eli was relieved, when he pulled up in Dad's borrowed car, to find Jenny sitting in her own and, apart from looking flustered and a bit harried, fine.

"There you are!" she said, getting out of her Audi. "It just won't start! I think it's the battery, it *tries* to turn over but it won't and I have the wrong number for the RAC saved, and—"

"Get Rob to pop the bonnet when he arrives, he might be able to start it," Eli advised. "He keeps jump leads in his boot if it's the battery, and—"

Movement out of the corner of his eye caught his attention, and he snapped his head around. Three figures loped out of the shadows by the call centre, faces obscured by hoodies and baseball caps, and they moved with a slow swagger that spoke danger.

"Jenny," he said quietly, "get in Dad's car."

"Nice rides," one of the figures said. "What d'you reckon they cost, huh? Twenty grand each?"

One of his mates sniggered; Eli put out an arm to shield Jenny, and began to inch her back towards the cars.

"A pouf and a preggers bird," the guy sneered, then coughed a dry laugh. "Give us your keys, then."

"No," Eli said.

"Oh for fuck's sake, he wants to be a fucking hero. Give us your keys, mate, don't be a twat."

"I'm not letting you steal our cars."

"Uh, yeah you fucking are, 'less you and your slag there want a good fucking hiding?"

The ringleader stepped forward into the halo of light pooling on the tarmac from Dad's headlights, the sickly light throwing his thin frame into sharp relief, a pointed chin jutting from the shadows of the hat—

And Eli caught the sinister glint of a crowbar hanging from a gloved hand.

CHAPTER 24

SHIT. SHIT, SHIT, *shit!*

"Jen, get in the fucking car," Eli breathed out of the corner of his mouth.

The ringleader sneered.

"How about you give us the keys first, huh? C'mon, mate, think straight. Give us the keys, nobody has to get hurt."

"She's *pregnant,* you stupid fucks."

One of them shrugged. "One born every minute, ain't there?"

Eli heard the catch of the car door give, then the heavy thud of Jenny shutting herself in.

"Lock the doors, Jen!" he yelled at her, but she'd—stupidly—gotten back into her *own* car, and if not even the electrics would start…shit, did she have manual locking?

"God, you're a dense fuck, aren't you?" the boy said. His voice was thin and reedy, barely having broken.

Eli backed right up against the frame of the car, the edge of the roof digging into his spine. His heart was beating a mile a minute, his eyes fixed on the glint of the crowbar and theirs on him, and—

Jenny screamed, and Eli was blinded. Something roared, someone swore, and then the headlights that had hit him full in the face swung around. Eli, who hadn't realised until he lowered them that he'd thrown up his arms to defend his face, blinked owlishly in the sudden gloom again. A familiar, battered car was rocking to a halt on the tarmac, windows down, music blaring, a passenger leaning out with familiar dreadlocks and a shit-eating grin.

And Eli relearned how to breathe, and inched further away from the lads as a huge frame unfolded itself from the driver's seat almost lazily.

"I think," rasped a familiar deep voice, "that you might wanna fuckin' rethink that, lads."

Eli's heart staggered in his chest. Thank fuck. Thank *fuck*.

The boys were less impressed. "Fuck off, mate, this don't involve you," their ringleader snapped, almost casually jabbing the crowbar in Rob's direction.

"Yeah? Kinda fucking does," Rob snarled. His approach was slow and idle, but relentless; he came to a halt almost casually between Eli and the boys, lounging against the roof of Jenny's car like a man turning up for a photoshoot, not a man disturbing a mugging.

"Fucking hurry up an' can 'em, Rob, let's go! I'm fucking hungry!" Danny bellowed. The door of the Suzuki slammed, and then a dark shadow hopped up onto the bonnet, toothy grin visible even in the shadows from the headlights. The music kept pounding, just as irrepressible as the Hawkes brothers.

"Good idea, mate! Yeah, why don't you and your boyfriend piss off," one of the lads said.

Rob's snort was nothing short of derisive.

"You sick wanker," he sneered. "That's my fucking brother, you perv. *That's* my boyfriend," he added, jerking his thumb over his shoulder at Eli. "So…no. I ain't pissin' off. Best thing for you to do is go home and give your mother another good fuckin', how about that?"

"Fucking faggots, man," one of the hangers-on sneered.

Eli slipped around the car. He wasn't fucking stupid. Rob was there to defend him, and if he was out of the way…

"Can 'em, Rob," Danny drawled.

Eli whipped back around, just in time to see the crowbar flash in the glare of the Suzuki's headlights. He cried out—but Rob was faster, almost casually batting it aside with a blow to the kid's wrist. He caught the hood in a fist and *slammed* the kid, head-first, into the roof of the car. The Audi rocked violently; Jenny screamed inside, and Eli saw the flash of her phone screen.

"Call the fucking police!" he yelled at her.

Rob let go, and the kid slumped boneless and keening to the tarmac.

"Either o' you two cunts wanna give it a shot?" he sneered.

"Fucking *shit,* Jamie, move your arse!" one of them yelled at the downed idiot, who was sitting up and swaying. Rob snorted and delivered a hefty kick to his ribs that sent him sprawling before idly loping back to the Suzuki and tossing Danny his phone.

"Thing is, lads," he said loudly, emptying his pockets of keys and wallet, too. Danny accepted them with a wide, gleeful grin that was downright disturbing. "You oughta pick your targets proper, like. Pretty blokes and preggers birds, that's bad karma, that. That's the kind of shit you get punished for before y'even fucking started. Now you pick on another little shit jus' like you, nobody'd come for 'im. That's how you play it. Not pretty blokes and preggers birds. They got people, they do."

"People like you, you fucking queer?" one of the lackeys sneered, but his voice was wobbling. "Fuck off, alright? We weren't gonna fucking 'urt 'em."

"Maybe not," Rob drawled. His accent was thickening into the heavy slur it had been in Scotland, only more steely. This wasn't Rob's fucked-out voice. It was his gonna-fuck-you-*up* voice. "I'm gonna hurt you, mind."

The ringleader staggered to his feet, wobbling drunkenly, and spat a gobbet of blood onto the floor. "You…fucking…pouf," he snarled.

Rob hit him.

It wasn't a graceful move—it was a single, hard, boxer's punch. It landed square in the centre of the kid's face, Rob's arm faster than a lightning strike, and Eli heard the sick crunch of the kid's nose. He dropped, for good this time, and Eli saw the advantage Rob had when the other two hesitated before attacking—they were already scared of him, despite Danny's lounging and non-interference, despite their being armed and Rob not.

One of them smashed what looked in the gloom to be a screwdriver down in a stabbing motion, but his aim was poor and his speed crap. Rob caught his wrist and snapped it with a deft twist, effortlessly bringing the kid to his knees. He cut off the yowl by kneeing the kid in the underside of the jaw. The clank of teeth didn't come; the muffled scream and the flood of blood down his chin said why.

"You don't," Rob snarled, before twisting and heavily introducing a knee to the side of his head, "fucking attack fucking pregnant women, you stupid fucking *fucks*!"

The kid scrambled to get away from Rob, who refused, briefly, to let go. There was a screech of pain as the broken bones of his wrist were jerked around. That sparked the third hanger-on, it seemed, who scrabbled in his hoodie.

It happened all in a blur. The wide-eyed, scared face of the last shit standing. The flash of metal in the headlights. The sudden flash of motion as Danny bellowed and launched himself bodily from the bonnet of the Suzuki. Jenny's scream from the car.

And Rob's sudden roar of pain as the kid ducked under his punch and buried the knife to the hilt in his gut.

"*Rob!*" Eli bellowed.

Danny bodily smashed into the kid, throwing them both sideways onto the tarmac. The knife clattered onto the ground in a spray of dark, wet liquid and Rob, for a brief second, merely cupped his fingers around the wound and looked down at the deep crimson flooding over his fingers.

"Fuck," he said, sounding…oddly surprised.

Then his knees buckled, and he went down.

Eli hurtled around the car, but not fast enough—Rob hit the ground with a sickening thud, head appallingly limp. Eli tore the knees of his jeans, and the skin of said knees, as he skidded across the tarmac and slammed his palms down over the shocking red flooding over Rob's white T-shirt.

Rob *screamed*.

He arched under Eli's hand and screamed, one boot scraping

loudly as he writhed. It was all Eli could do to keep his hands pressed as hard as possible over the wound, hot blood bubbling up between his fingers and tears blurring his vision.

"I'm sorry," he gasped. "Oh God, I'm so sorry, I'm sorry, I'm sorry, just hold on, they're coming, Jenny called, they're coming—"

Then the cavalry arrived.

In the form of a siren screaming down the main road, blue lights flashing off the buildings. One of the kids swore and bolted; Danny turned flawlessly on the other, eyes wild in his white face. Eli twisted to seize him by the shirt and haul him bodily towards Rob.

"Help me!" he shouted, desperate to get Danny to stop, to listen, to fucking *help* him because if Danny got nicked, if Danny...if Danny wasn't *here*...

"Fuck-fuck-fuck-fuck, you fucking fucker!" Danny shouted, ripping off his jacket. He ripped off his T-shirt, too, wadding it into a ball and crushing it over the bloodstains, slamming it onto Rob's gut so hard he received a heavy punch in the face. "Fuck off, you retard! I'm trying to fucking help you!"

"You're trying to finish me the fuck off!" Rob bellowed, then his voice cracked and he sagged against the tarmac again, eyes rolling in his head.

Eli flung Danny's jacket over Rob's upper chest and neck, then wrapped both hands into Rob's hair, smearing blood onto his greying skin.

"Stay with me," he whispered desperately. "Fuck, Rob, c'mon, stay with me, it's not that bad, it's not that bad..."

"Hand," Rob grunted, screwing his eyes shut. Eli caught Rob's hand, and promptly had his fingers crushed.

"Fuck!" Eli hissed, then steeled himself and weakly clung back.

A strong grip was good. If Rob was just...just reacting to pain, as long as he had strength in him...

"Get me a fucking ambulance!" Danny bellowed over his shoulder.

A stray copper skidded to his knees, a green first aid box in his hands.

"What the fuck use is that, he's been fucking stabbed!"

"Gauze," the copper said, not batting an eyelid. "It's better for packing the wound and stemming the flow."

Danny snarled, but allowed for the assistance.

Rob jerked and swore fluently as the bloody T-shirt was ripped aside—Eli nearly threw up at the sheer *amount* of blood soaked into the thin material—and a handful of gauze was slammed into place.

"Oh *Jesus*," Rob grunted. His hand started to shake violently in Eli's. "Fuck, fuck, fuck—"

"Don't you *dare* pass out on me," Eli demanded, shaking his face lightly. "C'mon, Rob, ambulance isn't far now, and then they'll hop you up on the really good stuff, and you—you *can't*, you can't do this…"

"Eli," Danny snapped. "Help me."

Eli swallowed and kissed Rob's knuckles before letting go and twisting back to Danny.

"Hands here," Danny ordered brusquely, clapping Eli's into place over the already bloody gauze. The copper laid his own hands, warm through the rubbery blue gloves he was wearing, over the back of Eli's to increase the pressure on the wound. Hot blood squished through Eli's fingers. Rob groaned deeply. Danny was bending over him and muttering very fast. Eli caught the word 'fucker' several times.

"He was defending me and my sister," he croaked to the policeman. "He was…he's my boyfriend, he's my partner, my sister broke down and texted me asking me to pick her up and I thought he might be closer so I texted him, too, and then…then he interrupted those kids…"

Eli talked, because it was better than listening to Danny swear at Rob and *not* hear Rob's replies. Then there was another scream of sirens down the main road, and a policewoman was running into the road to flag down the ambulance. It rocketed into the car park with less finesse than the abandoned Suzuki, one of the paramedics jumping out before it had even completely stopped, then Eli and the cop were roughly elbowed out of the way.

"What's happened?" the paramedic barked.

"He's been fucking stabbed, what d'you fucking think?" Danny shouted.

"If you want me to help him, I suggest you shut your lip and give me what I bloody well need to help him," the paramedic snapped back, not in the least bit perturbed by the attitude. "Conscious and breathing?"

"And in fucking pain!" Rob snarled. His voice was reed-thin, but still clear.

Eli's heart jumped in his chest. He scrambled up Rob's other side to cup his face in both hands and kiss his forehead, the skin cold and clammy.

"Where's the fucking drugs, eh?"

"I'm a paramedic, not a bloody pharmacist," the man retorted as his colleague dropped beside him. Despite his words, their gloves worked quickly over the wound. "Male, mid-twenties, conscious, breathing, aware, stab wound to the lower left abdomen, doesn't appear to have ruptured the bowel..."

"Fucking great, I'm not gonna shit myself to death," Rob groaned.

Eli slapped his cheek lightly.

"You're not fucking dying," he spat furiously. "You fucking jumped in front of an armed robber for me and Jen, I'll drag you back here myself if I have to."

"Whipped, bro. You're so whipped," Danny laughed hoarsely, his dark eyes wild. He was clutching at his jacket over Rob's shoulders, his lips bloodless and grey.

"Call ahead to Northern General, he'll need to go straight in, bleeding's not coming under control..."

"M'bleeding to death on a car park floor," Rob complained. "This ain't the bar fight you promised, Dan."

"Piss off, I *distinctly* said you'd be forty-five when you coughed it in the local," Danny snapped.

One of the paramedics vanished back to the ambulance with the cop. Rob took a deep, shaky breath.

"Hey, Eli?"

"Uh-huh?"

"I am never picking up your sister ever again."

Eli laughed, hating the high sound of his own voice. He swallowed against the heavy lump in his throat. "Me neither. And I'm never borrowing Dad's car either. I'll borrow yours. Nobody'd steal your car ever, it's a stinking piece of shit."

"Oh, fuck you…"

The stretcher was banged roughly on the ground and Danny and Eli were shooed away while the paramedics and the cop struggled to transfer Rob's heavy frame onto it. The thin quality to Rob's voice was passed over for his usual loud, coarse language. But when they finally lifted the stretcher, his skin was completely grey in the harsh blue lights of the emergency vehicles.

"Oh God, Rob…" Eli whispered. He started forward like a string was pulling him along, determined not to lose sight—or sound—of Rob's twitching and swearing, the proof he was still *here*…

"Eli!"

Danny's hand was firm on his shoulder; Eli tore his gaze away from the stretcher, and rested them instead on his own bloodied fingers.

"Eli, mate, your sister needs you, yeah?" Danny said. "She can't fucking come wi'me, she don't know me from fuckin' Adam and she's freaked enough. Go wi' your sister."

"But…Rob…"

"I got Rob."

Eli locked eyes with Danny's—the same shape, the same size, even the same way of flicking the gaze from left to right and back when staring at you, as Rob's. But *not* Rob's.

"I got him, Eli," Danny said earnestly, no trace of the usual joviality. "'E ain't fuckin' off and leavin' me. Ain't allowed. I *got* 'im, yeah?"

Eli's chest unlocked, and he squeezed Danny's wrist hard in his bloodied palm.

"Text me the minute you know anything," Eli said, and pushed Danny in the direction of the ambulance. "Don't let him go fucking *anywhere*!"

Danny saluted—and then he was swinging up into the back of the ambulance, the rear door was slamming shut, and—

And Rob was gone.

CHAPTER 25

IT WAS NEARLY forty minutes before Eli got to the hospital.

They'd had to call another ambulance. Eli was shaking too much to drive, and Jenny—of course, because the universe was fucking like that, wasn't it—had gone into labour. Her waters had broken in the car, and it took a policeman and another paramedic to get her out of it and into an ambulance.

"You best go with her, son, you might need a look-over yourself," one of the cops said kindly.

Eli cast a look back at the abandoned Suzuki—with its headlights still on and music still blaring inappropriately—and shivered.

"The cars…"

"We'll take them in. They'll be safe enough. G'wan. Get your girl there seen to."

"M'sister," Eli mumbled numbly, but allowed himself to be pulled up into the back of the ambulance with her.

They didn't speak, Jenny too focused on the baby and Eli too focused on the blood smeared into his hands and fingernails. Rob's blood. He'd never really gotten blood on his hands before, not like this, and the thick, almost fuzzy texture as it dried was both fascinating and unpleasant.

"He won't die, right?" he asked the technician, who simply eyed him before returning to giving Jenny instructions on relaxing and breathing.

Rob wouldn't die. Eli was—well, no, he wasn't sure of it, but…he'd still been conscious when they'd taken him away. And Danny was with him. Danny wouldn't let Rob go.

Right?

The hospital had no such cares for Eli's shock—they dealt with this sort of crap every day. They whisked Jenny away in a wheelchair, and pushed Eli to sit on a hard plastic chair with a cup of water.

"One of the nurses'll nab you in a minute, mate," the technician said before disappearing.

Eli clutched the water, the blood dried enough it didn't stain, and watched it ripple as his fingers shook. Somewhere Rob was here. And Danny. Maybe Danny was still slapping him and swearing, or maybe they'd been sep—

Eli screwed his eyes stuck against the fearful, knee-jerk terror that rose up in the back of his head at the thought that Rob and Danny might have already been separated. It was stupid to think Rob might die because Danny wasn't allowed to be with him, but…but the thought was there all the time.

"Sir? Are you alright, sir?"

Eli shook off the hand that clasped his arm, fumbling his coat pocket for his phone. He had to—someone. Call someone. Jenny would want Mum. Or…where'd she left Flora? Was Flora with the babysitter? Or—

The cold wash of air at the hospital entrance was a welcome slap to the face, and Eli took what felt like the first breath he'd managed in days. His fingers still shook as they dialled. He had to close his eyes and sink down the cold, concrete wall to the floor, dampness seeping into his jacket, as the sky spun above him dizzyingly.

"Eli? I'm at—"

"Dad."

His own voice sounded very hollow and far away; Dad's, tinny-sounding and even further, paused.

"What's happened?"

"I—" Eli whispered, and tipped his head back against the concrete. "You...you and Mum...someone..."

"Eli? What's the matter, love?"

Love. An endearment Eli rarely heard from his father, and one he usually hated. It wasn't a term for men. It was a term for your daughters, not your sons. And yet, in the cold dark outside the hospital entrance, it was like a warm blanket around the shoulders.

"Hospital," he croaked. "I...Jenny and I...we're at the Northern General. She's—shit, Dad, you have to...you or Mum have to get here—"

Something banged on Dad's end, but his voice—a copper's voice, deep and calm no matter what he was hearing—remained steady. "What's happened, Eli? Are you and Jenny alright?"

"Jenny's having the baby," Eli coughed. He ground the heel of his hand into his eyes. "I went—I went to pick her up, and these kids—and Rob came, and—shit, Dad, Rob's...I don't know if he's going to be okay—"

"Eli, love, I'm at work," Dad interrupted, still speaking so maddeningly calmly. "I just got on shift, I'll have to find cover, but I will be there as soon as I can. Your mother's at home, I'll send her a message, and she can come right up—"

"Jenny'll need Mum," Eli said numbly, then cracked. "Fuck, Dad, Rob's been stabbed. He's been stabbed, I don't—there was blood everywhere and I don't know if he's going to be *okay*—"

"Eli!" Dad's voice was suddenly sharp. "Eli, I'm sorry, but I need to go and get cover sorted, and then I will be *right with you*. Alright? I'll ring your mother. You stay with Jenny, alright? You stick with Jenny, don't you worry about Rob, and we'll be there as soon as we can."

Eli scrambled at the instructions, grasping them with greedy hands. Stay with Jenny. He couldn't *not* worry about Rob, but Mum and Dad were coming to look after Jenny, and then he could...then he could find Danny, and wait with him. Danny was with Rob. Rob would...Rob would be alright if Danny was with him. They'd always been that way, and they'd be that way now.

"Okay," he said. "I—okay."

"Alright. We'll be there soon."

For a long minute after Dad had hung up, Eli simply sat and clutched the phone, before slowly pulling it away and texting Danny. *Whats going on??*

They just took him into surgery n the cops have shode up 2 talk. theyll b lookin 4 u 2.

Eli swallowed, rolled his shoulders, and stood up. Of course the police would come. A man had been stabbed, and at least two others pretty seriously assaulted, by the way Rob had been fighting and Danny had whaled in at the last second like that. And Eli knew—far better than Danny did—the right way to put things, the buzzwords like 'defending us' and 'feared for my life' to get the boys in trouble and not Rob.

Talk to the police. Yeah. He could do that.

WHEN ELI'S PHONE next went off, it was Mum.

"I'm sorry," he said to the copper taking his statement. "Can I get that?"

"'Course." He was the kind of copper Eli wanted Rob to meet: young, earnest, and with a calming manner. And armed with this big smile that got the nurses to keep bringing cups of tea as Eli had reached the part where he'd seen the kid stab Rob.

He shuffled aside to take the call. They were in the back corner of a quiet-ish waiting area, as at that time of night there was nowhere really private left. "Mum?"

"Eli! Eli, dear, where are you?"

"Um, on the second floor. I'm giving my statement to the police—you need to—"

"Already?"

"I didn't want to wait." Eli swallowed hard. "Are you with Jenny? Jenny'll need—"

"Yes, dear, I'm with Jenny." Mum's voice was even more flustered than Dad's, and Eli felt a pang of…something. It was petty to feel a little resentful that Mum had found Jenny before even calling to check on him, because Jenny was having a *baby*, for God's sake…

But then a tiny, uncharitable part of Eli's mind pointed out that Jenny was thirty-eight weeks pregnant and had had a baby before. Eli, on the other hand, had been trying to hold all his boyfriend's blood inside to stop him just…just bleeding to death in the middle of a dirty car park. And he'd never…he'd never…

"Eli?"

"Sorry," he mumbled. "I…where are you?"

"Ward ten, darling. There's no maternity unit, but Jenny's a little far gone to be moved on now, especially after that shock the two of you have had. They're trying to get a midwife out here rather than take Jenny to her—"

Eli coughed. "Okay. Um. Let me…let me finish this, and… and I'll be up."

"Alright." Mum paused. "Eli? Darling? Are you alri—"

"See you soon."

Eli hung up, his fingers shaking around the phone. The copper took his elbow gently and pulled him back into his seat.

"You've had a bad shock," he said sympathetically. "We can finish this whenever suits you, Mr Bell."

Eli stared at his still-bloody hands. "It could've been me. Or Jen. What'll—what'll happen to them?"

"If they're convicted? Stabbing someone's not a light sentence."

"What about Rob? Rob hit him, Rob—"

"From what you've told me, Mr Bell, then it sounds like Mr Hawkes was acting in defense of another. And using reasonable force to protect another person from harm is perfectly legal."

Eli nodded, barely even hearing the words, and slowly closed his fingers. A little of the redness flaked and fell off. Paper rustled, and then the copper flipped his clipboard—borrowed off a nurse—shut and rose to his feet.

"Why don't we continue this another time, Mr Bell? Let's get you up to see your family."

"I need to see Rob," Eli whispered, "but he's in surgery."

"So let's go and see your family," the copper repeated. "Come on, I'll walk you up there."

The policeman's hand was firm and warm on Eli's elbow again, and Eli coughed a hollow laugh as he was steered towards the stairs. "You're the kind of cop I keep telling Rob exists. He thinks you're all bastards."

"Lot of people do," the man said amiably. "And, hell, I'm not blind. There's some cops deserve that label. But most of us, it's all that serve and protect stuff. Someone's gotta be there to protect the public."

Eli managed a watery smile. "Rob's the kind of guy you're usually protecting the public *from*."

"Hard lad, is he?"

"Hard-*headed*," Eli mumbled. "Shitty upbringing. Likes pub fights and weed. You know the type. He's a good guy, but he's…"

"See," the copper said as the lift doors closed and the floor jerked, beginning to inch them down towards the first floor, "funny thing is, they're the guys who go either way when they hit their teens. They become criminals, or they become cops. Funny how most people on either side don't see that."

The doors opened onto the melee of a busy corridor. Eli immediately saw his mother hovering outside a set of ward doors and wringing her hands.

"Mum!" he called—and promptly forgot all about the nameless, faceless copper. He walked right into her hug, folding himself into the smell of fabric conditioner and whatever she'd been making for dinner, and fought back the urge to cry.

"Oh *Eli*," she breathed, clutching him back. Mum hadn't hugged him properly for years, ever since he'd come out to them and that odd distance had evolved between him and his own family. And now, quite suddenly, the gap had snapped shut, and she was clinging to him as though he had never drifted away. "Oh, Eli, love."

"How's—how's Jenny?"

"Jenny's fine, dear," Mum said, stroking his hair like he was a child again. "She's just fine, the baby's a little upset by all the chaos but they're both doing fine. They just don't want to upset them again by moving them to a full maternity unit, so here we are!"

Her voice nearly snapped on the would-be cheery note.

Eli let go, stepped back, and scrubbed both hands over his eyes. "Fuck," he whispered.

"Eli, dear, your father rang, but he was very—confused, I suppose. What *happened?*"

"A couple of fucking kids tried to nick Jenny's car," Eli whispered.

"And—he said something about Rob?"

Eli's throat ached, and he shook his head. "Rob—I texted him. I was going to—I was…Rob asked me to live with him, Mum."

"He—*what?*"

"I was packing up my stuff and me and Dad were arguing and then—then Jenny rang me saying her car wouldn't start and could I pick her up, and I knew Rob would probably be closer so I texted him asking him to go, so…so he and Danny, his brother, they turned up just as these kids were gonna set on me and Jenny for Jenny's car keys and…and *fuck,* Mum, one of them stabbed Rob. He just—he literally—he took a fucking *knife* for me and Jenny, he's in surgery here somewhere and I don't know what's happening and—and—" Eli's face burned hot and damp,

Mum's face was a picture of startled horror and something…something else, lighting behind her eyes. She closed her fingers around Eli's wrists and began to tow him towards the toilets, murmuring something about getting his hands cleaned. Eli let her take over, his vision foggy and everything in him begging to be able to abandon Jenny and find Rob…

"Here, let's get these washed."

The water in the sink was hot, and Mum began to knead at Eli's skin, spreading the hand soap over his knuckles with gentle ease. She hummed lightly as she did, and Eli felt a little of the tension between his shoulders loosen. "He…he saved our lives, Mum. They'd have attacked me. And Jen. I refused to give them the keys. I—I said no, and one of them had a crowbar, and then this other one stabbed Rob…if he hadn't been there…if he'd not…"

"What we are going to do," Mum said softly, "is get you cleaned up and settled down in the ward with Jenny, nice cup of tea and a blanket, get you settled. And when there's some news about Rob, then we'll have you up to see him and make sure he's going to be alright—and then your father or I will come with you, and thank him in person."

"Oh, right, yeah," Eli mumbled hoarsely. "Because Dad is ever going to thank Rob for anything."

Mum squeezed his wrists.

When Eli looked up at her, her usually soft, genial face was firm and tight-lipped.

"From what you've said, Eli, then Rob Hawkes took a blade for my children and my grandchild," she said quietly. "And I never would have thought that of him. Which says to me that we have…rather dramatically misjudged him. And I will not waste time now I know that we've done that in trying to mend those bridges, and find out who this man really is."

The tears welled up again, and Eli balled his hands into fists. "I *told* you," he whispered fiercely. "I fucking *told* you."

"I know you did, darling," Mum whispered, "and I'm so, so sorry. But sometimes…sometimes it takes a shock for people to realise they've been…wrong. And we have. And we will fix it, I promise you—because I *do* know some things about your Rob, and that's that one little idiot with a penknife is not going to keep him down for long."

Eli laughed—then cracked, his chest heaving, and felt the shock shudder and buckle under the sudden sharp wave of grief. Mum hugged him tightly, murmuring nonsense, as he began to cry…In spite of his wet hands, the smell of antiseptic, and the ache in his chest that was made of pure fear for what was happening to Rob in some shadowy operating theatre…

Eli felt something, finally, after long years of chilly rejection and misunderstandings, begin to heal.

CHAPTER 26

EXHAUSTION MUST HAVE caught up to him, for the next thing Eli knew was his phone buzzing by his hip, and the dizzying tip of the gleaming corridor as he almost fell out of his chair. He had been settled in a chair in the main corridor of the ward, with the promised tea and blankets formed out of his and his mother's coats, and…he didn't remember sleeping, but he had. And his leg had gone to sleep. A passing nurse seized his arm and righted him, chuckling lightly. Eli groaned as he fumbled for the phone.

"You need to get yourself home, love," the nurse said.

"Can't," Eli mumbled, the brightness of the phone screen hurting his eyes, then—

Then he jumped up from the chair and was making a beeline for the door.

Out of surgery. ward 3 bay 2 theres a green curten by the door.

He forwarded the text to his mother and broke into a light jog as he headed for the stairs. It was irrational, the way his heart was pounding against his ribs. He knew Rob, he knew Danny—if there was bad news, Danny would have come and got him in person, or…or called, if he couldn't leave Rob. Neither of them said heavy shit by text, they weren't those kinds of guys, and yet…

And yet Eli's fingers felt hot and wet with Rob's blood again, the phantom sensation disturbing and chilling. It hadn't been that bad—Rob had still been conscious when they took him in the ambulance, after all—but then...how could that much blood not be bad? It had been *everywhere*, and Rob had been so white...

His shoes squeaked on the gleaming floor of ward two, his shadow flitting along the darkened bay windows like a phantom. Or like the grim reaper, which was a thought so chilling Eli forced it away and looked for the green curtain like a man in a desert looks for an oasis. He found it right down the end, and beyond it, quiet broken only by the beeping of machines.

But the squeaky shoes had done him a favour; a curtain twitched near the end of the bay. A dreadlocked head poked itself out—just as a hand clamped down on Eli's arm.

"Out," the ward sister said firmly.

"No, I have to see—"

"Family only, out," she repeated. She was tall and broad-shouldered, the uniform making her look as feminine and caring as a broody rock. Dark circles were smudged under her eyes, and she looked worn down but resolute. Eli was not staying.

"He is family." Danny appeared like a welcome mirage. "He's Rob's partner. He needs to be here."

The nurse eyed him suspiciously, and Danny turned on the weird charm, big dark eyes and hopeful smile totally disarming his usual looks.

"Please," Danny said. "Rob's—he's got some issues, yeah? And tonight'll have upset him, if Eli's here, he'll keep calm."

The nurse softened. "Alright," she said, and huffed at Eli. "You need a badge, though."

Eli hovered long enough to be presented with one, then shot into the cubicle. He had no time for Danny's lies and the nurse's badges. He only had time for—

His breath caught.

Rob looked...*small*. It was a ridiculous thought, but he did. His skin was chalk-white. He'd been dressed in a hospital gown, one of his tattoos peeking out from the green robe, the ink looking almost wet on his paler-than-pale skin. Eli wanted to touch him to feel the heat, to make sure he was—

But he *was* breathing. The gown was rising and falling in a gentle, familiar pattern. An oxygen tube had been taped under his nose, but there was no mask. He looked oddly fine, despite the colour of his skin. Eli sank gingerly onto the edge of the mattress, hands hovering in the air uncertainly.

"Is…is he…?"

"Out like a light—they had to do surgery to close the hole," Danny said, collapsing into the visitor's chair. He looked worse than the nurse, eyes ringed in black on the skin and red on the whites. His dreadlocks were sticking up every which way. "Twenty-six stitches and he'll need, like, blood tests and every piss he takes in the next week tested 'cause the knife nicked his liver."

"Oh God—"

"But he'll be 'reet."

"He's—?"

"Doctor said he'd be fine," Danny said, his face breaking into an exhausted smile. "He didn't black out. I mean, like, blood everywhere and he needed two transfusions, doc said, but he was still swearing at me when we got here. So I figured…you know, it couldn't be *that* bad, and the doc said unless something goes stupid wrong like he gets killer AIDS—"

Eli managed a hoarse laugh, daring to reach out and stroke his fingers gently through Rob's hair. When nothing happened, he petted a little harder and allowed those rough strands to soothe his jangled nerves. "The doctor did not say killer AIDS, Danny."

"He meant it," Danny defended himself. "He so fucking meant it. But yeah, he'll be alright, they said."

"Thank God," Eli whispered. He slid off the mattress to snag the second chair and drag it up to the head of the bed. Eli settled in to card his fingers through Rob's hair and kiss his boyfriend's forehead absently. Rob's skin was cool and slightly clammy. Eli rested a cheek against it to look down that long body and observe the way he breathed, the relaxed points of his feet at the very end, the gentle slope of his arm down his stomach to where—

To where Danny's hands were both clamped around Rob's. Eli frowned.

"Are *you* alright?" he asked quietly.

Danny shrugged. "Nurse looked me over."

"Not what I meant."

Danny gave him a look that said it was all Eli was going to get. Eli snorted.

"God, you're both emotionally constipated," he mumbled.

"How d'you think I am?" Danny grunted. "Imagine...like, fucking imagine having the one person in the world who ever gave a fuck about you, going down. Imagine that. Even when he were in prison, he were alright." He said *arreet* again, his accent thickened by fear and exhaustion. "But the doctor said he'll be fine, so I'm fine. S'easy."

Eli knew it wasn't quite so easy as all that, but let it go.

"How's your sister?"

Eli shrugged. "Upstairs having a baby," he said. "She was due in, like, three weeks anyway so I don't think there'll be a problem, but I don't know shit about babies."

"Aw, I'm not gonna be an uncle?"

"Me and Rob, with a baby? Are you kidding me?"

Danny sniggered, some of the weariness easing out of his face. The absence of his cheery demeanour was oddly even more unsettling than Rob sleeping soundless between them. His face resettled, then he whispered, "He started beating kids up for me when I was, like...five."

Eli blinked, cheek still rested against Rob's forehead.

"This girl at school made me a daisy-chain and I wore it 'cause that's what you're meant to do when a pretty girl makes you a daisy-chain, y'know? And this other kid laughed at me and nicked it, and Rob smashed his head against a door."

Eli grimaced. "Oh my God, seriously? When *I* was five we called each other booger-brains, we didn't commit GBH."

Danny laughed. "Yeah, well, you grew up in fuckin' Dore."

"*Touché.*"

"S'just weird seeing him out for the count," Danny mumbled.

"You can beat the shit out of him and he'll just smirk and spit the blood out. Dad used to do it all the time. Never touched me, 'cause Rob'd get in the way and sound off. And he tells me shit, you know, how you 'n' your old man keep clashing about it. I get where you're coming from, you know, 'cause he's not what everyone else reckons. Me 'n' you, we've seen Rob for real, yeah?"

"Yeah," Eli whispered, stroking Rob's upper arm gently.

"He used to blow off hanging out with his mates to take me places 'cause Mam and Dad flaked out on doing it. I remember being, like, nine and being dead upset 'cause Mam had promised to take me to the zoo and didn't, so Rob just got me up in the middle of the night and we broke in and went anyway."

Eli laughed quietly. "I can see that."

"It was awesome," Danny admitted, face lighting up. "When Rob left care and I was still there, I just kept running away to go to Rob's flat. He used to sneak me bus fare to hide in my socks when they'd come and get me, so I could go straight back the minute they left me alone. Even when he was in prison, he was there. Tonight's…tonight's first time he's really threatened to fuck off, y'know?"

"Yeah, but he didn't," Eli said quietly. "Didn't even threaten to, not if he was swearing at you all the way to hospital."

Danny half-smirked.

"You know, there's plenty of opportunity for revenge," Eli murmured. Rob's skin was a comfort, and the panic had washed away, leaving him tired and in need of sleep. "He'll be sore and stiff and in need of help when he gets to go home."

Danny's smirk turned vicious. Eli twisted his face to kiss Rob's hairline and whisper an apology to him for the hell Eli had just dropped him into.

"Eli?"

"Mm?"

"Thanks."

Danny's grip on Rob's hand wasn't quite so tight anymore.

❖

ELI DIDN'T REALISE he'd slept until the pillow stirred. And only when it stirred did he realise it wasn't a pillow at all, but someone's shoulder.

He sat up, and his jacket slid off his shoulders where someone had tucked it. Danny was gone. The cubicle curtains were half-open, sunlight streaming across the gleaming floor of the ward, and Rob—his shoulder having seemingly served as Eli's pillow—was shifting restlessly in the bed.

"Hey, ssh," Eli soothed, reaching out to stroke his hair with one hand and press the call button with the other. "It's alright, babe."

Grey-white eyes appeared through the slimmest of cracks between cheek and lid. Eli kissed one stern eyebrow, stroking Rob's hair and swallowing down the lump of pure relief in his throat, even as Rob made a faint noise of discomfort.

"I know it hurts, ssh," Eli whispered gently, as a nurse appeared. "He's in pain, I think," he told her.

She started fussing with the drip.

"D'n't...D'nny, where's D'nny..."

"Danny's gone home to get some sleep and a shower," Eli said. "He's alright."

"'N' you?"

"I'm alright, too—everyone's fine. Everyone's fine, babe, you're the only one who got hurt. I'm fine, Danny's fine, Jen's fine..."

The more he talked, the calmer Rob seemed to get—or maybe that was the nurse dialling up his drugs. Either way, awake and making sense was more than Eli had hoped for, so he petted and murmured until the anxious twist to Rob's expression began to fade. When Eli took his hand, those thick fingers closed like a trap, strong in spite of the weakness in the rest of him.

"I'm here," Eli crooned. "I'm here, savage."

Rob cracked a tiny smile at the pet name, and turned his face into the kisses Eli was lavishing over his eyebrow and forehead. His pupils were blown wide with the drugs, and he seemed to have difficulty focusing, but Eli simply smiled and offered more kisses.

"You 'n' Jen..."

"We're fine," Eli repeated softly as heavy boots sounded in the ward and the nurse slipped out again. "You wanna wake up a bit more? I could ask if you can have any breakfast, or a drink or something?"

The curtains rippled and Danny's tall form materialised. A smile did, too, his face switching from sombre to blindingly bright in a moment. "Bro!" he cheered and squeezed Rob's wrist. "'Bout fuckin' time, me 'n' Eli were waiting all night for you!"

Rob rumbled something that might have been a 'fuck off.'

Eli smiled, nuzzling Rob's hair as Danny dragged up the chair and lightly shook Rob by a hand in the middle of the chest, like a man aggravating a small kitten. Not that Eli was stupid enough to voice the comparison.

"Y'okay?"

"Me? M'fine, man, you're the only one dumb enough to get in the way of a knife," Danny said cheerily, settling down and squeezing Rob's wrist again. "You need to get better soon though, mate, the nurses in here are *not* the hot type."

"Fuckin' letch," Rob mumbled.

"Like you 'n' Eli can fuckin' talk, he's been molesting you in your sleep the whole time."

"I have not."

"'N' I missed it…?"

"You did."

"Fuck off, Danny."

"Mate, it were disgusting! In a *ward*, too, you perv—"

"Fuck *off!*"

The banter seemed to settle Rob more than their mere presence, although he made the mistake of laughing once and groaned so deeply that Danny was half out of his chair to summon a nurse before Rob could tell him not to bother.

It settled Eli, too. He'd had visions in his head of serious injuries or brain damage from blood loss—could that happen?—or shock-induced amnesia or something, but Rob was normal, if sluggish and sleepy, and…

The curtain slid back. For a split second, Eli presumed it was a nurse, until Rob's face twisted in a scowl and he mumbled, "What, m'I gettin' arrested for not bitin' it?"

Eli twisted; his father stared back, face split open in an expression of raw shock. Danny made a derisive noise and shifted noticeably closer to the bed.

"Dad?" Eli said, tightening his grip on Rob's hand. "What's up? Is it Jenny?"

"I—ah—yes," Dad said, looking hugely uncomfortable. His hair was all over the place, his clothes crumpled in a way Eli couldn't remember ever seeing before. "She's, ah, had the baby. A boy. She's, um…asking for you…you…you ought to come and meet your nephew, after all…"

His voice was drifting and vague; his eyes didn't waver from Rob.

Eli swallowed and kissed Rob's knuckles, deciding it would probably be best to separate them now, before any row could happen when Rob was still flat on his back in a hospital bed and drugged up to the eyeballs.

"You gonna be okay with Danny while I go see my new nephew?" Eli whispered.

"Mm."

"G'wan," Danny said, patting Rob's elbow. "I'll keep the fucker busy. Or steal his drugs, either or."

"Text me if anything changes," Eli ordered.

"M'still *here*," Rob grumbled.

Eli snorted, kissing him on the forehead before standing up and not bothering to dignify his complaint with any acknowledgement.

"Rob," Dad said quite suddenly. The name sounded funny. Eli realised with a jolt that he couldn't remember his father ever saying Rob's first name before. "I—thank you. For…for what you did for my family last night."

There was a pregnant pause. Then Rob screwed up his face, visibly struggling, and said, "What?"

"Not now, Dad," Eli said quietly, even as something tight and toxic unwound in his gut and disappeared. "He's on a lot of morphine. Let's go?"

He steered his father out of the cubicle—but threw a look over his shoulder to Danny that was returned in full force.

Was all it took for Dad to change his mind a fucking *stabbing*?

CHAPTER 27

THE MOMENT THEY left the ward, Dad turned on him.

To hug him.

Eli froze in the grip, his own hands stuck out awkwardly by his father's sides. They hadn't hugged since Eli was twelve. And suddenly his father was crushing him in a bear hug, Eli's ribs creaking under the pressure.

And then, just as quickly, he let go. And began to walk.

"Um," Eli said, then jogged to catch up. "Are you...alright?"

"Both of my children, and my grandchild, were in danger tonight," Dad said tersely. "I'm doing as well as you might expect."

Eli opened his mouth, then thought better of it. There was nothing he could say to that.

Dad was silent on the long walk to the lifts, the longer wait for—and then in—said lift, and then the thankfully short walk to the ward. Eli fidgeted, unsure of what to say or how to say it, and then was distracted by his mother's tired smile and warm embrace.

"Thank God you're alright," was all she said, and then Eli was steered into a curtained cubicle and pushed into a seat next to Jenny's bed.

"You look like crap," Eli said.

"Dick," Jenny mumbled. She did look like crap, hair sweaty and plastered to her scalp. But she was beaming a pleased smile, and sitting up, a bundle of blankets cradled in her arms. "How's Rob?"

"Alive."

"Don't—is he—"

Eli took pity at her stricken face, his usual wariness whenever his family asked about Rob easing. "He'll be okay," he said, and Jenny let out an audible breath. "The knife nicked his liver, and he lost a lot of blood, but he woke up about ten minutes ago and he sounded okay. The doctor…Danny said the doctor said he's gonna be alright."

Jenny reached out to squeeze his wrist, her eyes huge in her white face. "Good," she said earnestly. "And—are *you* okay?"

"Better'n you," Eli said.

"I only had a baby," she teased, and they suddenly sniggered like children. The blankets stirred and mewled. Jenny's face lit up, glowing despite the layer of sweat and sagging exhaustion. "Want to meet your new nephew?"

"Um—"

In truth, Eli wasn't the world's biggest fan of babies, especially newborn ones, but Mum was standing at the foot of the bed with her gleeful grandma face on, the same one she'd had when she'd held Flora for the first time, and Eli decided it wasn't worth it to refuse.

"Okay."

Mum arranged the passing of baby from mother to uncle. Soon a heavy weight was draped along Eli's forearms, a head lumpy and misshapen in the palm of his hand, and tiny starfish hands groping at empty air above the blanket melee.

"Oh," he said. "He's, um. Beautiful."

He was hideous, with a squashed nose and a mouth that looked like one of Rob's dodgy dealer mates had beaten him up. His eyes were firmly shut, too, giving him a proper grumpy-old-man expression. Eli jiggled the lump warily, and sighed with relief when the moody mewling stopped and the new baby curled into his chest comfortably. Good. Babies were one thing; *crying* babies were another entirely.

"He's not a bomb, Eli. You don't have to look at him like he's going to explode," Dad said.

Jenny giggled.

Eli seized on the flash of a good mood, and pulled a face.

"He looks like a red potato," he admitted.

"He does not!" Mum squawked. "He looks *gorgeous*! Doesn't he, Jenny? And he needs a name, we can't just keep calling him baby."

"I haven't decided," Jenny said. "And shut up, Eli, he *is* gorgeous. And he likes you already, look."

Eli pulled another face. He always felt like a gawky teenager again with babies. He just didn't like them. Even his own niece—and now nephew—had failed to get that whole rush-of-love, parental-instinct thing going in him. He was already itching to hand the baby back.

"Someone has to, I suppose?" he hazarded. Flora had screamed the house down when anyone but Jenny held her for the first five months of her annoying life.

"How *is* Rob?" Jenny repeated. "I mean, is he in bed, or—"

"Well, yeah," Eli said, surprised.

Jenny got her stubborn face on. "Then I'll have to go down to see him, won't I? Mum? Go and find that nurse and ask her if I can get washed and changed yet?"

Mum looked as bewildered as Eli felt. "Dear, you'll need to get some *sleep*, first and foremost! You've had a nasty shock, and—"

"And Rob and Danny saved our lives," Jenny said earnestly. "*Literally*, Mum, it could have been hours and hours before anyone came to help if they'd attacked us, Eli could have been hurt or killed and I'd have had the baby on the tarmac—I want to see him. And I want him to see the baby."

"Er," Eli said, going for diplomacy, "I don't think Rob'll be too cut up about having to wait a while to see the baby. He's not a baby person."

"I'm still going," Jenny said stubbornly. "I'll need to wash first, though. Mum, if she blows you off, just nick a basin and some towels out of the nurse's cupboard, like you did when I had Flora? There's a hairbrush and stuff in my bag—"

"Jenny, dear, really—"

"I am going!" Jenny snapped; the blankets wriggled against Eli's chest and wailed. "Rob saved our lives last night, Mum! And I am going to thank him in person, *today*!"

Mum took the baby; Eli awkwardly got to his feet and said, "Um, well…d'you want anything from the vending machine, then?"

"Twixes. Lots of them. Dad, you get out, too," Jenny said grumpily, glaring at their mother so hard Eli wasn't convinced she wasn't going to set fire to something. "I'm not bloody stripping in front of you all, bad enough I nearly had a baby in front of you."

"Let's, uh, let's find a machine, then," Dad said quietly, steering Eli out by the shoulder, the men for once united by Jenny's ferocious manner in the aftermath of giving birth.

Eli let him, and they retreated to the relative safety of the vending machines in the waiting room, where a couple of new fathers were anxiously chewing their thumbnails, and a harried-looking grandma was trying desperately to keep a sullen three-year-old entertained.

"Eli, uh…let's just…sit for a minute before heading back, perhaps. Let, uh…let Jenny get herself sorted, eh?"

Eli closed his eyes at the thinly-veiled—even for Dad—excuse, and exhaled. "Okay," he said, trying his very best to remain level-headed. "Just for a bit, though. I want to get back to Rob before too long."

"Yes, about Rob…" Dad said, slowly lowering himself into a chair.

Here it came. Eli braced himself.

"I…well. I may have been…mistaken."

Eli blinked.

"…What?"

Dad shifted in the chair, the plastic squeaking.

He looked horrendously uncomfortable, and something deep in Eli's chest softened. Slowly, Eli dragged another chair around to face his father, and sat down.

"What d'you mean?" he pressed.

Dad exhaled heavily. "Your mother told me everything that you told her when she arrived. Was it…was that what really happened?"

"Yes," Eli said shortly.

Dad swallowed. "Then I have been mistaken."

"I'm—mistaken?"

"About Ha—" Dad winced. "About Rob. I would never have...thought that of him."

Eli ground his teeth. "What, that he'd step in to protect his boyfriend and a pregnant woman?"

"That he would arrive at your request to collect Jenny," Dad corrected quietly. "That he would defend you to the point of being stabbed. Or that his brother would have come with him, and assisted. That...those are not the actions I would have believed from the Hawkes family."

Eli ducked his head to eye the tiles. "Yeah, well, you've all shut Rob out, but Danny's like his shadow and Danny likes me well enough."

"I—"

"Danny knows, too," Eli continued ruthlessly. "About me being trans. And their aunt in Scotland. We had a really nice time at Christmas. They welcome me well enough, and they're not exactly waving the flag for gay rights, you know? But they love Rob, what's left of his family, they do, and that was enough. If Rob loved me then that was enough for them. Why hasn't it ever been enough for you?"

Dad went very red, and ducked his head in a similar manner.

Eli licked his lips and twisted his hands over each other between his knees.

"I love him, Dad," he said quietly. "I really do. And it hurts that you and Mum are so determined to hate him and drive us apart, and—I already cut you out of the whole thing, and I'll cut the whole family out of it if it means not losing him. I *can't* lose Rob, Dad. He's the first person to *really* accept me. He *loves* me, he's helping fund my surgery even though Rob's about as comfortable with his gender as guys ever get, and I won't lose that. If you won't come out from behind your uniform once in a while and see him for what he really is instead of his mugshot and his police record, then you and I have nothing to say to each other anymore."

Dad's mouth worked silently.

Eli huffed an exhausted, exasperated laugh.

"You know," he croaked, "the copper who took my statement said guys like Rob…they hit their teens and they turn into criminals or cops. That deep down they're the same type of guy. And he was right, you know. He's stubborn and bloody-minded and he doesn't think nothing of pub brawls with other blokes but hitting a girl makes you total scum…he's just like you, really. And if it weren't for you being so insistent on calling him a criminal every time he's mentioned, and him having this stupid hatred of the police based on shitty experiences he's caused by being a tit, you'd probably get along really fucking well."

Dad was very quiet for a long minute, then leaned forward and sighed heavily.

"I'm sorry."

Eli was stunned into silence.

"I'm sorry you've felt unsupported. It wasn't my intention, or your mother's. We just had no idea what to do when you started saying you wanted to be a boy. And I honestly did think it was just…kids being kids. If Rob *has* given you that confidence and that support, then…I apologise for not seeing it. And for not listening. From what you've told me, I have…misjudged Hawk—Rob. And I will…apologise to him, too, when I can."

Eli snorted and managed a croaky laugh. "Right, yeah, I'd like to see that."

"Eli…"

Eli shrugged. "It'll take a bit of time, yeah, Dad? He doesn't like you either. And part of that is I've told him everything, what it was like growing up with your parents hell-bent on ignoring you and being forced to go through puberty even though even the *doctor* was offering hormone blockers. He knows all of that. It's not just the cop in you he doesn't like."

Dad made a face. "I can't promise we'll get *along*, Eli."

"I'm not asking that," Eli said flatly. "I just want you to stop *picking* all the time. Stop having a go every time I mention him."

Dad looked like he was swallowing a lemon, but slowly nodded. "Alright. I—alright."

"Hey!"

Jenny's voice was loud and demanding; both men twisted and saw her being pushed out of the ward in a wheelchair, the baby bundle cooing and wriggling in her arms. She hadn't had a bath, that much was obvious, but she'd washed her face and her hair was tidied up in a bun. She looked a little fresher, and a little more awake.

"Where's my chocolate?" she demanded.

"Should you be up yet?" Dad asked.

"Come off it, Dad, they'd already discharged me by now with Flora," Jenny said flippantly.

"Er," Eli said. "When was he actually born?"

"About two in the morning," Dad said, scrubbing a hand over his face. "Alright, alright. Let's, uh. Let's go up and see Rob."

Eli bit his lip, wondering if it really was a good idea to let them. "Um," he said. "How about you get Jenny her chocolate, and give me...ten minutes? Ten minutes to make sure he's up for it. He was pretty groggy earlier, and Danny's with him and Danny wears people out normally never mind..."

Jenny gave him an anxious look. "Okay," she said, "but even if he's asleep I want to see for myself he's alright."

Eli nodded, and slipped away. He took the stairs, unwilling to wait for the busy lifts, and near-ran back to Rob's ward with the full intention of giving the man as much warning time as possible. Rob would kill Eli later for letting Dad see him less than up and fighting, but Eli could see he wasn't going to get a second chance at this, so—

Danny jumped and nearly spilled his cup of orange juice when Eli slipped back into the cubicle and closed the curtains behind him. The smell of bleach was eye-wateringly powerful. "The fuck?" Danny demanded, hastily putting the cup down. A slow smirk crossed Rob's face, but his eyes were half-lidded and drowsy.

"Hey, savage," Eli whispered, stooping over the bed to kiss him gently. "How you feeling?"

"Sick," Danny supplied. "He's on fluids. They tried giving him OJ, so he fuckin' puked all over the floor, then nearly punched a nurse 'cause it hurt so fucking much."

Eli winced. "You feeling any better now?" he whispered, stroking both hands through Rob's hair.

"Mm."

"They upped his drugs," Danny supplied. "He's in and out a bit."

Eli grimaced. "Rob? You actually *with* me?"

"Uh-huh," Rob mumbled before yawning widely. "Sit m'up?"

Eli and Danny exchanged wary looks, then Danny shrugged and fumbled for the buttons on the bedframe. "Your funeral," he said.

Rob went a funny shade of grey as the head of the bed rose, but—thank God—he didn't throw up or pass out.

Eli perched gingerly on the mattress beside him, and slid his arms around Rob's shoulders in an awkward hug. But a needed one, judging by the way Rob turned his face into Eli despite his younger brother's presence.

"Jenny wants to see you," Eli said.

"Jen?"

"Mm. She's had the baby but she's worried about you. She's coming to see you."

"What, now?" Danny asked.

"Yeah."

"Is she bringing the baby?"

"Yeah."

"*Sweet*," Danny said, and grinned lecherously. "Fit bird with a new baby and no bloke in the picture? I'm *there*."

"Her old man ain't worth the trouble," Rob advised sleepily.

Eli laughed quietly, kissing the top of his head.

"Actually, Dad just apologised to me for ragging on you all the time and misjudging you."

"You what?" Danny said, and started sniggering. "The great Chief Inspector Bell apologised for something? Fuck off." The *off* was drawled into *orrrfff*.

Eli rolled his eyes even as he smiled at Rob's stuttered, painful laugh.

"He did," Eli said quietly. "And he's going to apologise to you, too."

"Mate, no fucker tell you it's fucking rude to lie to people who're high on morphine?"

"S'not morphine…"

"Might as well be fucking morphine, state o' you."

Eli smiled, pressing his nose against the crown of Rob's head, and slid off the bed when his phone buzzed. Undoubtedly Mum. "They'll be up in a minute," he said, and kissed Rob on the corner of the mouth. "Love you."

He got a fuzzily confused look in reply, and a snigger from Danny, but ignored them both and retreated. His family were clustered in the ward corridor, looking suitably confused. He steeled himself.

"He's really fuzzy," Eli said, looking his father right in the eye, "and if he reacts badly to you guys being there, you're out. He's got a scratched liver and a big hole in his side and I'm having him out of hospital and home *soon*, not in several weeks because you pissed him off and he ripped his stitches."

Mum made a little noise, but Eli ignored her and turned on his heel, returning to the cubicle. By the time Mum pushed Jenny through the half-open curtains, Eli had resumed his position on the mattress beside his boyfriend.

Rob stiffened and squeezed him tightly when his sharp wariness broke through the drugs.

"What're they doing here?"

"Jenny wanted to make sure you're alright," Eli said, "and Mum and Dad wanted to talk to you."

"*Why.*" Rob's voice was hard as stone, and Danny's face matched. Jenny snorted.

"Because I've just had a gorgeous little boy, *safely,* thanks to you, instead of being attacked and maybe losing him in a dirty car park," she said snottily. "So shut up and meet your new nephew."

"My—what? He ain't my nephew," Rob said, his voice slurring again.

"He's mine, though," Eli said, "which means he might as well be yours." He kissed the top of Rob's head, and grudgingly accepted the baby, cradling him against his chest so Rob could see.

The baby squirmed and opened a tiny maw of a mouth to mewl quietly before cuddling into Rob's hospital gown and, apparently, going back to sleep.

"It's fuckin' tiny," Danny said, awed.

"And he's safe and healthy and *here* because of you two," Jenny said firmly. "And I'll never forget it. Proper never, because I'm going to call him Robert Daniel Bell, after you two."

Rob baulked.

Danny hooted with laughter.

"Fuckin' hell, mate, you're fucked now!"

"Go fuck yourself, Danny."

Eli laughed as the baby stirred and clutched a tiny starfish hand into Rob's gown. He had a crop of dark hair, and Eli kissed Rob's ear and said, "If you're not careful, people will think he's your *son*, not your nephew."

"Eli, seriously, go open the fucking window and jump out," Rob grumbled hoarsely, but he pressed his head into Eli's neck. "S'a baby. Take it back."

Eli smiled and handed the baby back to Jenny, who cuddled him with an anxious look. "How *are* you, Rob?" she implored.

"Hurts," Rob mumbled. He was slipping again, the flash of awareness having worn him out.

Eli hiked the blankets a little higher and squeezed Rob's shoulders.

"Drugs're shit. Nurses're shit. And this bed's fucking crap."

Jenny giggled.

"Grumpy," Eli teased, stroking Rob's hair. "You'll be alright, though."

"Danny's already said he'll kick my arse f'I'm not…"

"Good."

Mum's voice was a loud surprise, and Eli felt Rob jump and hiss in pain. She didn't seem to care though, standing at the end of the bed with her determined face on, and fists firmly planted on her hips.

"We were wrong about you, Rob," she said flatly. "You saved both my children last night, and my grandson, and I won't be forgetting that. We've misjudged you badly, and for that I'm very sorry."

It was a simple, blunt apology, and Rob's face turned a faint pink. Danny coughed, going scarlet.

"You put yourself on the line for my son and daughter," she

continued, "and you've made my son happy, which he hasn't really been ever since he was small. So I'm sorry for the way we've treated you, and I hope we can start over again."

Eli waited patiently, curled against Rob's side, Rob's head cuddled below Eli's chin. He could feel the tension, could almost see Rob looking for the trap, but he said nothing. Whatever Rob decided, Eli had told his father the truth—he would walk away, if it meant keeping Rob. He was done.

Dad coughed when Mum elbowed him, and said, "Yes. As I, uh, already discussed with Eli…we have been…mistaken."

Danny went an alarming red and scowled, but subsided when Eli shot him an angry look. This was for Rob, not for Danny. Rob had the power now, and Eli would keep it that way.

"Er," Rob said eventually. "Right."

It seemed like that was all he was going to say, for he made a wobbly hand gesture in Danny's direction and said he needed more drugs now. Eli jerked his head at the curtains, and his father beat a hasty and grateful exit. Jenny tried to stay, arguing with Mum, but Eli ignored them and stroked a thumb over Rob's jaw, peeling himself away to look Rob in the eyes.

"I love you," he said firmly, uncaring that his mother and sister were still in the ward to hear him, "and no matter what you decide to do about starting over with Mum and Dad, I'm on your side. Okay?"

Rob's hand was shaky on the back of Eli's head, but his kiss was firm, albeit stale and foul-tasting.

"Okay," he rasped.

And it was. Eli knew it—he could feel it in his bones, in the way the anxiety and anger had fled down the hospital corridors. His world had reshaped itself around merely him and Rob, rather than having the whole world and both families in there with them.

It was all going to be okay.

EPILOGUE

10 MINS.

I'm nervous, Eli replied, and received a photo of Rob's face, one eyebrow raised in an unimpressed expression.

U have had tit surgery and a fuckin huge chest tattoo how the fuck r u nervous?

Because this is gonna hurt more!

"Is that Rob?" Mum asked.

It was Sunday evening. Eli always came home for Sunday dinner—something Mum had insisted on, because she was getting proper grandma since Bobby had been born and empty-nested like crazy now—and usually Eli would drive home or Jenny would drop him off. But tonight—

"Yeah. He'll be here in ten minutes."

"Ask him what ice cream he wants."

"We're not stopping, Mum."

"Ask him!"

Eli rolled his eyes. *Mum says what ice cream dyou want?*

Wtf im not stoppin! came the predictable reply.

"Mint choc chip," Eli lied. "but we're really not stopping, Mum. Rob wants to get going before it gets dark, you know what the Snake Pass is like…"

"I don't know why you have to go to Manchester," Mum complained. "Can't they do it in Leeds like your top surgery?"

"I'd have had to wait until September for Leeds," Eli said. "Anyway, Rob's booked a nice hotel in the city centre, so I can just sleep for a couple of days and not do anything after."

"And what's Rob going to do in Manchester while you sleep for a couple of days?" Mum asked, amused.

"I dunno, kick pigeons?" Eli suggested flippantly. "He'll probably watch the hotel telly for the first day then wander off. You know what he's like."

She did now, too. A little bit, anyway. Rob still didn't come around much, and it was still a crap idea to put him and Dad in the same room for more than half an hour—or ever, if unsupervised—but Rob came out on family stuff sometimes, like the day they'd taken Flora and Bobby to the zoo and made a proper big family day of it. Jenny came round to the flat occasionally, too, to see Eli—although Eli suspected she had a bit of a crush on Danny.

"Are you still anxious?" Mum asked as she rattled ice cream bowls.

"Yeah. Surgery , en't it?"

It was the long-awaited phalloplasty. Tuesday morning, eleven o'clock. Eli had struggled to find a surgeon willing to do the phalloplasty and the removal of his remaining female parts at the same time—most had wanted him to either keep his vagina and uterus, or remove them and push back the phalloplasty for another year.

And *yeah*, it was going to hurt, but Eli was mostly excited about finally getting it done. His nerves rested more on…well, more on Rob than the surgery itself.

Still, he wasn't daft enough to say it.

"It'll be nice to have a bit of a break though, just the two of you, before you start college, won't it?"

Eli curled his toes in his converse. "Yeah," he said, secretly thrilled she was saying it. "Rob got taken on at his gym, too, you know, the one he boxes at. They're starting this thing for troubled youth or whatever, and the guy who runs it talked to Rob and said he oughta help out, the kids'd respect him more 'cause he's been there, and they're gonna pay him nine quid an hour."

"Oh that's *good*," Mum said in heartfelt tones. "Oh that's wonderful, dear, he's really turning things around, isn't he?"

Well, mostly. Eli had found an iPod in Rob's bag the other day that definitely didn't belong to him. And he still sold a suspicious amount of stuff on Gumtree. But he wasn't burgling, and he didn't show up smelling of weed anymore. It was a start, and Eli would take the little starts he could get.

…And anyway, if he wanted Rob out of all criminality ever, Rob wouldn't fuck him in public places anymore. And that'd be crap.

His phone buzzed as Mum finished serving up the ice cream. A photo of the front of his parents' house greeted him when he unlocked it. He rolled his eyes. *Come inside mum's put out ice cream. I'll eat yours ;)*

Can we just go already????

INSIDE. NOW.

He heard a car door bang.

Mum flitted to the window to pull the curtain back and peer out down the driveway. "Oh, it's your Rob!" she trilled, just as the bell rang.

Eli laughed as Flora gallumphed out of the living room.

"I'll get it, Gammar!" she bellowed at the top of her lungs. The door crashed off the wall, and then—"Uncle Eli! It's your tree man!"

"Seriously, something's wrong with you," Rob was telling her gravely when Eli went into the hall to rescue him.

"No there's not!" Flora shrieked.

"Flora, shut up," Eli mumbled, and kissed Rob on the mouth before taking firm hold of his wrist. "Come and at least say a quick hello to Mum. She's been dead nice about you today. Seems to think you're becoming a good citizen."

"That's your fucking lies."

"Mind your language."

"Fucking lies!" Flora echoed cheerfully.

"Flora!" Mum shouted from the kitchen.

"The tree man said it!"

Rob levelled Eli with a flat, unimpressed stare. Eli just gave him an obnoxious smile, firmly closed the front door, and hauled towards the kitchen.

"Rob, dear, have some ice cream!"

Rob grunted a hello, and stuck his hands in his pockets. Eli tipped Rob's bowl out into his own and attacked both portions when Mum's back was to him.

"Are you all set for going to Manchester, then?" Mum chirped, busying herself by washing her hands.

"Yep."

"Eli says you've booked a hotel—it'll be nice to get away for a bit, won't it? And he said about your new job at the gym! That'll be nice, won't it, helping those less fortunate?"

"Guess so."

"You know, you ought to come to Sunday dinner with Eli more often, dear. Flora's your biggest fan, she's always asking about you, and Bobby's getting so big!"

"Maybe."

Eli rolled his eyes and kicked Rob under the table. "Dad's not home," he said pointedly, and Rob's shoulders visibly relaxed.

"So when are you heading off?"

"When Eli's done shovelling ice cream."

"Eli!" Mum scolded, finally turning and realising what he'd done.

"What? Rob doesn't like it," Eli said defensively.

Rob sniggered.

"So I'll be finishing this, and then we'll go. Did you bring my suitcase?" Eli added.

"No shit. 'Course I did. M'not retarded."

Little shoes slapped on the tiles. "What's retarded?" Flora asked.

"Stupid" Rob said.

"A nasty word," Mum said at exactly the same time.

Eli smirked around his spoon.

"What about fucking retarded?" Flora demanded.

"Flora, why don't you and I go and get little Bobby from his playpen so Uncle Rob can say hello to him, eh?" Mum said quickly, seizing her chubby hand and turning her around.

"Baby Bobby!" Flora cheered, her voice carrying powerfully as Mum led her away.

"Quick," Eli whispered. "The playpen's in the study, we can escape."

"Thank fuck," Rob muttered. He shot out of his chair like he'd caught fire, and Eli stifled his laugh with his hand as he dumped the half-empty bowl in the sink and chased after him.

"Eli!" he heard Mum yell just as they reached the car, but Rob flung the door open and started the engine anyway.

"Go, go, go!" Eli shouted, then collapsed into fits of laughter as the Suzuki shot off the grass and barrelled down Heather Lea Avenue, Rob fighting to drive and slam his door at the same time. "Oh my God, poor Mum. That was awful. I blame you, you're a shit."

"I blame babies, for being shit," Rob corrected. He pulled over at the corner of the avenue to put his seatbelt on. "Right. Suitcase is in the back. Bag of snack food is behind your seat. I nicked Danny's laptop and a bunch of DVDs so we have something decent in case the telly's crap. Owt else?"

Eli settled, the laughter giving away to the anxious gnawing in the pit of his stomach that had started up about ten days earlier, when he'd made the final payment to the surgeon. He rummaged in the glovebox for Rob's sunglasses and handed them over at a set of traffic lights, fidgeting to keep himself busy. He hadn't lied—he was nervous. And now, en route, he was feeling faintly sick.

"No," he said quietly.

"Sure? I ain't fucking stopping once we get out of the city."

"M'sure."

Rob made a huffing sigh and shook his head. "You going to tell what's got you twitchy?"

The question made Eli look at him, and he swallowed anxiously. Rob's voice was lazy and casual. He practically lounged in his seat, one hand on the wheel and the other arm draped out of the open window, fingers tapping on the top of the wing mirror. There was the very faint shine of sweat on his neck, and Eli absently wanted to lick it. He was fucking incredible, and the sudden shadowy threat to having him...

"Oi! Focus!"

Eli laughed. "Sorry. You're looking a bit unfairly fuckable."

"You really complaining?"

"When I can't fuck you? Yes."

"Lies," Rob drawled. "But answer me—what's up?"

Eli chewed on his lip absently, watching the jagged views of the Peaks as the city bled away behind them in silence for a minute before murmuring, "I'm…I'm a bit…worried."

"About?"

"You."

"Me?" Rob's voice sounded genuinely surprised.

"I'm worried this'll…change things."

"Well, yeah, I'll not have to watch where my fingers go."

Eli snorted. "That's not what I meant and you know it."

"I don't, fucktard," Rob responded. "What's got you worried? I *have* figured out you're a tranny. Newsflash for you and all."

Eli rolled his eyes. "But you've never…you've never seen me have surgery, you've never seen me changing, this is all you know. I'm worried…I'm worried you're going to look at me differently. Or *be* with me differently. I mean, I may not ever be able to have a proper physical orgasm again, and I'm going to look and feel different down there, and—"

"And, again, yeah, I know? I came to your fucking consultation with your psychiatrist, Eli, I *know*," Rob said firmly.

Eli squirmed. His psychiatrist had asked to meet his partner, and have a discussion with him, too. Eli liked his psychiatrist, he was friendly and funny and very up-front about what was concerning him about Eli's transition, and this new relationship had had the psychiatrist watchful for a while. And when the appointment had happened, Rob had been on his best behaviour, and—to Eli's enormous surprise—they'd gotten along like a house on fire. They'd spent half the session ragging on each other's football teams.

Then the psychiatrist had gotten down to business and given Rob a pretty brutal talk about what it meant, being the partner of a transman having full bottom surgery. Rob had actually sat and listened, even asked fucking questions, and—

Eli had taken Rob home after and pretty much played sex slave for the whole evening, intent on rewarding him for it.

But Rob hadn't really mentioned it since, or gone again. He'd reverted quickly enough to his vaguely uninterested approach to the whole thing…until now.

"But—"

"Shut your face. I know what's happening here, yeah? I ain't thick. Things'll change, permanently, that's the whole fucking idea, and if I had a problem with it, you'd know by now, fuckwit." Despite his language, his voice still rolled and rumbled in its usual rasping rhythm. It was…not quite soft or gentle, but it was at ease, and Eli slowly relaxed. "The fact I can't get my end away for at least a month is *seriously* going to make me pissy, and then I'm probably gonna throw a fit one night and you'll beat the shit out of me with that belt, and I will admit I'm going to miss going down on you because you really do taste fucking awesome, girly bits aside. And I'm hoping that's not going to change too much. But at the end of the day, it's not about me. S'about you. And if this is gonna make you happy, gonna let me drag you to Robin Hood's Bay in August for me and Danny's piss-up trip because you're not so wary of wearing board shorts in case someone realises you ain't got nothing in 'em, then fine."

Eli swallowed.

"Eli. It's. *Fine*," Rob repeated in a softer voice. "You're gonna feel like what you want. You're gonna have a dick and the right number of holes. Stop worrying, okay?"

"What if I can't…get off anymore?" Eli whispered.

And that was the crux of his fear. His relationship with Rob had started from sex. There'd been sex long before there'd been love. And without that sex life—that varied, incredible, passionate, sometimes painful life—there was a tiny part of him that wondered if Rob wouldn't…get bored?

Rob snorted.

"What?"

"Get real," he said. "You don't get off physically in most of the scenes you control, babe. You've never come *any* of the times you've beaten me. It's not about that for you. So what if you can't anymore? You still enjoy it, right?"

Eli chewed on his lip. "Would you still…you'd still sleep with me, right, even if you couldn't get me off anymore?"

"Yeah, if you want me to."

"Of course I fucking want you to!"

"Then I will, Jesus," Rob said, and laughed. "You are worrying way too fucking much about it, babe. You don't get off on anal, you know what I'm saying? But you still like it. You still want me to do it, and the surgery won't change that."

Eli swallowed. "Pull over?"

"Eh?"

"Pull over. Next layby or parking area. I want a hug."

"Oh hell," Rob grumbled. "Are you gonna cry on me? I ain't stopping this fucking car if you're gonna fucking bawl."

"No, I want a *hug,* open your ears."

Rob chuckled. Eli carefully blinked to ensure he *didn't* cry, and waited semi-patiently until a parking area came up on the left. Rob pulled haphazardly over, not bothering to indicate or really slow down. The moment the handbrake was on, though, Eli's seatbelt was off and he wrapped both arms around Rob's shoulders tightly.

"Tell me—really, honestly, no repercussions—"

"Reaper-what?"

"Um, bad consequences."

"Okay."

"—if this is going to change anything. Because if this is going to change anything between us—"

"It's gonna change *some* things," Rob said. A heavy hand settled on the back of Eli's head and began to stroke his hair. "We're going to get to re-learn what makes you feel good in the sack. And I get to snap your trunks when we go to the beach in August, 'cause you'll be able to come. And that's pretty much it."

"Yeah?"

"Yeah. Look—and fuck you for making me go fucking mushy here—but this thing between us, there's a fuck-ton of sex and that's fucking awesome, but…it's not everything. Not for me. If it was just sex, I'd have walked a long time ago after all that crap with your old man, yeah? But I didn't. The sex, that's just a part of it, and it'll adapt and carry on anyway. That whole…I'm here, I'm supporting what you want, that bit? That's not changing. After this surgery, you're gonna *be* what you look like. You'll be what you seem. And that's what you want, and because of what this is between us, that bit where I support you, that's what I want, too."

Eli swallowed and kissed Rob's neck. "The bit where you love me."

It wasn't a question.

"Yeah," Rob said. "The bit where I love you."

ABOUT THE AUTHOR

MATTHEW J. METZGER is an asexual, transgender author from the wet and windy British Isles. Matthew is a writer of both adult and young adult LGBT fiction, with a love of larger-than-life characters, injecting humour into serious issues, and the uglier, grittier edges of British romance. Matthew currently lives in Bristol, and—when not writing—can usually be found sleeping, working out at the gym, and being owned by his cat.

Find more online at matthewjmetzger.com.

Made in United States
North Haven, CT
26 April 2022

18602397R00147